11502

☑ **W9-AND-114**

DATE DUE

DATE DUE			
APR 2 5 20			
GAYLORD			PRINTED IN U.S.A.

TIMOTHY HOLME

A Funeral of Gondolas ✓

Futura

A *Futura* Book

Copyright © Timothy Holme 1981

First published in 1981
by Macmillan London Limited

This edition published in 1986
by Futura Publications, a Division of
Macdonald & Co (Publishers) Ltd
London & Sydney

ISBN 0 7088 3078 1

Printed and bound in Great Britain by
Collins, Glasgow

Futura Publications
A Division of
Macdonald & Co (Publishers) Ltd
Greater London House
Hampstead Road
London NW1 7QX

A BPCC plc Company

For Chiara and Simona

A pride of lions,
A gaggle of geese,
A school of porpoises,
A funeral of gondolas.

Playing psychological associations most people, it seems, when faced with 'gondola' would hit back instantly with 'death'.

Gondola, Gondolier

The Historical Regatta in Venice is a two-oar race. I have presented it as a single-oar event to sharpen the narrative focus. That it is popularly considered a one-oar race is demonstrated by the enormous acclaim that used to be showered upon Strigheta—the great Regatta hero of the 1950s and 1960s, who is in no way connected with the Bull of this story—rather than upon Strigheta and his partner.

T.H.

Part One

THE UNDERTAKER

Pantaloon appears upon the scene,
masked.

Mémoires
Carlo Goldoni

ONE

The old man with the word GANZER in faded gold letters on his cap was in startling contrast to his surroundings. He had a long, much patched and filthy overcoat which almost reached his ankles and a pair of ancient boots without laces. He was unwashed with at least a week's growth of beard and gave off an odour to match his appearance. The tourists and the native Venetians gave him a wide berth. He was the only blot on an otherwise idyllic landscape, and nobody any longer even knew what the word on his cap meant.

The Rialto Bridge humped regally over the Grand Canal as though posing for a postcard photograph. The water of the canal chopped and glinted in the sun. A huge low-lying craft piled with colourful rubbish swung out from under the bridge while a water-bus, overcrowded beyond the limits of the most elastic safety regulations, churned water in mid-stream.

Then a long black craft with a silver bow prong swept with cheeky magnificence in front of the water-bus and in towards the shore. It rode lop-sidedly in the water, sported a pink plastic rose on its fore-part and was propelled by an oarsman with a permanent, involuntary grin upon his face which had earned him among his colleagues the nickname of Smiler. In this craft, oblivious of everything except each other, sat a couple who had been married the previous morning in Didcot.

The boat was a Venetian gondola and, as it nosed in to the shore, the old man with the word GANZER in faded gold letters on his cap shuffled to meet it.

Probably none of these people noticed an unusually good looking southerner who was sitting at one of the cafe tables by the canal drinking a glass of Chivas Regal whisky, smoking a black market English cigarette and glancing occasionally at a copy of

9

The Times. If they had noticed him, they would almost certainly have assumed he was a tourist, for he had a knack of taking on, almost unconsciously, whatever appearance suited a given situation.

It would have taken a very detached observer and a shrewd physiognomist to recognise in this meridional tourist Achille Peroni, the man referred to in the more cliche-ridden newspapers and magazines as the Rudolf Valentino of the Italian police.

In spite of what most people would have regarded as idyllic surroundings and perfect weather, the Rudolf Valentino of the Italian police was not in a good mood. Indeed, he had been in a fairly bad mood on and off ever since he had been transferred to Venice on what was tactfully described as a 'temporary mission'.

This temporary mission, in fact, represented an awkward political compromise. Peroni had previously been in Verona where he had been in charge of an affair involving the Red Brigades and two prominent local families. The truth of this matter had never come out, but following the murder of the Veronese police chief by Red Brigade killers there had been an orgy of leaking (in both senses of the word) in high places and a lot of more or less accurate journalistic guesswork. And this had led—as such things inevitably do in Italy—to a major political row. The left swung pro-Peroni for no better reason than that the right had swung anti, and it quickly became evident that he would have to be moved, at least temporarily, away from Verona.

But where to? Milan, Turin or Rome would have looked like promotion and would have aroused an outcry from the right. On the other hand, Peroni's native south would have appeared to be punishment, calling forth the rage of the left. So Venice had been decided on as a compromise, and everybody had been more or less contented.

Everybody except Peroni. He had an almost unprofessional passion for crime. He liked it as highly spiced as his native Neapolitan cooking and such crime, taken in combination with his personality, called forth the oohs and aahs of the media which then proceeded to polish and enhance the great Peroni legend.

But crime was non-existent in Venice. There were investigations, interrogations, even arrests and convictions, but not what you would really call crime, the boiling and bubbling sort. The only exception to this seemed to be a wave of petty—and in some cases perhaps not so petty—blackmail. But, for what they were worth, these cases had not been entrusted to Peroni, and ever since his arrival in the Serenissima Republic, Queen of the Adriatic, he had felt reduced to the status of a glorified hotel detective. Indeed, he reflected bitterly, what was Venice itself but one vast, crumbling hotel? And now the sheer banality of it all had reached the bathygraphical maximum. Word had come to the *Questura*—the police headquarters—that certain gondoliers were taking bets on some sort of annual gondola race held in Venice. It was a technical illegality, and that only because the state wanted to reserve all gambling for itself.

Peroni had been instructed to observe the gondola ranks at the Accademia, Ca' Rezzonico and the Rialto, where bets were reported to be taken, and to find out if there were an organiser behind it. So it was that Achille Peroni whose outrageous and dramatic exploits had often kept the Adriatic boot on tiptoe with suspense had been reduced to watching Venetian housewives placing 1000 lire bets with gondoliers.

He had quickly spotted the bookies at the Accademia and the Ca' Rezzonico without finding any sign of an organiser, and now he had come to the Rialto where the bookie—a genial looking, tubby gondolier who indulged in back-chat with the passers-by and joked with their children—had been no more difficult to pick out.

Peroni glanced at his *Times* of which, to be frank, he understood very little. Some years had passed since his six months' special posting to New Scotland Yard, and his English, erratic at its most pristine, had become about as practical as a pioneer telephone in a museum case. But there had been no diminishment in his love of what he fondly conceived to be England—a largely mythical world where bobbies beamed, Big Ben boomed, bacon and eggs sizzled and tea tasted like elixir.

So now Peroni glanced through the largely incomprehensible headlines with nostalgic affection. But when he looked up from them he found that the tubby, genial gondolier had vanished into the aquatic air.

If the circumstances had been less dull, this could have been dangerous carelessness. He went over the crowded scene with economical rapidity and was just in time to catch a glimpse of the gondolier's stout behind disappearing, like Alice's rabbit, down a narrow *calle*, one of the hundreds of little, usually dark alleys with which Venice is veined.

Peroni put down 2000 lire for his Chivas Regal, folded *The Times* and set off in unobtrusive pursuit. The tubby gondolier scuttled along the *calles* without looking right or left. Wherever he was going, it was plainly a route he had followed before. He might, of course, just be going home, but Peroni thought not. Gondoliers didn't just stop work like that peremptorily in the middle of the afternoon.

Up and down over bridges they went, the gondolier's zig-zag course seemingly programmed in his mind like an ant's. And then suddenly he reached his destination and went in. Peroni halted in surprise. It was a church.

A very minor Venetian church, its facade set square with the buildings on either side. You had the impression that it was disguising itself—a sort of architectural Peroni—so as not to be recognised by tourists. But its most curious feature—undisguisable—was that the three steps leading to the front door went down and not up.

Peroni waited outside for a couple of minutes looking in a shop window full of chocolate hedgehogs. Then he went in.

The door announced him with a complicated creak that sounded like a phrase you just couldn't catch. Inside, the church smelled musty and would have been dark if it hadn't been for a small forest of candles burning before a fresco of a female saint Peroni couldn't place. But of the genial gondolier there was no sign.

Prompted by *The Times*, Peroni was an English tourist, scrupulously doing Venice. He examined a cluster of silver votive hearts as carefully as if they'd been a Tintoretto.

And then he realised where the gondolier had got to. From a wooden box at the far end of the church there came a little wavelet of whispering, followed by silence, and then another little wavelet. He was confessing.

The picture Peroni now studied, for all the world as if he'd

12

been in the National Gallery, was puzzling. It was a sort of strip cartoon of the late 18th, early 19th century, stiff and naive in style and obviously of no artistic value, but oddly fascinating. It showed four scenes. In the first a man was asleep in bed while another man with a spectacularly malignant face was climbing in through the window. In the second scene the villainous man was standing over the sleeper holding a blunt object with which he was obviously about to dash the other's brains out.

The genial gondolier came out of the confessional and, without so much as glancing at Peroni, bobbed a genuflection and went out. Peroni debated following him, but decided against it. The gondolier's traces could easily be picked up again. Rightly or wrongly, it was the church which absorbed Peroni's interest now.

Silent and invisible, the priest in the confessional seemed to loom over it as though his presence were hatching it. Peroni wondered whether the priest were observing him. Wondered, too, what he should do next.

Then he decided to put off the problem a little longer and continue with his tourism. In the third scene the two men were in the same positions, but now the ceiling was rent in two to reveal the celestial figure of a girl, presumably the saint of the fresco. The attacker was looking at her in terror and the blunt object had fallen harmlessly to the floor. Then in the fourth and final scene, the villain was clambering out through the window and the sleeper was reverently on his knees before the heavenly vision.

The door from the street creaked open again, and this time the creak seemed to be a crotchety, elderly servant announcing to its mistress, the silence within, the arrival of a caller. Heavy footsteps were interrupted for genuflection and then resumed. Peroni looked round and was just in time to recognise the gondolier who had been taking bets at the Accademia before he, too, disappeared into the darkness of the confessional and once again little wavelets of sound started to ripple out across the silence.

So the church was the headquarters of an illicit betting ring.

And the picture was an *ex voto* offering. The sleeper had been attacked in bed, but just as his assailant had been on the point of murdering him the saint, whoever she was, had appeared, terrifying him away. In gratitude the man who had so narrowly escaped having his brains dashed out had caused the picture to be painted. And there it hung in the church today, though probably nobody any longer had even an inkling of who the two men were or what precise reality lay behind this drama which had been played out in Venice two hundred years before.

The Accademia gondolier's confession came to an end and he, too, left the church. The immediate problem could be postponed no longer. But how does a policeman approach an unknown priest in a confessional? Does he just pull aside the curtain to reveal the sacerdotal inmate? Certainly not if he is Neapolitan.

Peroni went to the confessional and read the card outside with the priest's name, don Amos. Then, feeling awkward, but at least not iconoclastic, he knelt beside the grill.

There was a pause during which he felt irrationally as though the silent and invisible priest had somehow rumbled him, rather than the contrary. This was heightened by the sensation that, although he could make out nothing of the priest's face behind the grill, the priest could somehow see his.

'Jesus Christ be praised.' The voice which spoke the formal opening phrase of confession was down to earth and clothed in dense Venetian dialect.

'May he always be praised,' replied Peroni.

'How long is it since you last confessed?'

Peroni forced himself to a decision. '*Questura*,' he said.

The best way to arrive in Venice is via the railway station. If you come from the Marco Polo Airport or leave your car in Piazzale Roma you are Venetianised by degrees. But if you arrive by train, the very minute you emerge from the station you are immersed in the city's quintessentiality. The Grand Canal lies before you, gondolas ply, water-buses chug and churn and, without being sensational, the church of the Scalzi on your left is as Venetian a piece of architecture as you are likely to find.

Mr Cornelius Ruskin knew this well and had organised his journey accordingly, so as he stepped out of the station he paused for a second in delight to take in the shining scene. Venice hadn't changed. That was the marvellous thing about it—it sank into the Adriatic, it crumbled, it decayed, but it never changed.

Mr Ruskin was, in fact, a sort of honorary Venetian with what you might call a corner in the city. For he was the greatest living expert on the 18th century Venetian playwright, Carlo Goldoni, and his period, and back in the States he had published many books on the subject.

This year he had organised his annual study-holiday to coincide with a festival of Goldoni plays which was to open the next day. So now, as he moved down the station steps, he instantly recognised the poster advertising it, a copy of which had been sent to him at the college where he taught.

It depicted a slim, nubile figure. She was wearing an 18th century dress with a flowered skirt, and she was holding a broom, though it seemed she was not very intent on her sweeping, concerned rather with some young gallant moving towards her, out of sight of the viewer behind the frame of a doorway, while her lowered eyes were doing their demure best to pretend he wasn't there.

The choice of picture was appropriate, thought Mr Ruskin, for Goldoni's plays were crowded with female figures like this little maidservant for whom their author had felt considerably more than literary passion.

The only name on the poster, apart from Goldoni's, was that of Maddalena Spinelli, Italy's leading actress and a foremost interpreter of Goldoni heroines. La Spinelli was famous on the stage of life as well, and Mr Ruskin knew all about her from a weekly magazine which he also received at the college. With scholarly interest he had followed her tempestuous amorous adventures which had involved leading politicians, jet-set figures, artists, film stars, businessmen, athletes, racing drivers and, on one occasion, a gigantic dustman from Cagliari.

He also knew that this succession had been interrupted lately when Maddalena Spinelli had announced her forthcoming marriage to Prince Attilio Cattamini, a noted member of the Roman black nobility who had also made a fortune out of manufacturing electrical household appliances.

But far above these ephemeral flutterings there towered the fact—for Mr Ruskin—that Spinelli was the greatest Mirandolina in the *Locandiera* since Duse herself, and he was awaiting the performance with almost religious awe.

He stood for a moment, uncertain as to whether he should take a taxi-boat or a gondola. But the indecision was brief, for his

Venetiaphilic heart insisted it would travel no way but by gondola. So he had his luggage loaded and then settled himself on one of the shiny leather-seated chairs amidships.

'*Il Vivaldi, per favore,*' he said in his precise, but accented Italian and prepared himself to plunge, metaphorically, into the Grand Canal, unaware that, in the words of his favourite author, he was soon to become 'a character of secondary importance who complicates the play of events and prepares the catastrophe.'

'You're quite sure you wouldn't like to confess?' enquired the priest, apparently unperturbed by the revelation that Peroni was a policeman.

'Quite,' said Peroni. 'Thank you.'

'It's an underrated sacrament these days. In an age of hypochondria people ignore its therapeutic value. I once knew of a woman with a goitre the size of a football which vanished at the moment of absolution. *Ego te absolvo a peccatis tuis* and pop it went like a pricked balloon. Still, if you won't, you won't.'

Peroni opened his mouth, but the priest cut in before he was able to speak. 'From Naples are you?' Peroni admitted it. 'Guessed as much from your accent. And I suppose, like most Neapolitans, you place your confidence exclusively in the hands of St Janarius. An excellent saint, of course,' he went on rather as though he were recommending a good butcher, 'though far from being the exclusive channel of divine grace. However, God made you Neapolitans, so he will doubtless wink at a little excess of local patriotism.'

Peroni was taken aback, for he did in fact tend to rely on St Janarius, the patron saint of Naples whose blood still miraculously liquifies twice a year to the rapturous awe of the Neapolitans. But the interview, he felt, would have to be placed on a more orthodox footing.

'If you don't mind,' he said, 'there are some questions I must ask you.'

'Hum.' The priest seemed to be considering it. Then he said, 'I'll be with you immediately.'

He murmured in Latin before drawing back the confessional curtain and then, stepping out himself, Peroni was at last able to see his interlocutor. He was a heavily built man with large, powerful hands, wearing a threadbare cassock which looked none too clean.

'We can talk better in the sacristy,' he said and led the way, pausing half way up the church before the forest of candles, the fresco and the picture.

'The liquifying blood of your St Janarius is all very well as far as it goes,' he said, 'but it's nothing to what she used to do.'

'She?' said Peroni, curious in spite of himself.

'St Angela. The patron of gondoliers. As a matter of fact, she's not in the official calendar of saints, but the gondoliers venerate her as one just the same and the hierarchy have to lump it. She lived in Venice in the 13th century, and when she couldn't get a boat to take her to mass, she used to walk across the Grand Canal.'

'Across the bridge?'

'No, no, no—on the water. Countless other miracles she did, too, or people say she did which amounts to the same thing in the end. You see that casket?' Peroni noticed a bejewelled casket in a glass case below the fresco. 'That contains her right index finger. During her lifetime she always used to make the sign of the cross over the competitors in the regatta. And after she died, her finger continued doing it on the day of the regatta. Went on for centuries.'

'And now?'

'It stopped in 1852 when the Cardinal Patriarch of Venice forbade the ceremony which had naturally grown up about the event on the grounds that Angela was not a canonised saint.'

He raised one of his large hands in a gesture of salute, whether at the finger or the fresco Peroni couldn't tell, and continued on his way up the church. Behind the main altar was a doorway through which they passed into a dark and fusty sacristy. The priest went to a high cupboard which he opened to produce a bottle and two glasses.

'Wine,' he announced pouring for them both, 'You mentioned questions?'

'Two gondoliers,' said Peroni, feeling at a disadvantage for some reason, 'went into your confessional just now.'

'That's right.'

'To confess?'

'Also right.'

'What else did they come to do?'

'Pass me betting slips and money.'

Peroni felt as though he were in a tug of war and the person at the other end had suddenly let go. He took a gulp of the wine which was excellent.

'So you run a betting organisation on the Historical Regatta?'

'And on all the other regattas.'

'How long have you been doing this?'

'Just over a year.'

'What made you start it?'

'Oh, I didn't *start* it. It's been going on as far back as anybody can remember. The Venetians have always bet on their various regattas and gondoliers have always taken their bets. But gondoliers are a disorganised race of men and the betting wasn't always as scrupulously run as might be hoped, so they asked me to take it over.'

'May I see?' Peroni held out his hand and the priest drew a wad of banknotes and betting slips out of his cassock. The money amounted to 175,000 lire. 'How many gondoliers collect bets?'

'About thirty on and off.'

'There must be a lot of money involved.'

'A goodish sum, though it's not so profitable as you might think. There are the winnings to be paid, of course, and a commission to all the gondoliers who collect the bets. Such profits as remain I hold in trust for needy gondoliers and their families.'

Peroni looked at him amazed. 'You do it for charity?'

'Well, of course.'

Peroni glanced at the betting slips which he found puzzling. They carried the name of the bettor, the sum bet and the odds offered. This information was followed by names or what appeared to be nicknames bracketed with a colour, a number, a place name or, perplexingly, the word pig.

'Perhaps I'd better explain,' said don Amos, as though Peroni were a slow but willing altar boy, 'betting in Venice has always been a dominant passion. Not so very long ago the children used to learn their alphabets from cards with aces and knaves upon them. And Venetians will bet on anything. The old story of the men wagering upon the precise point at which a fly will alight originated in this city. And betting upon the regattas is an ancient, complex and in many aspects an almost ritualistic affair. The Venetians would never be content with betting merely on the gondoliers to arrive first, second or third. They bet on every place. The colours—white, yellow, violet and so on—are the colours of the different racing gondolas which are drawn by lots.'

'So "The Bull—yellow" means that this person is betting that the Bull will draw a yellow gondola?'

'Exactly.'

'Why is he called the Bull?'

The priest stared in amazement. 'You mean you've never heard of him? The Bull is the greatest regatta champion of all time, so nicknamed because of his extraordinary strength. He's won nine historical regattas consecutively and no power on earth can stop him winning the tenth on the Sunday after next.'

'This one says Accademia Abracadabra Three. What does that mean?'

'The person is betting that the gondolier nicknamed Abracadabra will pass in third position under the Accademia bridge.'

'And the pig?'

'That's a bet on the fourth position at the end. Traditionally the fourth prize is a sucking pig.'

It all seemed very harmless, thought Peroni, but the machine of officialdom had ground into motion and now don Amos as much as himself was caught up in its workings. 'I'm afraid I'll have to ask you to come to the *Questura*,' he said.

The priest gulped down his wine, shrugged and said that if he must he must.

The *calles* of Venice, crowded with people, were a chiaroscuro of sunlight and shade, and as Peroni walked through them with the large priest on their way from the church to the police launch a lot of people stared and even turned round to observe the oddly matched couple.

At first the cause of this seemed to be curiosity and Peroni felt no more than self-conscious. But after a while he had the strange impression that curiosity had given way to menace, and the needle of his own reaction shifted towards fear.

The affair of don Amos and the bets took up the rest of the day. Tactful enquiries among the ecclesiastical authorities revealed that he was considered guilty of nothing worse than eccentricity which manifested itself among other things in his championing of the unofficial St Angela. But he was popular, especially among gondoliers, and no action had been taken against him.

It soon became evident that no action was going to be taken by the police either. The affair was a trifling one. Moreover, a priest is always a priest and nobody wanted trouble with the Cardinal Patriarch of Venice.

The problem was, what was to be done with the betting ring? Now that official action had been taken, it could hardly be allowed to continue uninterrupted. After a hasty conference between Peroni and *dott*. Amabile, the *Questore*, or police chief, of Venice, it was agreed that don Amos should be released immediately on condition that the whole business was wound up and the stake money returned to the punters.

The priest shrugged once again on hearing of this decision. 'It'll only start up again somewhere else,' he said.

'I know it will,' said Peroni, offering his hand. And that settled, he went home.

Home for Peroni in Venice was a large, damp, uncomfortable apartment on the second floor of a crumbling palace not far from the Rialto on the fruit and vegetable side of the bridge. The rooms were high and wide and crowded with all the furniture the landlord had been unable to get rid of elsewhere, so that Peroni lived in the company of several large empty glass cases, a dark and looming cupboard which looked as though it had had ambitions to be a coffin, an excessively frilly dressing table, a broken rocking chair which bucked convulsively when you sat in it and a book-case containing ill-assorted junk shop items including a trumpet, a broken pair of opera glasses, a sombrero and a doll with one eye which, due to a curious flaw in its mechanism, said 'Mamma' apparently of its own volition.

Peroni lived here in a manner of speaking, for crowded with unsuitable furniture though the apartment was, it was in another sense far too empty for his taste. His Neapolitan soul craved for company. He had no family of his own, but until recently had lived with his sister who had married a rolling, jolly northerner and given birth to two children. Peroni doted particularly on his niece, Anna Maria, and felt the loss of them all sadly.

The children's homework and quarrelling, the plates of spaghetti clashing like cymbals at meal times, the television turned on too loud and above all the impassioned family—and extra-family—discussions that went on about confidential police affairs were things which had occasionally irritated him when they were part of his life, but which he now thought of as a desert traveller thinks of cool shade and water.

Women could and did come into the flat, but he had not succeeded in finding one capable of making it feel less empty. Indeed, for some while now he had been feeling that pre-storm unease which comes before love, but so far, though he had had cause to recognise that Venetian women could be lovely, there had not been the smallest flicker or rumble on his horizon.

Meanwhile the flat was to be avoided as much as possible, and he had only come to it now to change his shirt before going out for a pizza and returning to the *Questura*. He went into the bedroom, pausing to look out of its window at the pigeon which lived opposite. The *calle* outside this window was so narrow that you couldn't open an umbrella in it, and across it he often observed this pigeon which talked importantly and incessantly to itself in the window opposite, reflecting that if he stretched across quickly enough he could have roast pigeon for supper.

And as he looked out at the pigeon, he felt a little stab of the fear he had experienced earlier in the company of don Amos. Why he couldn't tell, for it seemed to be as motiveless as the doll's cry of 'Mamma!'

TWO

Tortuosity is endemic to Venice which explains why the inhabitants, when you ask them the way, always reply 'Straight on'; anything more specific would require a full-scale lecture. This tortuosity was reproduced in miniature in the lawyer's office. Such space as there was among the furniture weaved drunkenly in and out, just like the Venetian *calles*, and books, documents, letters, files, ancient letters and photographs lay everywhere, apparently without rhyme or reason.

Yet the lawyer could lay his hands on any single item blindfold, for this office had been his kingdom for all of forty years and he knew his way about it as well as his fellow Venetians knew theirs about the labyrinthine city.

But now it was dark in the *calles* and canals outside and time for the lawyer to go home where he would rapidly munch the meal prepared for him by the daily woman before she left. And as he munched he would flick crafty, accurate looks at a copy of the Venetian daily, the *Gazzettino*, folded beside his plate. He went through it word by word every night and often came across interesting information.

He collected the material on his desk, rose creakily and opened the door behind him. Normally he would have put the material in a bank, but it was too late for that, and his private safe deposit was just as effective.

Having dealt with that, he went back into the office, locked the door behind him, collected his hat, coat and newspaper and went out, locking also the main office door with another of the keys which hung from a chain in his waistcoat pocket.

He didn't merely follow the same route home as he followed every night, he even put his feet in exactly the same position on the paving stones, looking neither right nor left, but occupying himself with the thoughts that rustled in his head. On the whole they were satisfactory thoughts; things were beginning to go well. This new business network had required time and effort, but at last he thought he could flatter himself it was thriving.

And as for the last particular deal, that promised richly. Most richly. There was good reason for cautious optimism.

He didn't notice the figure which was standing round the corner on his left as he came up to a small intersection of *calles*. The first he knew of its presence, indeed, was a blow on the back of his skull which struck with the force of all the stones of Venice forged into one.

But by then it was too late.

By some strange anomaly of leasing there intervenes at street level, between the offices of the Venetian police and the headquarters of the flying squad, a hearing aid centre. To Peroni it was as though the defect catered for at this centre had somehow seeped into the fabric of the building causing wadded dullness which made life in Venice so flat.

The view out of his office window did nothing to cheer him. The Fondamenta San Lorenzo is a desolate backwater of Venice, only visited by those tourists who get lost on their way somewhere else. There is a still, narrow canal and, on the side opposite the *Questura*, a dismal looking geriatric home and the church of San Lorenzo which is plainly going to collapse at any minute. Dramatic cracks zig-zag about its facade like a gigantic spider's web.

But somebody had been foolhardy enough to stick on its facade that same poster for the Goldoni festival which Mr Cornelius Ruskin had observed on his arrival in Venice four days before, and the sight of this did give Peroni a little cheer. And it was while he was studying the little maidservant with a mixture of fondness and drowsy lasciviousness that one of the telephones on his desk rang.

'*Pronto*?' he said, picking up the receiver.

'*Pronto*,' said the voice at the other end which he recognised as that of the about-to-retire *maresciallo* on the desk downstairs, 'There's just been a 113 call—a woman says there's a male body in Corte Balbi near the Fenice Theatre.'

There were laws governing the speed of canal traffic, for without them the centuries-old palaces would topple prematurely to their watery graves. But *Madonna Santissima*, thought Peroni as they chugged along at the speed of an elderly and infirm whale, what happened when there was an emergency?

'Very hot the sun in Venice,' said de Benedetti, the Venetian detective who was also in the launch.

Just like them, thought Peroni, even the sun in Venice had to be different from what it is anywhere else. And what about Peroni's own Neapolitan sun which was hot enough to cook a pizza by? But de Benedetti was a pleasant individual so Peroni conceded that the Venetian sun was indeed very hot.

23

The boat nosed its way under a bridge and out into the lagoon. For a second it seemed to stand still on the water, and then suddenly it thrust itself forward like a jet taking to the sky and roared ahead in a great, soaring arc, spray rising up on either side of it like the wings of an archangel.

Peroni, who was hiring a motor boat privately, decided to try the trick himself one day.

Now the boat seemed to be heading for the island of San Giorgio, but then the curve of its arc became apparent and the nose moved in towards the dome of the Salute. They passed it on their left and, as quickly as it had started, the flight came to an end and they were in the choppy waters of the Grand Canal.

After a couple of minutes the boat turned right into a dark side canal. It seemed deserted, but then from somewhere ahead of them they heard a melancholy, echoing cry of '*Ole!*' which by now Peroni had come to recognise as the centuries-old warning cry of the gondoliers announcing that they were coming round a corner. And sure enough a silver bough-prong reared into view followed by the gondola's long, black body.

'How do they manage to make such tight turns with such long boats, *dottore*?' asked Peroni admiringly.

'It's quite a skill, *dottore*,' said de Benedetti sounding pleased. They were all *dottore*—*dott*. for short—at the *Questura*. This didn't mean that they could practise medicine, but simply that they had degrees—usually in law which is the shortest and simplest of all. 'As a matter of fact, this is just about the trickiest part of Venice for the gondoliers. It's where they do their test.'

'They do a test, do they?'

'Indeed they do,' said de Benedetti, politely shocked at such ignorance, 'They have to be every bit as much specialists in their own line as we do.'

The specialist now rowing towards them, Peroni couldn't help reflecting, had a villainous look about him, but he handled his craft with consummate skill, flicking it almost contemptuously past the police boat with only a few centimetres between them.

Shortly after this they chugged to a halt at a landing stage. 'It's quicker to walk from here,' said de Benedetti.

They didn't have far to go. They crossed over a canal where a notice said '*No Swimming*' which made Peroni wonder who in their senses would want to swim in such water; they turned into a *calle* and saw just ahead of them one of those knots of silent, open-mouthed humanity which indicates the presence of tragedy. When they came up to it, Peroni observed that it was spilling out of a low, narrow archway bearing the name *Sotoportego e corte Balbi o Morosini*.

Headed by Peroni, the cluster of detectives and uniformed police pushed its way through the crowd with the magic word '*Questura*' and passed under the *sotoportego*, lowering their heads as they went, into the *corte*. It was a tiny courtyard, surrounded on three sides by the backs of houses and enlivened by geraniums on the window sills and washing hanging out to dry, including some surprisingly delicate female underwear which aroused the attention of that reprehensible, Neapolitan Peroni who lurked within the commissario.

When they had got through the crowd they saw a human shape lying on the stone flagging almost entirely covered by a piece of tarpaulin which somebody had pulled back to reveal the face of an elderly man which for some reason put Peroni in mind of Pantaloon; not the slapstick, Commedia dell'Arte Pantaloon, but one of Goldoni's crusty, sober, Venetian businessman-type of Pantaloon.

De Benedetti knelt down to pull the tarpaulin off him, revealing an austere, prim looking man in his mid sixties, dressed in a manner that was almost a caricature of old-fashioned conventionality with a black suit and waistcoat with gold watch-chain, a shirt with starched collar and cuffs, a silver-grey tie, black boots and, improbably, spats. His face was as wrinkled as a prune and wore a disapproving expression.

This disapproval may have been caused by the fact that the back of the elderly man's head was missing. In its place was a gaping, cavernous hole, caked with blood where the skull had been shattered.

Peroni lit a black market English cigarette. 'Telephone the magistrature and get hold of a doctor and photographer,' he told one of the uniformed policemen.

'*Si, dottore.*'

With a humming of voices and a shuffling of feet the crowd allowed itself to be dispersed. And then Peroni noticed that de

25

Benedetti was staring at the body in incredulity.

'It's *avvocato* Bixi,' he said, as though in answer to a question.

'A lawyer?' said Peroni with interest. The hotel detective routine gave signs of looking up.

'I don't know him well,' said de Benedetti, 'but I've seen him in court occasionally.'

'We'd better have a look at him,' said Peroni.

A preliminary examination revealed the presence, in an inner pocket, of the lawyer's wallet containing an identity card and 27,000 lire in notes. It also revealed the absence of any keys which looked as though they might have been ripped off a chain dangling against his waistcoat. De Benedetti and Peroni looked at each other when they saw this.

'Maybe he knew something about somebody,' said de Benedetti.

'Lawyers often do,' said Peroni, 'What sort of a lawyer was he?'

'Just a lawyer,' said de Benedetti, and then stopped as though taken by a thought.

'What is it, *dottore*?' Peroni prompted him.

'Nothing really. It just made me think of an old Venetian anecdote. Somebody saw a tombstone with the words "Here lies a lawyer and an honest man" and commented "How can two people be buried in the same tomb?"'

'You're not suggesting that *avv*. What's his name—?'

'Bixi,' said de Benedetti, 'No, no. It only illustrates a popular view of the legal profession.'

'And not altogether unfounded,' said Peroni. He viewed the battered luminary of the Venetian forum speculatively. 'I suspect,' he said, 'that Bixi wasn't killed here at all. For one thing, I would expect more blood and brain spattered about with a massive wound like that. And for another, the heels of those boots are scuffed as though he'd been dragged here. Get some men to look around, *dottore*, will you, and see if they can find any traces?'

'At once, *dottore*.'

'And we'd better get his home and office addresses, too. If we're right about the keys, we might still get a line onto what somebody was after.'

When de Benedetti had gone off on these errands the police doctor and photographer arrived. The doctor was a plump, moist looking Sard, and he and Peroni shook hands with the cordiality of two southerners meeting in the north.

'Well, you won't have to wait for a post mortem to establish the cause of death, will you?' said the Sard, 'Blunt, heavy object. Some time last night I should say off hand.'

Peroni thought of the blunt, heavy object in the picture in the church. St Angela certainly hadn't appeared to frighten off *avv.* Bixi's assailant.

The doctor also tentatively confirmed Peroni's theory that Bixi had been killed elsewhere. 'I'll be able to tell you more exactly when I've had a proper look at him,' he said.

'I'm waiting for the examining magistrate at the moment,' said Peroni, 'Then he's all yours.'

'*A posse ad esse.*' A hoarse, whispery voice seemed to materialise beside Peroni who turned and saw a very tall, thin, tree-like man with dense foliage of prematurely grey hair.

'I beg your pardon?' said Peroni.

'Tron,' said the man, offering his hand which Peroni took hesitantly.

'*Dott.* Tron,' explained the police doctor, 'The examining magistrate.'

'Oh, forgive me,' said Peroni. Everybody shook hands cordially this time including the photographer.

'It's I who should apologise,' said Tron, 'subjecting you to a burst of unannounced Latin. It's a habit I got into at the *Liceo*. People find it tiresome, but it's hard to control. *Dott.* Peroni, I take it?'

Peroni wondered how he knew, but then assumed he must have been told on the telephone.

'*Avv.* Bixi,' said Tron, looking at the motive of their convocation, '*Clarus et venerabile nomen*, an illustrious and venerable name.'

'You knew him?'

'Distantly. We were in different fields.' He looked more closely. '*Fors Clavigera*,' he murmured.

The unlettered looked at him interrogatively.

'Fortune the Club-bearer,' he translated apologetically. 'It

27

looks like a case of that, doesn't it? Well,' he went on more practically, 'I'll be getting the details we want and then I'll give you formal authorisation to remove him to the police morgue.'

Peroni supplied him with such information as the police had gleaned, including an interview somebody had had with the woman who had discovered the body. While he was doing this, de Benedetti returned. 'His office is in Calle della Cortesia,' he reported, 'and his residence is in Calle dei Barcaroli. It looks as though he was going from one to the other when he was killed. And I've got men searching the area.'

'*A verbis ad verbera*,' came a raucous whisper behind them. They turned to the source of it. 'From words to blows,' translated *dott*. Tron, 'that is the process someone appears to have followed with the late *avv*. Bixi.'

'It would certainly appear,' agreed Peroni, 'that there *were* words on some occasion previously. He wasn't assaulted gratuitously or the killer would surely have taken his wallet and gold watch and chain which must be worth a lot with the price of gold today.'

'Words then,' agreed *dott*. Tron, 'and high words at that. Thereafter *furor arma ministrat*. Rage,' he explained before they had a chance to look bewildered, 'furnishes arms.'

'But what arm?' said Peroni. 'That seems to be the next thing to discover.'

'*Hoc age*,' confirmed Tron.

'I know that one,' said the Sard doctor, 'I remember it from school. This do.'

Tron smiled on him benevolently, and then after some further Latin sprinkled exchanges gave Peroni authorisation for the removal of *avv*. Bixi and took his leave, remarking '*Fugit hora*.'

'Is he always like that?' Peroni asked de Benedetti.

De Benedetti nodded. 'He's an odd sort of person,' he said, 'and he has a curious habit of popping up apparently out of nowhere.'

'That was how he appeared just now.'

'But he's able. Very able.'

Peroni was organising the transport of the body when a uniformed policeman brought confirmation of Peroni's theory that the lawyer had been killed elsewhere.

'Just round the corner,' said the man, 'There's a good deal of blood splashed on the wall. The only reason you don't notice it straight away is that the brickwork is a dark red.'

'So why bring him here?' said de Benedetti.

'This isn't a thoroughfare,' said Peroni, 'Here he could be fairly sure that the body would stay hidden overnight, giving him time to get clear.'

The site of the killing was less than half a minute's walk away at an intersection of two narrow *calles*.

'So if he was going home,' said de Benedetti who knew his Venetian geography, 'he would have been walking along here.'

'And the killer could have been waiting for him round the corner in this *calle* here,' said Peroni.

'That's what it looks like, *dottore*.'

'Then when he arrived just here, out steps whoever it is and—poum!'

'With what, *dottore*?'

'I was wondering about that,' said Peroni, 'and it occurred to me that when we were on the way here . . .'

He retraced the brief route they had come, but instead of turning off left under the *sotoportego*, he darted down an equally small and even darker turning which bore the name of Calle de la Madonna. Following him, de Benedetti heard a brief Neapolitan outburst of satisfaction and then saw Peroni coming towards him with a large piece of rock in his hands.

'Not this particular one, of course,' said Peroni.

Behind him, down the *calle*, was a little builder's shed, erected for some work that was being done with gas pipes there, and beside it was a heap of rocks extracted from the pavement of the *calle*.

'And then when it was good and done,' went on Peroni, 'what could be easier than to dump it into the canal there?'

'We can soon see,' said de Benedetti, 'If a rock was dropped into the canal last night, it won't be fully sunk into the mud yet. Venetian mud,' he added characteristically, 'is very dense. It'll be enough to drag it under the bridge.'

'And in the meantime,' suggested Peroni, 'Let's go and look at *avv.* Bixi's office.'

They had just set off when de Benedetti halted in his tracks.

'I've just realised an odd thing,' he said.

'What's that?' asked Peroni.

'The name of this street where he was killed. It's called Calle dei Assassini. Killers' Way.'

THREE

Stray cats are an integral part of Venice. Even the canals seem to imitate their silent, liquid glide. For centuries these cats have lived their independent, rapacious lives in the damp and murky guts of the Serenissima Republic, and the fact that Venice is a pre-eminently fishy town has made them sleek and, all other things being equal, contented.

They don't require human assistance, but they get it. Countless vestals, mostly elderly, minister to them, carrying out little dishes of milk or food at regular hours which the cats expect to be observed punctually.

One of these vestals was Signorina Letizia Fritti. Her truly alarming physical appearance having ruled out the more normal sentimental relationships, she spent all her capacity for love upon the cats. So this morning, before going to work, she went out with a carton of milk, a specially prepared risotto and various plates.

The cats were waiting for her, silent with green and yellow eyes fixed unblinkingly on her as she came out of the front door. The majestic ginger was sitting on the rim of the well, the cheeky grey and white with a battered right ear was lying on a window sill, the elderly black sage was curled up under a dust cart while the stripy Jezabel whose tempestuous love life did so much to keep the Venetian cat population up to par was licking her paws in the morning sunlight that was just slanting up to the steps of the well.

Signorina Letizia prepared the meal in an unfrequented corner where the cats could eat in peace, took in their dirty plates from the previous evening and set off for work.

She crossed over Campo Sant'Angelo into Calle Mandorla and so to the office. The door was unlocked, but this did not surprise her unduly, for he often arrived before she did. What did surprise her was the sight that awaited her inside.

The inner door leading directly into the *avvocato's* room was open, and it looked as though the room had been hit by a tornado. She stepped forward tremulously and looked in.

The room was scarcely recognisable. All the drawers had been pulled out, papers were scattered everywhere, all the books had been toppled from the shelves and even the seats of the chairs had been ripped open.

Then she went into her own little cubbyhole and found that it was in a similar state. She collapsed, stunned, into her chair and looked about her unbelievingly. Burglars, she thought. But where was the *avvocato*?

Faintly she reasoned that he must have arrived first and gone for the police. But no, surely he would have telephoned them?

And then she heard footsteps coming in through the outer door and froze with panic. If it were the burglar returning? But why should he return? More probably it was the *avvocato* himself. She forced herself to get up and walk towards the door, but when she reached it she was surprised to see neither the *avvocato* nor a burglar. Two men were standing there, and long experience in a legal office enabled her to recognise them as policemen. One was a pleasantly ugly young man, obviously a fellow Venetian, with fair hair and freckles. But it was the other who enmeshed her attention.

Early in life Signorina Letizia had reconciled herself to the fact that as far as men were concerned she was a non-starter, and having accepted this it was possible to proceed cheerfully enough along the years. There were just occasional moments when she wondered with a sudden pang what she had missed. This was one of those moments.

'Can I help you?' she said, a tremor in her voice revealing the powerful emotions within.

'Peroni,' said the policeman, his hand outstretched, '*Questura.*'

Of course! The famous commissario Achille Peroni! The living legend of the Italian police! Now she recognised him from the newspapers and television.

'Fritti,' she replied, even more tremulously, giving him her hand, and then repeating the gesture with the second policeman who introduced himself as de Benedetti.

'It looks as though there's been an earthquake here,' said Peroni.

'I've only just discovered it myself,' quavered Signorina Letizia, 'I got here just a moment or two before you . . .'

Suddenly it was all too much. She staggered and nearly fell. Achille Peroni caught her in time, laid her down on a sofa in the entrance, sent his colleague out for a brandy and generally shored her up with solicitude. He made her think of the younger brother she had always wanted.

Peroni's chameleon skill turned him effortlessly into a younger brother. Once he had consciously developed this faculty of divining and assuming the role best suited for every situation. Now it was second nature to him.

When the brandy had brought a little colour back into her cheeks, he judged the moment ripe to proceed. But she forestalled him. 'Where is *avvocato* Bixi?' She looked bewilderedly at the two policemen. 'It wasn't he, then, who called you?'

'I'm afraid we have bad news,' said Peroni, '*Avv*. Bixi is dead.'

'Dead? But he was perfectly well when I left him last night . . .'

'His death wasn't natural.'

'You mean—killed?'

Peroni nodded and paused to let her get accustomed to the idea. Then he said, 'If you're feeling strong enough we might start at the beginning.' She nodded. 'I gather you're his secretary?' She nodded again. 'How long have you been with him?'

'Seventeen years.'

'When did you last see him?'

'Last night when I left the office at seven o'clock.'

'And he stayed behind?'

'That's right. He always did stay in the office after I went home.'

'For long?'

'Usually. I sometimes had to telephone or call during the

evening as late as ten o'clock, and he was always here.'

'Do you know what he was going to do last night after you left?'

'No.'

'Did he have any appointments?'

'I'd have to look in his diary.'

She got up and made for Bixi's office with Peroni and de Benedetti solicitously flanking her.

'He always kept it on his desk, but—' She gestured weakly at the desk which had been swept clear of everything. 'Somewhere here—' And she started to sort through the chaos on the floor.

Peroni looked about him. 'Where does that lead to?' he asked, indicating a door behind the desk.

'Nowhere,' said Signorina Letizia, 'I mean it just goes out onto a canal. It was used when people had their own private gondolas.'

There was a window in the same wall and Peroni went to look out of it. He saw the dark, still water of a narrow canal with a cabbage-stalk floating motionless on it and, immediately outside the door, he could just make out the corner of a small, stone landing stage.

He turned again to observe the office, listening with his Neapolitan inner ear to catch its echoes. The waves of anonymous violence still rolled about the walls, but behind them Peroni thought there was the hint of something else: an older, long established, dry sound, the sound of the dead lawyer's thoughts scratching and rustling in the air. The parsimonious, businesslike thoughts of a solid, bourgeois Goldonian Pantaloon? Or was there something other, something counter and strange about them that might entail the thinker having the back of his skull shattered in a *calle* named Killers' Way? Unfortunately these thoughts were on a wavelength Peroni couldn't catch. Like the cries of bats.

'Here it is.'

Signorina Letizia Fritti was holding out a diary bound in dark blue imitation leather. Peroni flipped through the pages to the previous day. There were four names written in a precise, elderly handwriting, three with times against them and one with a telephone number. All would have to be checked. But the one that came last would take priority.

'Tonino,' it said with linear simplicity, '8.00 p.m.'

Signorina Letizia was baffled. She knew of no Tonino.

'A relative?' suggested Peroni.

To the best of her knowledge he had no relatives.

Peroni asked de Benedetti to visit all the apartments in the building enquiring whether anyone had seen a man entering around 8 p.m. the previous evening or leaving subsequently.

'You might enquire at the bar opposite, too, *dottore*,' he added. 'It looks straight onto the front door.'

'Very good, *dottore*.'

Peroni continued to question Signorina Letizia, but learned little of value. He had largely been involved in civil law, she said, and she knew of no client or opponent whose passions the lawyer might have whipped up to homicidal pitch; nor did she know of any information for which somebody might so viciously plunder the office.

'There's just one thing that sometimes struck me as a little peculiar,' she said. Peroni looked at her in absorbed fraternal attention. 'Just lately I've had a strange impression that he was—well, involved in some other activity. Something distinct from his legal business.'

Peroni pressed the point. But the nature of this hypothetical activity remained a mystery. Signorina Fritti had had no clue of it from the letters or documents she typed or the telephone calls she received.

'Signorina,' said Peroni, trying another tack, 'What sort of a person was *avv*. Bixi?'

She thought about it. Her relationship with the lawyer had been strictly formal. In seventeen years they had never spoken to each other with anything except the polite *lei*—a *tu* would have been unthinkable between them. Their exchanges had been made up of countless *Buon giorno, Signorinas* and *Buon giorno, avvocatos*, *Per favores*, *Grazies* and *Pregos*, and at the end of them all she had really no idea of what sort of person he had been.

So Peroni let her go home. Then, just as she was at the door, he thought of something else. 'Did *avv.* Bixi employ anybody except yourself?'

'There's a man,' she said, 'who took messages by hand and ran other odd errands.' She looked at her watch. 'He should be in any minute now.'

'What's his name?'

'It must seem very silly,' said Signorina Letizia, 'but I don't know. He's always known by his nickname.'

'And what is that?'

'The Undertaker.'

FOUR

De Benedetti had spoken to an old lady living alone, to a dentist's receptionist with a lisp, to three friendly girls at the Ca' Foscari university, to a glass-blower with a broken ankle and to a bleary-eyed lady in a dressing-gown who said she had been working late the night before. None of them had seen anybody who might have been Tonino entering or leaving the night before.

So he went to the bar opposite. It was one of those tiny bars, scarcely bigger than cupboards, that are a Venetian speciality. There was just about room for an espresso machine, a perspex container with brioches in it, the necessary bottles, a squawking transistor and, with a tight squeeze, a customer or two. It was empty at the moment except for an overblown lady doing her nails behind the cash register.

'*Buon giorno*,' she said.

'*Buon giorno*,' said de Benedetti, '*Questura.*'

That made her sit up for a second. Then she decided it was something to do with her licence and began to look wily. '*Si?*' she said.

'Were you in here last night?'

It didn't sound like the licence. 'I'm always in here except when I'm closed. Wouldn't be economical to hire a waiter.'

'Round about eight o'clock last night, did you see a man going into that door over there?' He indicated it.

35

'Yes, I did.'

'You did?'

'Why d'you look so surprised? Want me to say no?'

'How can you be so certain?'

'Well, I know it was eight because the radio had just said it was. And there were no customers then, so I was looking out of the window. And I saw him go in.' She suddenly looked concerned. '*Mamma mia*! He hasn't done anything, has he?'

'I've no idea,' said de Benedetti honestly.

'Well, I certainly hope not—he was such a nice looking boy!'

'Boy?'

'Well, young man. In his early twenties I'd say.'

'Can you tell me anything else about him?'

'One thing for sure. He was a gondolier.'

'Now that,' said Peroni, 'is a coincidence. Tonino is the second gondolier to be inscribed in our books in the last half hour.'

'Who's the other, *dottore*?'

'A man known as the Undertaker. Signorina Letizia told me about him. Strictly speaking he's an ex-gondolier. He had to give up his gondoliering for health reasons about six months ago and Bixi employed him as a messenger. By the way, how did the lady in the bar know the man she saw was a gondolier?'

'Striped shirt, straw hat and black trousers. Everything short of the gondola itself.'

'Well, it should be easy to trace him.'

'I'm not so sure, *dottore*,' said de Benedetti, 'Tonino is a common name.'

'After St Anthony, presumably.' St Anthony, as far as Peroni was concerned, blew neither hot nor cold. He had a high reputation, but wasn't even in the same class as the patron of Naples whose image on a chunky medal hung beneath Peroni's Pucci tie. 'What's the easiest way of running him down?'

'Send a launch discreetly round all the various gondola stations, I should suggest, *dottore*.'

'Get them to organise it at the *Questura*, will you?' said Peroni.

While de Benedetti was on the phone, the office door opened and a man appeared. There could be no doubt as to his identity. Indeed, he seemed deliberately to play the part of an undertaker, for he wore a black suit and tie. Nature had rendered him gaunt and cadaverous, but the expression of grim mourning was his own.

Like Signorina Letizia Fritti he recognised the police at once and looked as though he would have liked to withdraw. But at the same time he took in the chaos.

'What,' he asked in a hushed voice, 'has come to pass? And where is my employer?'

'*Avv*. Bixi is dead. He was murdered last night.'

Peroni watched a shifty expression pass over the Undertaker's face like a cloud over a shadow. It couldn't be more precisely defined, but it certainly wasn't of grief.

'May he rest in peace,' said the Undertaker unctuously, raising his eyes to the electric light bulb, 'I had best be going my way.'

'Just a minute,' said Peroni, 'One or two questions first.' He had instinctively assumed a military manner which sliced through the Undertaker's mournful evasiveness. 'Name?'

'Beltrame, Luigi.'

'Address?'

The Undertaker answered this and the other formal questions with an expression that suggested he was giving away funeral trade secrets. He confirmed that he had started to work for the lawyer about six months before in the capacity of what he described as a 'personal assistant'.

'How did he come to know of you in the first place?'

'My late employer,' said the Undertaker still looking at the electric light bulb, 'had handled numerous small legal matters concerning gondoliers and was cognisant with the ambience.'

'When did you last see him?'

The Undertaker fetched a windy sigh. 'Yesterday after luncheon. He entrusted me with some documents to deliver to the court.'

'You didn't come back?'

'He intimated my presence would not be further required.'

'Why should somebody kill *avv*. Bixi?'

'Only the good Lord could divine.'

But Peroni felt certain that the Undertaker could divine too, if he wanted—that the Undertaker, in fact, might be privy to that part of Bixi's activities which had baffled Signorina Fritti.

'*Avv.* Bixi used to work late in the evening. Were you ever here on those occasions?'

'My late employer sometimes availed himself of my services in the evening,' he allowed cautiously.

'What for?'

'The conveyance of communications to clients and colleagues.'

'Only legal matters?'

The Undertaker looked as if Peroni had advocated the use of plastic coffins. 'With what other matters should my late employer be concerned?'

Evasion stood out as plainly as a stranded whale in the gulf of Naples, and Peroni was pleased, for where people evaded, there was something to evade.

De Benedetti came over from the telephone. 'Settled,' he said.

'Last night at eight o'clock,' Peroni went on, 'the *avvocato* had an appointment with somebody called Tonino. Who could that be?'

'My late employer did not inform me.'

'You were a gondolier yourself until recently. Did you have any colleagues of that name?'

'The name is not uncommon.'

Cut, thrust and unctuous parry, it went on until finally Peroni let him go, watching him make his exit with an expression that suggested he was walking behind a third-class funeral.

'Try and find out something about these legal matters that Bixi handled involving gondoliers,' said Peroni when he had gone.

'*Si, dottore*,' said de Benedetti, making a note of it.

'And I want to know more about the Undertaker, too,' said Peroni, 'Birth, life and miracles.'

'Check,' said de Benedetti who had picked up the word from television.

The police launch chugged to a halt at the gondola station on the Riva degli Schiavoni and *dott*. Muso—Milanese, unmarried, running to fat and fury—got out. He dabbed irritably at the sweat on his neck and then went up to a tall gondolier.

'*Questura*,' he said unnecessarily.

The tall gondolier nodded in a disrespectful way.

'Are there any gondoliers at this station named Tonino?' Muso asked.

'Two.'

'And where are they?'

'One of them's dead.'

'If he's dead he can't be on the station.'

'Oh yes he can, because his boat's still being rowed on behalf of the widow by a substitute. So Tonino's still on the establishment until his widow dies.'

'And the other?' said Muso impatiently.

'Tonino!' called the tall gondolier. 'There's a gentleman from the *Questura* would like a word with you.'

A wizened little gondolier with gnarled hands and a leathery, almost black face appeared from a little hut near the jetty. 'Well?' he said, sounding as though he'd been disturbed in the middle of a drink.

Plainly this couldn't be the Tonino they were looking for who was said to be young and good looking. Prickling with irritation, Muso took the second Tonino's name and address and, with the gondoliers' silent, mocking looks pinging into the back of his neck like children's arrows, went back to the police launch which then swung out into the lagoon around the vast bows of a ship carrying machine tools from the Soviet Union.

Back in his office, Peroni stared at *avv.* Bixi's dark blue imitation leather diary. It would have to be gone through carefully, day by day, copying out the names in it on one of the *Questura*'s weary typewriters. This list, when completed, would be divided up among the detectives so that everyone who had had dealings with *avv.* Bixi could be checked.

But in the meantime, Peroni allowed himself a sneak preview. Flipping quickly through the winter months he was confirmed in his suspicion that a lawyer would not confide anything revealing to an office diary. Names, telephone numbers, addresses, but, at a quick glance, all well within the confines of the legal citadel.

Until, at the beginning of July, Peroni saw something which made the little hairs at the nape of his neck bristle in wild surmise. At the top of the page, above the date, were hastily scribbled three place names. Accademia, Ca' Rezzonico, Rialto. The three places where don Amos's pious gondoliers had been taking bets.

He pondered this, then returned to the diary. Nothing more in July, and now he was in August almost up to the lawyer's death. And then, exactly a week before the murder, another place name scribbled above the date. Harry's Bar.

Peroni knew Harry's Bar well. The unofficial branch of the American Embassy in Venice. The place you went to when somebody else was paying the bill. The place where Ernest Hemingway had drunk such a legendary quantity of those wonderful dry martinis which blast multi-coloured rockets into the sky of your head. But there was something else about Harry's Bar.

For it, too, was a gondola rank.

'Is there a gondolier named Tonino here?'

Muso had reached San Silvestro, having bagged five more Tonino's, not one of whom could remotely be called young or good looking, and by now the sheer fatuousness of the question seemed to call down ridicule on his head.

'That's right!' said a fat gondolier cheerfully, 'he's just coming in now. Over there!'

Muso looked across the gleaming water of the Grand Canal and, for a moment, couldn't believe his luck. There, standing on the poop of a gondola, rowing in towards the mooring poles, was a gondolier, a Tonino, unquestionably young and good looking.

'Name?' he demanded when this gondolier was free of his customers.

'Pasquetti, Tonino,' said the gondolier looking alarmed.

'And where were you last night?'

'In Padua.'

'In Padua?' What would a gondolier be doing in Padua at the height of the season? 'I suppose,' with irony, 'you can prove it?'

'Of course he can,' said the fat gondolier, 'and so can I—*and* several hundred other people who saw us give a concert in Padua.'

'A concert?' repeated Muso, frustrated and baffled.

'That's right,' said Tonino Pasquetti, 'I'm a tenor with the Singing Gondoliers Choir.'

'Have you come back to confess?'

Don Amos was in front of the fresco of St Angela, removing the white stubs of the candles that had been consumed in the forest fire of devotion.

'No,' said Peroni, 'I've come back to ask some more questions.'

The grey luxuriance of don Amos's eyebrows rose in ironic interrogation.

'Do you know anything of *avv.* Bixi?'

'I know that he was murdered.' He crossed himself and murmured, '*Requiem eternam.*'

'But did you know him when he was alive?'

'No.'

'He never approached you?'

'No.' Don Amos seemed to hesitate, then he said, 'He approached some of the gondoliers who took bets.'

Peroni drew an inaudible sigh of relief. He had taken a step, perhaps a stride, towards the truth.

'Why did he approach them?'

'He wanted to know who organised the betting.'

'But they didn't tell him?'

'No.' Don Amos hunched his black arms like a crow's wings in a deprecating shrug. 'Not that I was ashamed of it, but one didn't want the whole of Venice chattering about a gambling ring run by a priest. His Eminence would be most distressed.' His tone suggested that the last consideration didn't bother him unduly.

'You told me at the *Questura*,' said Peroni, 'that the betting was only run at the Accademia, Ca' Rezzonico and the Rialto. You didn't by any chance overlook Harry's Bar?'

'No.' Don Amos was quite firm about this.

They seemed to have reached a dead end. But was it as dead as it seemed? Peroni thought he would like to know more about the big priest. He glanced up at St Angela and contemplated lighting a candle to her in exchange for the truth about him, but decided against it.

She would have been on don Amos's side.

41

Muso had reached the Rialto. And how many more Toninos could there be between there and the railway station? And even then he would only have covered the Grand Canal.

He climbed wearily out of the police launch and made his way up the Riva Ferro towards a little cluster of gondoliers standing near their bobbing, black mistresses.

'*Questura*,' he said yet again, 'I'm making enquiries concerning a gondolier named Tonino.'

Knowing smiles passed from gondolier to gondolier. 'There are two here,' said the senior of the group. 'One of them's home with a bad back. The other's doing the ferrying.'

Apart from the normal gondola rides, which is where the gondoliers make their money, there is also the chore of ferrying the general public backwards and forwards across the Grand Canal. This is shared among the gondoliers at those ranks which are also ferry points.

They all now looked across the Canal to the ferry gondola, and Muso suddenly saw surprise and bewilderment billow over the gondoliers' faces. A second later he understood the cause. At the other bank was a gondola full of passengers, all staring, with expressions he could guess at rather than see, at an empty poop.

With a rumble of fury, Muso charged heavily towards the Rialto Bridge. Scattering alarmed tourists and Venetians carrying comestibles on their heads or bumping trolleys up and down the steps, he ran up and along the top of the bridge between the expensive jewellery shops and down the other side.

But even before he got to the bottom he knew he was wasting his time. In the confusion of the fruit and vegetable market with the crowd heaving and jostling like the pigeons in St Mark's Square at feeding time, and with narrow *calles* leading off in all directions, as numerous as the quills of a porcupine, it was difficult enough to find someone who wanted to be found, impossible to find someone who didn't.

There was little doubt he had come upon the right Tonino at last. And lost him.

FIVE

Gemma had her daytime being in a zoological garden of glass.
About her groups of dolphins leapt skywards, black bulls pawed
the ground, lions and tigers stalked, monstrous fish swam silently
in the air. There were less substantial flora and fauna, too,
brightly coloured and small enough to fit into a match-box,
produced with two or three deft flicks of the blower's tube.

For Gemma worked in one of the innumerable glassware
shops of Venice and, as she had the delicacy and fragility of the
products she sold, it had occurred to more than one tourist that it
would be nice to wrap her up and take her home as a souvenir of
Venice.

It was nearly closing time which was a relief because this
evening she would see Tonino. She was worried about Tonino
because just lately he'd been preoccupied, his mind constantly
reaching into another world which she couldn't see.

Men in general, she knew, and gondoliers in particular did
have areas of their lives which they kept closed from their
womenfolk, and being an old fashioned type of girl with generations of Venetian femininity behind her, Gemma accepted this
uncomplainingly. But she wished he would tell her nevertheless,
if only because she might be able to help. Perhaps this evening.

'Gemma!'

She looked up and saw her young brother, Renatino, a twelve-
year-old with uncharacteristic red hair. He never came into the
shop, a don't-touch world of glass and a small boy being mutually
inimical. This, coupled with the fact that he was swelling with
drama, worried her.

'What is it, Renatino?'

'Tonino—' Her breath checked in fear. 'He's run away and the
police are looking for him. A lawyer was killed last night, and
they say Tonino did it.'

The sun in Gemma's private sky was suddenly extinguished.

The boat glided silently over the black water except for a whispered drip as the oar was lifted. It wasn't a gondola, but a sandolo

43

which is a more modest craft, lacking the magnificent silver bow-prong, but with the same characteristic iist to starboard.

The Undertaker had chosen it because it was less obtrusive. Not that he had much fear of being seen at this hour; and even if he were seen, he was hardly likely to be recognised.

He was satisfied to find that he still had his old dexterity with the oar. The sandolo responded with smooth docility to his handling of it, slipping easily round corners, riding the water with flowing ease as he shifted his weight instinctively at the right moment.

Within minutes he was in the canal he had been making for and had spotted the back of *avv.* Bixi's office which gave onto the canal—the only possible approach now that the office itself was sealed and guarded. He edged the boat in towards it. Now was the dangerous moment. There was a policeman in the building and the nosy old cow who lived upstairs had hearing as sharp as splintered glass and would be quite capable of looking out with a torch if she heard an untoward noise below.

He tied the sandolo up at the little stone landing place from which a door led into *avv.* Bixi's office and then climbed out of the boat. He knelt quickly and felt in the darkness for the chain which was on an iron ring just below the water level. He found it, grasped it with both hands and pulled gently. By the weight he could tell that the box was on the other end.

Avv. Bixi had thought nobody knew of the existence of this waterproof metal box which he had used as a sort of private safe deposit for documents or valuables that reached him when the banks were closed. No burglar indeed would think of looking on the canal bed (once every papal death they drained the canals for cleaning and the stink of it was almost tangible in the Venetian sky, but ample warning was given of this).

Quite early in his career as lawyer's clerk the Undertaker had spied out the secret of this box, and now he was to exploit it for the first time. Provided, of course, there was something he could exploit. What Bixi hid away there was always valuable to him; it remained to be seen whether it could be made valuable to the Undertaker.

He pulled again at the chain. It was more difficult than he had suspected, but it came up and surfaced, for all his caution with a dripping that sounded torrential in the Undertaker's ears. He put the box gently on the landing stage, forcing himself to wait for a moment to make sure nobody opened a shutter to look out.

There was no question of breaking open the lock here, but he hoped with the aid of a screw-driver he had brought with him to prise away the ring that attached the box to the chain, and in fact a few minutes of silent levering did it. The Undertaker edged the box as gently as he could into the sandolo, got in himself and rode back through the darkness with his prize.

Night was draped over Venice like a sheet that might at any moment become a shroud. It draped over a palace near the fruit and vegetable market where a vulnerable Neapolitan policeman was dreaming of a girl he had not yet met. Over the *Questura* mortuary where, in a large drawer, there lay a dead lawyer, his beard still growing and the whiteness of his prune-like face livid with patches of darkish purple. Over one house where a young gondolier was in hiding and another where a girl, as delicate as a glass ornament, lay awake and in anguish over him. Over the Vivaldi Hotel where Mr Cornelius Ruskin was dreaming that he had to give a lecture on Goldoni in the basilica of St Mark's, but had dropped his notes in the Grand Canal.

But at last fingers of light felt their way across the lagoon to twitch at the sheet and slowly pull it off. The Queen of the Adriatic stirred and found herself alive for yet another day. Then, her toilette accomplished, she prepared herself to face the tourists.

Dott. Amabile, the *Questore* of Venice, who had just opened his regular morning conference, was a native of Friuli and possessed the solid, down-to-earth quality of the inhabitants of that region. He also had the air of an old fashioned headmaster whose occasional gruffness, you suspected, was a result of shyness. And as he was very tall and invariably wrapped in a cloud of pipe-smoke, he made you think of a mountain enveloped in cloud.

'And then, *dottore*?' he prompted Muso with a slight inclination of his peak within the eddying smoke.

'And then,' said Muso, 'I went to the home of this Tonino, but he hadn't been there since yesterday morning. A watch has been kept on the house all night, but he hasn't been back there.'

'What family has he?'

'There's only a mother. A bit of a Germanic type—she comes from Bolzano. The father was a gondolier. He died when Tonino was seven.'

'Did the mother know he was going to see *avv*. Bixi?'

'She says she didn't.' Muso's tone was vindictive. 'But then she tried to pretend he was with her all the evening. But I knew she was lying, and I managed to get two reports from neighbours who heard him coming home at two in the morning!' He seemed to get personal satisfaction from this.

There was a pause while *dott.* Amabile replenished the cloud about him.

'Girl?' The word issued from the smoke as though pickled in contemplation.

'I beg your pardon?' said Muso, off balance.

'Does he have a girl?' Headmasterly patience. 'If he does, she might lead us to him.'

'I'll get onto that right away, *dottore*.'

But Peroni saw the twitch in Muso's cheek and correctly diagnosed it as having been caused by exasperation at not having thought of the girl angle himself. Peroni had been following the exchanges with a certain gloom. The Tonino development had stifled the exhilaration he had felt at being involved in something with headline potentiality at last. His only satisfaction was that his theory about the rock had proved correct. One had in fact been dragged up from underneath the bridge, and the Scientific Squad had found traces of Bixi's hair and blood on it.

One of the telephones on the *Questore's* desk rang. Amabile picked it up, at the same time rumbling his surname into the mouthpiece. The rest of the conversation consisted of quackings at the other end, punctuated by impassive umms from the *Questore* and terminated by a '*Grazie, dottore.*'

'The full medical report is on its way,' he said, 'but the salient point is that *avv*. Bixi was killed not before eleven o'clock on Monday night and not after one a.m. yesterday morning.'

'And Tonino got home at two,' said Muso, letting the sentence fall into the conversation like the rock that had smashed *avv*. Bixi's skull and fallen into the canal.

The Undertaker's mother had been bedridden for the last ten years of her life, but her personality had continued to dominate the top floor apartment where they lived in a dilapidated building near the Fondamenta Nuova. Her bed had been by the window, and through this she hauled up baskets of provisions on a rope and then, on the kitchen stove, which was by the other side of her bed, she had cooked for her son and herself.

Two years previously she had died, but her personality had so strongly imprinted itself on the atmosphere that it was as though she were still in command there. The Undertaker talked to her—he had no other intimate—and if he had been asked whether he really believed her to be there, he would probably have found it hard to answer.

So it was the previous evening that he had showed her the metal box from the canal bed, and she had watched in silence while he broke open the lock.

The contents came as a shock to him. He had been hoping for cash or documents containing exploitable information. But this was in no predictable category.

'What is it, mamma?' he breathed into the dark room, but she didn't answer, no doubt engaged in puzzling over the problem herself.

He examined it carefully from all angles, then observed it like a cat at a mousehole as though he expected it to stand up on the table and explain itself. Then finally he raised his head in an attitude of listening.

'True,' he said unctuously after a minute, 'True, true. A wise mother always knows what is best, and it is a foolish son indeed who disregards her counsels. As you say, mamma, we shall sleep upon the matter and trust that the morrow will bring a fresh vision.'

So he had put it carefully away, wished his mother goodnight, switched out her bedside light and gone to his own austere bedroom dominated by a painting of an Arcadian funeral procession he had picked up in a junk shop.

And now this morning he was back with the problem again. But for once his mother had been wrong, for the morrow had brought no fresh vision. The contents of the metal box remained as baffling as ever.

'Whatever shall we do with it, mamma?' he said, 'It appears the best course is to dispose of it. "What doesn't earn its way, doesn't deserve house stay," as you always put it yourself, mamma.'

And at that moment there was a sound which might have been a little gust of wind, or the flapping of a pigeon's wings outside, or a mouse stirring a piece of paper. But to the Undertaker it sounded exactly like the whisper of an elderly female voice.

'Sell it!' said the voice, 'Sell it!'

In the first moments of terrified shock, it never occurred to Gemma that Tonino might really have killed the lawyer. The idea was wicked and impossible. Tonino would have been no more capable of murder than flying.

But as the night wore on the doubts began to creep into her room like small demons attracted by her anguish. There was another side to Tonino of which she knew nothing; he had another life from which she was barred. How could she be sure that in that other life he had not done something frightful which the lawyer had learned of, and that Tonino had then killed the lawyer to prevent a criminal charge?

By dawn the new monstrous Tonino whom she didn't believe in, but hated just the same, had become more real for her than the old Tonino.

She couldn't face the shop, so her mother telephoned to say she was ill, and Gemma sat staring out of the window at the diabolical Tonino who hovered on the air wherever she looked.

The telephone rang and she jumped to answer it. '*Pronto*?'

'Gemma—'

The single utterance of her name by his voice dispelled the other Tonino as a black cloud is dispelled by a strong wind.

'Tonino—'

'Listen carefully, Gemma . . .'

She listened, nodded, said '*Si*', several times, then '*Ciao*' and put the telephone down.

Her mother disapproved vociferously, but Gemma was adamant, and a few minutes later she was half-running, half-walking through Venice. When she got to the house, she ran up the stairs to the second floor and knocked three times slowly, twice quickly

48

on the door of the apartment facing her.

Immediately it was opened and she allowed herself to be pulled inside and wrapped in a tremendous embrace which, for all the glass-like fragility of her appearance, she not only survived but adored.

'What is this place?' she asked when they paused for breath.

'It's a flat belonging to some people my mother cleans for. They're away on holiday.'

'But why hide, Tonino? Why run away? It only makes things worse!'

'Once the police get hold of you they never let you go. But if they don't find me, they'll have to look for whoever really did kill *avv.* Bixi.'

'But did you know him, Tonino?'

'I'll tell you about that another time. For the moment it's enough that I didn't kill him. I didn't kill him, Gemma!'

She knew he was telling the truth.

By overwhelming mutual consent they resumed the interrupted embrace, and there was no telling when it would have ended this time if it hadn't been for an interruption which was not of their choosing.

A gunshot blast exploded into the lock of the door, the door burst open and suddenly the room was filled with police.

SIX

When the boy from the *Trattoria alla Conchiglia*, just a few doors down from the *Questura*, arrived with *dott.* Peroni's coffee he was intercepted by Policewoman Sofia Michelangelo who said not to worry, she would take it to *dott.* Peroni. Policewoman Sofia Michelangelo was always on the look out for such indirect approaches to *dott.* Peroni.

Her flat was only a couple of minutes from his palace just the other side of the Rialto Bridge, and she would often find herself, without having taken any conscious decision, making lengthy deviations in order to pass near it. Her ambition was to be invited into it. Not so much for carnal orgies, however, but simply to tidy the place up—she was sure it must be in an awful mess—and cook a delicious meal for two.

Policewoman Sofia Michelangelo's feelings for *dott*. Peroni were passionately unpolicewomanly.

But she was from Vicenza and she had the innate respectability of nicely brought up girls from that city, and this prevented her from showing the smallest sign of what she felt. *Dott*. Peroni himself was unaware of it. Even *dott*. de Benedetti, who was a walking x-ray unit, had guessed nothing. Which was just as well because *dott*. de Benedetti was always on the look out for raw material for jokes. Altogether Policewoman Sofia Michelangelo found *dott*. de Benedetti quite exasperating.

She knocked at *dott*. Peroni's door and then, when he called out 'Avanti!' went in with the coffee. He was looking out of the window.

'Good morning, Michelangelo,' he said, 'That's a very pretty skirt you're wearing.'

She chimed with inner delight. 'I got it at Luisa Spagnoli,' she said.

There was no knowing where they might not have gone from there if somebody hadn't knocked at the door. It was *dott*. de Benedetti. It just had to be him.

'Michelangelo on the team?' he said. 'Then it's as good as settled—the rest of us might as well pack up and go home.'

The worst of *dott*. de Benedetti's facetiousness was that there was no answering it. Michelangelo did the next best thing and ignored it.

'It's Tonino, *dottore*,' he said, 'they've found him—Amabile's theory about the girl worked. He's downstairs now.'

'Have him brought up here, will you, *dottore*?' said *dott*. Peroni, 'and sit in on the interview yourself. You, too, Michelangelo—I'd like you to take notes.'

Better than nothing, she supposed to herself, sitting by the window and carefully smoothing out the skirt which *dott*. Peroni liked.

A couple of minutes later Tonino was brought in. Not really a murdering sort of person to look at, she thought. Tall and dark, with powerful hands and arms, the classical young gondolier.

And if she hadn't had such a very elevated standard of comparison, she would probably have considered him handsome, too.

Peroni was the very image of paternity, severe but benign. He called Tonino 'My boy', waved him to a chair and offered him an English cigarette. If you had been able to follow the scene without sound track you would have sworn that Peroni was informing himself of the boy's final exam results before buying him a motor-bike.

'Let's go to Monday night,' said Peroni when the formal questions were done, 'You had an appointment with *avv*. Bixi at eight o'clock. Why?'

Tonino licked his lips. 'On Monday,' he said, 'he came to see me at the Rialto where I work—only I hadn't any idea who he was, of course—but he seemed to know all about me. And he'd heard—'' He checked in confusion.

'Well?' Peroni prompted gently, paternity aloft.

'He'd heard—he said he'd received complaints that I'd been overcharging. He said he would have to take official action against me. I begged him not to because it would have meant my losing my licence.'

Peroni glanced at de Benedetti. 'Overcharging by gondoliers is viewed very seriously by the municipality,' de Benedetti explained.

Which didn't stop it being just about as common as nose blowing, thought Peroni. Aloud he just said, 'And had you been overcharging?'

Tonino hung his head. 'Yes,' he said. Then suddenly his expression went dark. 'Everybody overcharges in Venice, and the higher up they are the more they overcharge!' he spat furiously. 'The politicians take graft—the whole of Venice is floating on a sea of bribery! And nobody says anything, nobody cares. But when a gondolier overcharges, everybody gets up on their hind legs and starts shouting in horror! And remember we only work properly from May to September. We have to make enough in that time to live for the rest of the year. And most of us with families. That's how it's always been in Venice—the gondolier's made the scapegoat for the whole city!'

His face was distorted with hatred at the injustice of it. Then, all of a sudden this drained from him and he seemed to go limp. 'I was saving up to buy my own gondola and get married,' he said flatly. 'I know I shouldn't have done it, but I'm not the only one. Why did he have to pick on me?'

Why indeed, thought Peroni. 'What happened next?' he said.

'He said he'd speak to the people who'd complained and see if he could persuade them to withdraw their complaints. He told me to come to his office that evening at eight o'clock.'

'And you went.'

Tonino nodded. 'This time he was different. Very friendly and smooth, like. He said there was a chance that perhaps it could all be forgotten. All I had to do in exchange was—well, tell him things.'

'What sort of things?'

'Things I saw, things I heard. Gondoliers do get to know one or two things that people would prefer to be kept secret. He said that if I brought him bits of news like that, not only would he forget about the overcharging, but he might pay me a bit as well.'

'And you?'

Tonino hung his head again. 'I said I'd try. Well, what else could I do? He'd got me on a hook!'

'And that was the end of the interview?'

'Yes.'

'What time did you leave him?'

'About half past eight.'

'And what did you do then?'

'Oh, I just walked about—had a few glasses of wine and thought about it.'

'Till two o'clock in the morning?' Peroni's paternal voice was suddenly hard.

'Oh, no,' said Tonino, 'Till I went to dinner.'

Peroni and de Benedetti looked at each other. 'What dinner?'

'The pre-Regatta dinner.' In spite of his situation, Tonino almost reared with pride. 'You see, I'm rowing in the Historical Regatta for the first time, and this is a special dinner they have for the competitors and judges and everybody connected with it.'

'What time did you get to this dinner?'

'A bit late because I was trying to think what to do about *avv*. Bixi. About half past nine.'

'And what time did you leave it?'

'Oh, a bit late. Dinners like that always go on a while. Quarter to two, I should say.'

For the second time Peroni and de Benedetti looked at each other. *Avv*. Bixi had been killed between eleven and one and throughout that time—subject to checking—Tonino had been under the eyes of probably twenty or thirty people at a crowded dinner party.

On the balcony of his room at the Vivaldi Hotel overlooking the lagoon, Mr Cornelius Ruskin poured himself another cup of coffee and spread a buttered rusk with apricot jam. The water glinted in lazy splendour before him, the sky was very blue, a water-bus was just leaving for a round tour of the islands and tourists were milling, compact and ant-like but happy looking, up and down a bridge on the San Marco side of the hotel.

The thought of New York somewhat ruffled the serenity of Mr Ruskin's Venetian happiness. Soon he would be back there where the streets weren't full of water and the prospects were not pleasing. He would have liked to live in Venice, but economically the idea just wasn't on. Fortunately he still had two weeks in which to revel in canals, *fritto misto* at the Madonna restaurant, and Campari and soda and 'Hello Dolly!' (selections from) outside Florians. And of course the Goldoni festival with the incomparable Maddalena Spinelli. It was a lot to be thankful for.

Mr Ruskin picked up the Gazzettino (he always made a point of reading the Venetian paper while in Venice). There was a surprisingly large headline this morning. *Avv. Tullio Bixi Assassinated between office and home*. Odd. Venice was scarcely a murderous city. He could recall no outstanding murders in the 18th century. Passions ran high as in the famous battle between Goldoni and the *Abbé* Chiari, but nobody ever got hurt. Not physically.

Just as Mr Ruskin was reading that the investigation was under the brilliant direction of Commissario Achille Peroni (*The Rudolf Valentino of the Italian police*? They wouldn't swallow *that* in the States!) the phone rang in his suite within. Mr Ruskin went to answer it without particular curiosity; a lot of people knew he was here.

'*Pronto*?' he said, lining up his careful, academic Italian just in case of need.

'Professor Ruskin,' said the desk clerk who didn't let foreigners speak Italian, 'somebody wishes to speak with you on an outside line. A Signor Rossi.'

Mr Ruskin frowned; he didn't know any Rossis, the Italian equivalent of Smith. 'OK,' he said, 'put him through.'

There was a click, a pause and then another click.

'Professor Ruskin?' The voice was male and pronounced his name Rooskeen.

'*Sono io*,' he said, '*Cosa desidera*?'

As the voice started to speak again, Mr Ruskin recognised the musical Venetian dialect, but it hadn't been speaking for more than a couple of seconds before all reflections on the manner of speaking gave way to incredulous astonishment at what was being said.

It was a hoax, of course. It had to be a hoax. Such things just didn't happen. But why bother to play such a complicated hoax on a visiting American?

Just suppose it were true, though? If he let a chance like this go by he would be consumed with regret to the day of his death.

'*Va bene*,' he said. '*Cosa debbo fare*?'

The voice told him to listen carefully, then proceeded with the instructions.

Outside Harry's Bar a bright looking boy of about sixteen, wearing black trousers, white shirt and crimson waistcoat, was polishing the brass of the door. He made Peroni wonder why so many of the brightest young men in Venice became waiters—a tradition that went back at least as far as Goldoni, as *The Servant of Two Masters* demonstrated. The bright looking boy held the door open with a flourish and Peroni went in.

Tonino's alibi was being checked and cross checked, but if it held—and there was now every reason to suppose it would—they were way out in the open again. At once Peroni had thought of the enigmatic reference to Harry's Bar in Bixi's diary. The other three place names had had their significance, so why not this? Peroni had come to see if he could find out what it was.

He ordered himself a dry martini because dry martini is part of the Bar's mystique and then sat on a high stool at the bar tuning himself in to the jangling chorale that was being performed around him in every imaginable variety of American accent.

'How much is that in dollars?'

'So this gondolier said he'd take us to the Giudecca and back for 50,000 lire which seemed a Hell of a lot of money to me . . .'

'It's not just the clothes, it's everything! I've never seen such perfect taste!'

'Napoleon took them!'

'American Express'll fix the whole thing.'

'I'm all out of cigarettes. Where can I get a pack of Chesterfield?'

The last speaker was a lady at a table near the door with a pekinese on the chair opposite her which she was feeding with scraps of chicken. As far as Peroni could make out, the question about the cigarettes had been addressed to the pekinese which was her only company. But, as if by magic, the bright looking boy who had opened the door to Peroni appeared at her side with a packet of Chesterfield.

'That's great,' she said looking surprised, 'How much is that?'

'Two thousand lire, Signorina.' The 'Signorina', Peroni noticed, was as calculated as a move on the Stock Exchange.

She opened her bag and gave him a 10,000 lire note, waving away the change and thus showing Peroni why so many of the brightest young men in Venice become waiters. The boy, in fact, reminded him of himself at the same age in Naples.

'Just a minute—' It wasn't difficult to catch the boy's attention; he seemed to have eyes in the back of his head.

'*Si, commissario*?'

Peroni was accustomed to being recognised, but not so quickly as that, and it took him aback.

'How did you know me?'

'I've seen your picture in the papers, commissario!'

There was a tang of hero-worship, and Peroni imperceptibly became Himself, a sort of meridional Superman, as once portrayed on the front cover of a scandal magazine.

'You keep your eyes open.' A pleased shrug which seemed to say, 'In this crazy life you have to.' 'Have you ever noticed the man in this photograph round here?'

'The lawyer who was murdered?'

'The same.'

'I saw him once.'

'When?'

'Early last week. Monday, maybe Tuesday.'

'In here?'

'No, outside—near the gondola rank.'

'Did you notice what he was doing?'

'He was talking to one of the gondoliers.'

The pekinese had moved on to mountain strawberries soaked in red wine.

'Any particular one?'

'Yes, the one they call the Lion.'

'The Lion? That's an odd sort of nickname.'

'If you ask me, Commissario, it's a sort of joke. They *call* him *il leone*, the lion, but they *mean il lenone*, the pimp.'

The central post office of Venice, an enormous classically-built stone hall, made Mr Ruskin think of Roman baths, and in fact like most Venetian public buildings, it did have something distinctly watery about it.

At first Mr Ruskin had wondered why his caller had fixed the appointment for the post office. Now he understood. Not only was it enormous, but it was crowded and had a complexity of smaller offices and halls running off it. An ideal place for a transaction such as this.

The second pillar on the right as you went in. No trouble locating that. Now behind it there should be a bench. And on the bench . . .

Although a scholar in his late fifties, Mr Ruskin felt a boyish leap of the heart when he saw the parcel. At the same time he felt a frisson of fear. From now on until he left the building, the caller had warned him, he would have a gun covering him. He had not been in contact with anything more deadly than a water pistol since the war, and one gets out of the habit. Fortunately, he had

56

an adventurous streak or he wouldn't have risked the enterprise at all.

He looked quickly about him to see if he could identify the caller, but the crowd made it impossible. So he picked up the parcel and sat down. He had five minutes to decide. He couldn't stop his hands trembling as he undid the parcel and pulled out the contents, and he wasted a good thirty seconds just staring at the thing. Then he started to examine it more closely.

In exactly three and a half minutes he had reached his decision. He wrapped it up quickly in the paper and put the brief-case with the money on the bench. That done, he had to get out quick, the caller had said, looking neither right nor left. He obeyed his instructions.

Outside, in the crowded Campo San Bartolomeo, he looked up for an instant at the statue of Goldoni striding like a benign country squire through the heart of his own Venice, and flicked him a brief, literary prayer. Then he hurried back towards the Vivaldi Hotel to gloat over his treasure.

SEVEN

The man was like an enormous scarecrow, and so untidy that he seemed to scatter bits of himself whenever he moved. He had a vulnerable moon-like face surmounted by waves of grey hair which pitched, heaved and tossed like a stormy sea. His patched and ancient clothes rode his frame like quarrelsome children, the shirt escaping from the trousers, the tie throttling the shirt, the jacket playing leap-frog with all three of them and the shoes trying to catch their own laces. Yet he had an air about him which explained why the *maresciallo* on the desk had told Peroni that a gentleman—and not the customary man—was waiting to see him.

And as soon as this gentleman saw Peroni his component parts momentarily resolved their differences to make a more or less united surge forward, and the right hand was charged by its fellow members to seize Peroni's and pump it up and down with enthusiastic reverence.

'What an honour to meet the great Commissario Peroni! What an honour!' For a moment Peroni suspected irony, but the jostling crowd in the large frame was so unfeignedly enthusiastic that he had to dismiss the suspicion.

'Partecipazio,' the man went on, announcing himself without losing his bear-like grip of veneration on Peroni's hand, 'your servant, Commissario, unworthy, but your servant!'

Ridiculously extravagant and straight out of a Goldoni comedy, but you couldn't help liking him. 'What can I do for you?'

'Too kind, too considerate, too condescending! I shan't take up more than a moment of the great Commissario Peroni's time! I wanted to speak to you on behalf of a wretched, unfortunate lad named Tonino.'

Oh? thought Peroni. 'Shall we go to my office?' he said.

When they got there and Partecipazio, with many protestations, was finally seated in the client's chair, he produced an enormous wooden snuff-box decorated with hand-painted flowers. 'No, of course not,' he said when Peroni had declined the offer, 'the habit of a bygone age. Will you permit me to indulge?'

Peroni waved Neapolitan consent and, when Partecipazio had sniffed a large quantity of the tobacco up his hairy nostrils and assisted a large red handkerchief to flurry busily about them, he reminded him gently of his mission.

'Tonino,' said Partecipazio. 'Yes, indeed. It has reached my ears, Commissario, that you are holding the thoughtless lad in connection with the wretched late *avv.* Bixi. May I make so bold as to ask, Commissario, if I can afford him any assistance?'

'To the best of my knowledge,' said Peroni, 'he doesn't need any. But might I in turn ask you why you interest yourself in him?'

Partecipazio smote his breast in penitence. 'How remiss of me not to have mentioned it before,' he said. 'What a wretched idiot the great Commissario Peroni must think me. My family, Commissario, the Partecipazio family which has played some small, perhaps not altogether trivial part in the history of this great Serenissima Republic—my family, I say, has been known amongst other things through the generations for the assistance which it has rendered to gondoliers in their moments of need. A modest tradition handed down over the centuries from father to son.'

'In that case,' said Peroni, 'I see no harm in telling you that Tonino should be completely free by evening.'

Partecipazio rose, came round to Peroni's side of the desk, took his hand once more and shook it silently in solemn reverence for a good five seconds.

'Let no more be said,' he pronounced at last. 'Let no more be said. Unless—unless—'

'Unless?' said Peroni, fascinated.

'Unless your humble servant might be so bold as to issue a poor invitation to dine. Though it is not my place to say it, I can offer you dishes such as perhaps you have never tasted in your life—treasures from the Venetian culinary thesaurus, many of them secret recipes belonging to the Partecipazio family. May we have the honour, Commissario, of expecting you this evening?'

The promised food, the opportunity to learn more of this eccentric visitor and the enigmatic 'we' which presumably indicated a wife were all tempting, but under the circumstances it would have been culpable frivolity.

'A gondola will be waiting for you at eight o'clock.'

'Then I accept with gratitude.'

It was out before the Commissario was aware of it.

A dead man's dwelling, like a dead man's clothes, can tell you a lot about him if you know how to observe it properly. And if one thing was clear, they needed to know more about *avv.* Bixi. Which was why Peroni was now standing in the muddled, dusty flat at the top of an old house entirely owned by the lawyer.

He listened to the silent room with an inner ear attuned, years ago in Naples, to catching nuances of atmosphere. First nothing. Then the sounds that were there all along, but which you normally never caught—a muffled '*Ole!*' from a gondolier rounding a distant corner, a flutter of pigeon's wings on the guttering outside, the distant hoot of a water-bus, somebody practising the piano in another house. And then at last the sounds he was waiting for. A furtive rustling of footsteps that weren't there, a crackling of paper that sounded like old, dried banknotes.

Slowly the sounds began to evoke an image, seeming to take shape in the air. At first it was the image of the old Pantaloon mask, then it disintegrated like the face of a man long dead being exposed to the air. And behind it another face started to emerge. Its features were not yet clear; a few seconds more, though, and they would be. In the meantime, Peroni could only tell it was a face he didn't like, a face whose owner perhaps merited having his skull smashed in an alley. Here lies a Lawyer and an Honest Man. How can two men lie in the same tomb? There's your answer—they can't, for the Honest Man is only the Pantaloon mask which will soon have crumbled away altogether, revealing only the lawyer, so that at least, but also at last, Peroni would know who was dead.

'*Gradu diverso, via una,*' came a hoarse, whispery voice dispelling the revelation, 'Our pace may be different, Commissario, but it seems that we follow the same way.'

Peroni had been so caught up in the atmosphere which the dead lawyer had left behind him that he had not even heard the door opening to admit the examining magistrate, *dott*. Tron. The two men shook hands, and Peroni did his best not to let exasperation show through, for it is always prudent to keep on the fair side of the magistrature, even when it quotes Latin at you.

'You, too, are here, I take it, in search of some light on *avv*. Bixi's personality? It's extraordinary how little we know about him—*hiatus valde deplendus*. A gap to be deplored indeed, but, I trust, rapidly filled in.' As *dott*. Tron moved about the room, his long limbs swayed like branches in the wind.

'The trouble was,' said Peroni, 'that we all jumped too quickly to the Tonino conclusion. Or at least,' he added quickly, 'I did.'

'I, too, *dottore*,' said Tron, 'I, too. *Humanum est errare*; we can merely do our best to make up for it now. It certainly begins to look as though we should search for an answer in the late *avvocato*'s life and character.'

'Which is rapidly emerging as altogether different from what we thought it to be.' Peroni judged the first person plural safe this time as it was Tron himself who had described Bixi as illustrious and venerable.

'*Frontis nulla fides,*' said the magistrate, nodding his prematurely grey top, 'no trusting appearances. A basic rule for both of us, Commissario. Have you been able to learn anything of interest at Harry's Bar?'

Peroni looked up quickly. He had thought Tron was unaware of this angle. Then he decided that probably he had heard of it from *dott*. Amabile. The magistrate seemed unaware that he had said anything even remotely unexpected. He had taken a volume in Latin from one of the book cases and was studying it absorbedly.

Peroni told him about the Lion-pimp.

'Pandering,' said Tron. 'The most ancient of gondoliering malpractices. And last week you uncovered a gambling organisation run by gondoliers.'

'Exactly,' said Peroni, 'And that's not all, *dottore*. I've been talking to one or two colleagues at the *Questura*, and they tell me that the wave of blackmail and attempted blackmail which they haven't been able to get to the bottom of could perfectly well come from gondoliering sources. Which ties up again with *avv*. Bixi's asking Tonino to collect "information" for him.'

'*Tria juncta in uno*,' said Tron. 'Three in one, indeed.'

'And if we go a step further, *dottore*, and put those three together we get an organisation which could be potentially very profitable. And such an organisation would obviously need somebody to coordinate and direct it.'

'And you believe, Commissario, that *avv*. Bixi, who was unquestionably involving himself in gondoliering affairs, had discovered the identity of this somebody as a result of which . . . ?' He let the sentence hang in pregnant suspension.

'It's a possibility,' said Peroni.

'Would you then propose,' said Tron, 'detaining the suspected pander of Harry's Bar for questioning?'

'No *dottore*,' said Peroni, 'subject to your approval, I wouldn't. If I hadn't interrogated don Amos prematurely—without, of course, realising what was going to happen—I should now have another possible avenue of approach leading towards our hypothetical organiser. No, in this case I should prefer to find out first exactly what the Lion is up to at least before we detain him.'

'*Cuicunque in arte sua credendum est*,' said Tron, 'and in this particular case I have the fullest confidence Commissario, in you and your own art. So I leave the decision entirely to you. And in the meantime, shall we proceed to our examination?'

They went carefully through the apartment, but found nothing of interest and, although Peroni kept his inner ear open, it caught none of the whisperings he had heard before, and he concluded that they must have rustled into hiding before the more classically flavoured whispering of *dott*. Tron.

They gave it up after about an hour and went down the dark and creaking stairway together.

'Of one thing it seems we may be certain,' said Tron giving Peroni his hand when they were in the *calle* outside, '*Latet anguis in herba*. A snake is hidden in the grass. Or given our particular circumstances, should I say the water?'

EIGHT

The gondola was indeed waiting at eight o'clock sharp, by which time Peroni had come to regret the whole thing. But as soon as Partecipazio, who was in it, jumped out like a bear onto the canal-side to help him in with a courtly extravagant gesture he found himself once again intrigued by the outing, even if it was a waste of time.

'Be careful, Commissario!' warned Partecipazio, apparently terrified lest Peroni should slip, 'The water in Venice is very wet!'

Peroni would have considered this remark as another mark of Partecipazio's extravagance if similar statements by de Benedetti hadn't accustomed him to this habit of the natives of considering all things Venetian as unique.

Their passage along the canals was dream-like and silent, except for the dripping of water and small nasal explosions as Partecipazio took snuff. There was something sensuous, reflected Peroni, about gliding through the water in this long, black, lop-sided craft.

Partecipazio seemed to sense Peroni's enjoyment, and a contented smile on his large face indicated that he was pleased to have introduced the great Commissario Peroni to one of the supreme delights of Venice.

Then, after a while, he began to talk, pointing out the buildings they passed, relating anecdotes about the families who lived in them. He was a walking encyclopaedia of Venice, and Peroni found himself being entertained for the first time since his arrival.

The gondola crossed the Grand Canal and then slid into a network of little canals on the other side, eventually coming to a graceful halt before a wooden landing stage embellished by two of those mooring posts which look like majestic barber's poles sticking out of the water. On the landing stage was an old man with the word GANZER in faded gold letters on his cap. He had a hook which he used to pull their gondola in and hold it so that the passengers could alight.

Partecipazio gave him 500 lire and Peroni, observing the old man, realised that he wasn't in fact old at all, but just appeared to be so because of the dirt, the beard and the ragged clothes. He probably wasn't much above fifty.

'Poor fellow!' said Partecipazio, leading Peroni by the arm across the landing stage and the canal-side walk to a massive gate, 'Poor fellow! Dumb from birth and moreover . . .' He tapped his head significantly. 'When he was in his thirties he was left without any means of support, his parents and all his relatives having died. But his father had been a gondolier, so how could the Partecipazio family let him go unaided in such straits? Happily, I found a solution. Once there was a race of men in Venice—mostly retired gondoliers—known as *Ganzer* or hookers. Their job was to pull the gondola in as he did just now. Nowadays the *ganzer* has been made redundant by time, but I revived the function to provide a living for him. And we keep an eye on him, finding him accommodation when necessary and so on.'

'Extremely good of you,' said Peroni.

'Nothing, my dear Commissario, nothing! The humble duty of a Partecipazio—no more, no more! Shall we go in?'

Many of the older palaces in Venice give the impression that they are about to crumble from one minute to the next, but the palace which Peroni saw when they passed into the ample private courtyard looked as though it were already actively engaged in doing so. Once it must have been magnificent. It was four storeys high with marble balconies bright with geraniums (Signora Partecipazio?) before graceful ogival windows on the second floor. Over the arched front door was a marble high relief, so worn by time that you could no longer distinguish its subject, though Peroni thought he could just make out a dragon's tail.

Nervously bending his head for fear that the high relief should reduce him to the same state as that of *avv*. Bixi, he allowed himself to be ushered through the front door into a large stone hall, echoing and dusty, in which a circular staircase swept its way upstairs.

'If you will do me the honour of climbing the stairs,' said Partecipazio. 'We have been obliged to close up most of the house. We live on the second floor—what used to be known as the noble floor. Ah, Commissario, if this old house could reveal some of the splendours it has seen in the past when the Partecipazio family played its modest part in the doings of the Serenissima! How times have changed, Commissario, how times have changed! Here we are!'

Having reached the second landing, they turned off down a corridor and then into the first room leading off it. It was an enormous, high-ceilinged room with large windows opening out onto one of the balconies overlooking the canal. The room was sparsely furnished with battered, moth-eaten but authentic 18th century pieces—high-backed armchairs and a sofa with its innards dangling out, a low sideboard with candles in candlesticks, a mirror over the open fireplace and, under the chandelier in the centre of the room, a round table laid for three. On the walls were some vividly coloured naif paintings of Venetian scenes, and though they were out of keeping, Peroni liked them.

Indeed, they would have made a greater impact upon him if something else had not been in ambush to capture his entire attention. Standing by one of the windows was a girl who seemed the quintessence of Venetian femininity. She was slight with very dark hair cropped short, and she was wearing jeans and an open-necked Western style check shirt. But in contrast to these clothes, her face, with an expression flickering between gravity and amusement, might have been one of those faces which hid, or pretended to hide, behind masks during the endless Venetian carnival of the 18th century.

'My daughter,' said Partecipazio. (So that was the we, thought Peroni), 'Estrella. A most talented girl, a very—'

'Don't start, papa,' she said moving towards Peroni with her hand outstretched. 'You mustn't listen to him,' she went on, giving him the hand, cool and firm, 'By his account, all the people he knows of are models of intelligence, skill and virtue. I'm not really talented at all.'

'I can't believe that,' said Peroni, holding the hand far longer than was necessary while un-commissario-like thoughts swarmed in his head like flies.

Then she smiled and with a shock Peroni realised that it was a great deal more than the smile of a hostess welcoming a guest. She had rumbled him, that was what the smile said; she had recognised the individual who lurked within the commissario-like facade, and she found his presence irresistibly amusing. Gently she took her hand from his, but not before having given his hand an imperceptible squeeze which seemed to say, 'Don't worry though—I shan't let on.'

In his confusion, Peroni snatched at the first subject to suggest itself. 'Estrella,' he said, 'it's a delightful name, but surely not Italian?'

'Estrella, my dear Commissario—' began Partecipazio.

'After supper, papa,' ruled his daughter firmly but affectionately, and Peroni intercepted a look pass between them of such tenderness, he thought, as must be rare between fathers and grown daughters. 'It's too long a story to tell standing about on one leg when the Commissario must be hungry,' she went on. 'Shall we go straight to table?'

After fish hors d'oeuvres with Italian Tokai ('Such a Tokai, I dare predict, Commissario, as you have never drunk before!'), Estrella brought in the main dish, steaming and inky black.

Peroni's alarm must have shown, for she smiled once again. 'Don't worry, Commissario. The colour *is* a bit off-putting, but I think you'll find the taste will make up for it.'

'I'm sure I shall, Signorina,' said Peroni. 'What exactly is it?'

'A dish, Commissario,' said Partecipazio, 'unique rather than rare! The masterpiece of Venetian culinary art! A dish—'

'Cuttle fish,' cut in Estrella matter of factly, '*alla Veneziana*.

It's a famous local dish, but the Partecipazios have their own variant—they always have.' She flashed a look of mocking affection at her father. 'Simple enough, though—you just pop oil, salt, pepper and garlic clove into the saucepan, then add the cuttle fish and cook till they're tender. Put in half a glass of dry white wine and a couple of sacks of the cuttle fish ink. That's where the black comes from. Cook for a few minutes and serve piping hot with polenta. *Buon appetito, Commissario.*'

'*Grazie, Signorina,*' said Peroni.

'What a girl!' said her father, 'What a cook!'

'I hear you got poor Tonino out of the mess he'd got himself into,' said Estrella while they ate. 'I think that's wonderful!'

Peroni bloomed noticeably. 'He got himself out really,' he said, and went on to tell them about Tonino's alibi while father and daughter followed him as though he were performing a particularly brilliant conjuring trick.

'Has anybody taken Tonino's place as the Bixi basher?' asked Estrella when he'd finished.

'Really, child!' said Partecipazio, spluttering ink. 'You mustn't ask questions like that! Highly confidential! Professional secrecy!'

'Nonsense, papa,' said Estrella, 'the Commissario wouldn't dream of telling me anything confidential, would you, Commissario?'

But the look she gave him was gently mocking as though she knew that he knew that there was no secret in the entire *Questura* of Venice that she couldn't smile out of him if she tried. He did his best to keep up an appearance of dignity, merely saying that the movements of another gondolier were being followed.

'*Another* gondolier, Commissario!' she said in mock horror.

'They seem to be all over the place in this affair,' said Peroni.

'Nothing ever happens in Venice, Commissario,' said Partecipazio sententiously, 'without a gondolier being involved somehow. They are the very stuff of the place! An extraordinary race of men, Commissario, and often much maligned! The American writer, Henry James, said of them—I quote from memory—"I know them only by their merits and I am grossly prejudiced in their favour."'

'Henry James was a sentimentalist,' said Estrella, 'and so are you, papa. The simple truth is—'

'The truth is never simple in Venice,' interrupted Partecipazio.

'There are good gondoliers and bad gondoliers,' went on Estrella ignoring him, 'just as there are good and bad taxi drivers.'

'No, no,' said Partecipazio, pouring wine for himself and Peroni (Estrella only drank mineral water), 'that's an old argument—gondoliers are just the same as taxi drivers and so, by inference, as butchers, bakers or candlestick makers. But I'm not having that! No, Estrella! No, my dear Commissario! I may be a foolish old man, but I will believe to my dying day that there is something different about them! The canals, the lagoon, the very craft they row, the love of so many young couples which flowers beneath their eyes—'

'Oh, come off it, papa!'

'—all these things contribute to make the gondolier different from other men. They give him a touch of magic!'

'There you are!' Estrella said to Peroni. 'Incurably sentimental!'

'And proud of it!' said Partecipazio taking snuff.

Estrella took away their fish plates and served the fruit.

'I like these Venetian naifs,' said Peroni, indicating the pictures.

'There you are!' exclaimed Partecipazio blowing snuff in his excitement. 'Didn't I say she was a girl of rare talent? All Estrella's, Commissario! All the work of my daughter!'

'Stop it, papa! I just have fun with it,' she went on to Peroni rather defensively, 'I like throwing paint about.'

The fact that they were Estrella's made them even more delightful in Peroni's eyes. He examined them closer. St Mark's Square, the fruit and vegetable market, two old women outside a swirling rococo church facade, all in flaring colours. You could see that she used her pallet knife to mould the oils so that in places the pictures seemed almost sculpted rather than painted; and she suggested details of dress or architecture or light with deftly placed blobs which did not so much depict as guide the viewer's fantasy to see what Estrella intended. They were good, and Peroni said so.

'Thank you, Commissario,' she said, half pert, half embarrassed. 'Maybe I'll do one for you one day.'

'I should like that,' said Peroni, meaning it.

There was a pause, and Peroni had the impression she didn't want to talk about her paintings any more.

'You were going to tell me,' he said to Partecipazio, 'about the name Estrella.'

'I'll get the coffee then,' said Estrella and went out.

'The original Estrella,' said Partecipazio, 'was the only daughter of Venice's tenth doge, Angelo Partecipazio.'

'You mean—?'

'Precisely. My family goes back to the very earliest dawn of the Republic. And Angelo Partecipazio was the first of three doges to come from it. Not to mention great naval commanders—a Partecipazio fought at Lepanto—warriors, scholars, scientists, men of letters. The line of Partecipazio runs through the tapestry of Venetian history like an uninterrupted gold thread!'

It was not the first time that image had been used, Peroni guessed. But that took nothing from the reverence with which it was produced. For Partecipazio, his family, stretching back through time, was a single unity, living and present, a passionate cult. And then Peroni noticed two enormous tears, one on each side of Partecipazio's nose, like white mice on the moon.

'Estrella?' he prompted gently.

'Forgive me . . .' Clumsily he wiped away the tears with his sleeve, sending drastic charges of snuff up each nostril. 'Yes, Estrella. Daughter of the tenth doge, as I say. Eight hundred and ten, and Pepin, son of Charlemagne, was leading an attack against the Republic. He had taken the island of Malamocco which was then the capital, while the Venetians were holed up in the little island group of Rivo Alto—what we now call Rialto. Pepin started to build a causeway from Malamocco to Rivo Alto which would have meant the end for the people of Venice. But at this point, just when he was ready to launch his attack, Estrella, entered upon the scene.'

It was at this point, too, that her namesake entered with the coffee. She smiled as she gave them their cups, but didn't interrupt.

'Rowed by two gondoliers, she set off for Malamocco where—

68

because of her great beauty, the story says—she was received by Pepin and pleaded the cause of the Venetians.

'Pepin found himself in a dilemma familiar to men of power throughout the ages. He was reluctant to deny a girl as beautiful as Estrella, but he was also adamant that his political purpose should not be deflected. So he compromised by letting her talk on without committing himself—which was just what she wanted. She talked and talked and talked, and all the while the waters of the lagoon rose up around Pepin's causeway. At last when she knew that it had been entirely swamped by the tide, she took her leave.'

The sun had gone down during the course of the narrative, and it was already quite dark in the room. Estrella went over to the sideboard where she lit two candles and brought them over to the table.

'The delay was sufficient,' her father went on, 'the defenders had time to make their preparations and the Republic was saved. But the ending was not so happy for Estrella herself. On the way back, her two gondoliers somehow took a wrong turning which brought them within range of the Venetian firing line where a boulder, catapulted by the defenders, smashed into Estrella's gondola. She and her two gondoliers were drowned. It is said that the Rialto Bridge rears up over the very stretch of water where she died.'

Once more Partecipazio assisted the large red handkerchief to deal with his be-snuffed nose. 'So,' he said at length, 'when my wife gave birth to a daughter, I thought that if I gave her the name of Estrella she might do something to revive the spirit of the old Venice, so long, so lamentably dead. And maybe she will, Commissario.'

'I don't see much chance,' said Estrella.

'Nor did the other Estrella,' said her father, 'until Pepin came. Nobody can tell what they're capable of until the challenge comes.'

'I can't see Venice being threatened by any Pepins nowadays.'

'Pepins can take many forms . . .'

Soon afterwards, Peroni said he must go and they accompanied him down and out onto the landing stage where the same gondola was waiting for him.

'It has been a great honour, Commissario,' said Partecipazio swaddling his hand once more. 'You must come whenever you like. Don't wait for invitations—just arrive. You will always be welcome.'

'I don't back all my father's invitations,' said Estrella, giving him her hand again, 'but I do this one. We shall be expecting you.'

They stood on the landing stage as he went, two forms in the gathering dark, one bulky, the other slight and feminine, their hands raised in salute.

On Peroni's emotional horizon, the flash of sheet lightning and the clap of thunder were simultaneous.

He was standing at the top of a great stone tower which reared up into a leaden sky and he was looking down over a wide expanse of water which mirrored the lowering sky. And somewhere below him on the water was a gondola being rowed by two gondoliers.

Although the tower on which he was standing was so high he could see, quite clearly, as though in close-up, the passenger in the gondola. It was Estrella, but which Estrella he couldn't make out. The long dove-grey dress and the plaited hair falling down her back were those of Doge Angelo Partecipazio's daughter, but the face was the 20th century Estrella's. And as she looked at him, she smiled a smile which said that she had rumbled him on his high, stone tower.

Suddenly Peroni felt an acute pang of danger. At first he couldn't tell where this danger lay, but then his dream eyes looked up from the gondola and saw, across the water, a fortress, behind the battlements of which loomed a medieval catapult machine. And the soldiers of the fortress were loading a huge boulder onto it.

From the top of his tower he yelled down to Estrella and her gondoliers to turn back while there was still time, but they didn't hear, and she continued to smile.

Then the soldiers sprang the catapult and the boulder shot through the air, a megalithic bearer of death. It spun unerringly towards the gondola and Peroni felt racked with impotence. He could only stand there and watch her die.

But suddenly a crazy inspiration lightninged into his mind. If

70

he could fly through the air he could perhaps deflect the boulder in time. Logic said he would only plummet into the water, but just the same he jumped from his tower into the air. And incredibly found himself soaring towards the boulder. But would he reach it in time?

On the enormous book-case in the room next door to where Peroni was sleeping the defective mechanism inside the doll with one eye set itself in motion, and four identical syllables sounded, inane and monotonous, in the pitch dark apartment. 'Ma—ma Ma—ma—' Then it stopped.

Peroni was still arched convulsively in his impossible flight, unaware that he had just dreamed of Estrella for the second time.

Part Two

THE LION

A charlatan of a most rare species . . .

Mémoires
Carlo Goldoni

NINE

The Undertaker had quarrelled with his dead mother. When at first he had come home with the proceeds of the sale, she had seemed pleased with him, and he had hidden the bottle of whisky he had bought to celebrate in the cupboard of his room. But she noticed its effect on him just the same from some slight thickening in speech and unsteadiness in gait; she had always been a sight too sharp for signs such as these. And so an evening which had started under such happy auspices had degenerated into a bickering match which grew more acrimonious every time he paid a surreptitious visit to his own room.

This morning he had awoken with a hangover and a niggling sense of rancour. And so he oiled his way out of the house without paying the customary morning visit to his mother, lacking the courage to make a noise about it lest he should be enmeshed by the all too familiar reproachful whine from her room.

'May she stew in her own broth,' he opined unctuously when once he was safely outside.

But now the problem arose as to what he should do with himself. As a free man with a wallet full of money, the world was at his feet. He contemplated going to the cinema, but didn't even know if they started in the morning and anyway found that the idea held no particular appeal for him. Then he thought that he might go to the station and catch a train. He could go to Rome, Milan, Florence . . . He watched the idea float slowly away from him into space; he just wasn't interested. In the end he went to a bar near Campo San Bartolomeo. He could have gone to *Florian*'s or *Quadri*'s, but he chose this one because it was dark and smelly and familiar.

'*Giorno*,' said the fat woman behind the bar. (It was run by two sisters, one fat and one thin, and this morning the fat one was on duty.)

'*Giorno*,' said the Undertaker and ordered a whisky.

He took it to a greasy table in the corner and sat staring up at a large portrait hanging on the wall. It must have been painted half a century before, and it showed a muscular looking man with a meaty face and no neck holding an oar. Written at his feet was a couplet.

'Praise regatta hero Zorzi in song and in rhyme—
His fame will go down to the end of time!'

Who had ever heard of him today? thought the Undertaker, who, unlike most gondoliers, had always held that regattas were a waste of time.

He was reflecting morosely on regatta hero Zorzi when a group of three gondoliers he knew came into the bar. Hitherto, from his privileged position as lawyer's clerk, he had looked down on them. Now he envied them.

'*Ciao*, Undertaker,' they said irreverently, but amicably, crowding about him.

'Coming back to us now that your boss has been done in?' said one of them, a mottled, stubby man who needed to watch his blood pressure.

The Undertaker half wished he could, but it was out of the question; for one thing they'd never give him back his licence.

'What will you partake of, gentlemen?' At least in that he might have a spurious sense of belonging again.

'That's handsome of you, Undertaker,' said another, a gondolier with a squint, known as Abracadabra. 'What are *you* drinking?'

'Whisky,' the Undertaker pronounced solemnly holding his glass up to what little light there was.

'Whisky?' said Abracadabra. 'That's unlike you.'

'Drowning your sorrows for your dead boss?' enquired Blood Pressure. 'I'll take whisky, too.'

'Me, too,' said Abracadabra.

The third gondolier indicated with a slight nod that he also would have whisky, and four glasses were ordered. When they arrived, the others began to talk about the coming Historical Regatta.

'I'm aiming for second,' said Abracadabra who was a competitor. 'With the Bull rowing that's the best you can hope for.'

'He's drinking a lot,' pointed out Blood Pressure.

'He always has drunk a lot,' said Abracadabra. 'That hasn't stopped him winning nine Historicals on the trot.'

Bored, the Undertaker downed his whisky in one and ordered another round.

'It isn't only the strength, you see,' went on Abracadabra, airing his knowledge, 'it's the dirty tricks he can do—'cos when all's said and done that's what wins a regatta in the end—always has done!'

The door from the street opened again and the gondoliers, turning, saw the Hooker shuffling in with his shabby, ankle length overcoat and laceless boots.

'Trust him to turn up when there's whisky about,' said Blood Pressure.

It was an unwritten law, obeyed by even the meanest of gondoliers, that you always bought a drink for the Hooker. So now the Undertaker signed to the fat sister to give him a glass and, while she was at it, to fill up theirs.

The whisky was making him feel less isolated, and everything about him—the dim bar, the Hooker dribbling whisky down his chin, the gondoliers discussing the Regatta—began to take on a cheerier glow. It was an amiable world, and the Undertaker belonged to it once more.

So when the party gave signs of breaking up, he felt no qualms about paying the bill. He opened his bulging wallet with a flourish that still had something of the funereal about it, as though he were opening the door of a hearse with a particularly distinguished corpse inside, and produced a hundred thousand lire note.

'Lawyer leave you something in his will?'

It was the first time the third gondolier had spoken.

Life in a tax office is always second-hand, and people are the forms they have filled in. This was the experience of Enrico Cambiasi who worked in such an office on the first floor of a building next to Harry's Bar. By nature Cambiasi was timid, but he viewed all the excitement that had passed him by with the hopeless nostalgia of an old man looking at a pretty whore.

This explained the shudder of excited anticipation that had passed through him the previous day when he learned that the *Questore* of Venice—no less—had telephoned his office chief to ask if the police might keep a watch from their premises.

Speculation had exploded like a rocket among Cambiasi's colleagues as to what the police would be keeping a watch on. After some discussion, it was generally agreed that it must have something to do with drug smuggling and was probably in connection with the large, pale blue Cypriot vessel which was moored in the lagoon.

Cambiasi himself, having ascertained that the cover underneath his desk was sufficient in case shooting should start, pulled a pile of forms towards him and prepared to work as little and observe as much as possible.

Shortly after this a detective had arrived. He shook hands with everybody politely, announced his name to be de Benedetti and took up a position near the window only a few metres away from Cambiasi's desk.

While apparently studying the tax returns of a Sicilian restaurant owner with three houses who claimed he had only earned a million lire the previous year, Cambiasi observed the observing detective. The first thing he noticed was that his attention was directed, not to the left where the Cypriot ship was moored, but to the right in the direction of the Grand Canal. Nor was he looking out over the water, but down at the pavement which, in that direction, came to an abrupt end just beyond Harry's, at which point you either had to turn right or jump into the water. And the only thing that seemed worth observation in that small stretch of pavement was a gondola rank.

But the detective called de Benedetti hadn't seemed to get much satisfaction from his observation. He had the expression of a man who isn't seeing what he expects to see. After about an hour of this Cambiasi began to think that the professionally groomed mendacity of the Sicilian restauranteur might have the edge on the police watch as far as excitement went.

And this morning, when the same detective had returned, it

had been no better. The staff of the tax office felt they were not getting their returns. But then about mid-morning Cambiasi saw the detective stiffen with sudden attention. He was following the movements of something. Or somebody. Cambiasi would have liked to go to the window and look out, but he didn't have the nerve.

Then the detective got out a pair of binoculars and looked through them. The action had moved away. A few minutes more and he put them down. The action must have disappeared from view.

At this point a very striking southern looking detective arrived wearing the sort of tie Signora Cambiasi would never allow. The two detectives talked together in a murmur and, strain though he might, Cambiasi couldn't catch a word of it.

But then the detective called de Benedetti grabbed his binoculars again and trained them in the direction of the Grand Canal. 'That's odd,' he said, forgetting to murmur, 'he's coming back—and with the man. They usually drop them off. And anyway, there's not time for—'

'Maybe they fell out over terms.'

'Doesn't look like it. The Lion's still chatting away and the customer's listening as though he were interested.'

Cambiasi felt frustration like an itch. He could hear them now, but for all the good it was to him the detectives might have kept up their inaudible murmur. Who was the Lion? Where did he usually drop off who? What wasn't there time for? The questions poured into his mind, and not an answer to dry them up.

The inaudible murmuring was resumed, and then after a minute or so de Benedetti left the office as though bound on some errand, and the southern detective took up his position at the window.

With a sigh Cambiasi returned to his Sicilian restaurateur.

The whisky was beginning to tell. Somehow—just how the Undertaker wasn't sure—Abracadabra, Blood Pressure and the Hooker had taken themselves off, and he was alone with the third gondolier who had got him another whisky.

'Lawyer leave you something in his will?' this gondolier repeated.

The Undertaker felt a temptation to confide, but resisted it; better nobody should know.

'No, no,' he said in a tone of whisky soaked piety, 'my late employer, God rest his soul, was not the most generous of souls.'

'Another drink, shall we?'

The Undertaker was about to say no, but the other somehow didn't give him time. There was the drink, a large one under his nose, and it would have been rude to leave it. His little finger cocked, he raised the glass as though in a toast to the dear departed.

'Didn't realise you earned so much as a lawyer's clerk. I must get a job like that myself.'

'Oh, but I didn't acquire this money in the employ of the late *avv*. Bixi,' said the Undertaker. 'Dear me, no! At least,' he corrected himself with a nice regard for the truth, 'not exactly in the employ.'

'Oh?'

The monosyllable was shot through with amiable and innocent curiosity.

And after all, what harm could there be in telling the story now? It would be pleasant to confide and also, he felt, it would put his mother's nose out of joint.

He looked about him. The bar was empty except for the fat sister, well out of earshot behind the counter, absentmindedly feeding herself with fried fish. On the wall, regatta hero Zorzi stared out over their heads. But he wasn't listening. The Undertaker started to talk with slurred unctuousness.

It was the first time Peroni had been able to observe the Lion properly. If it hadn't been for the elided *n* in his nickname which transformed a lion into a pimp, monkey would have been a more appropriate epithet. His wrinkled, cunning face was pure monkey and so were the bright, quick eyes. He was less heavily built than most gondoliers, but the arms and hands were as powerful. Peroni noticed that he also had a slight limp.

He was walking slowly up and down by the water's edge smoking a cigarette with an air of simian innocence. But he was up to something. According to de Benedetti's report he had taken out a male foreign tourist and started talking with him in what appeared to be a persuasive manner. The man had listened intently, apparently favourable to whatever was being proposed.

And so far so clear. Pimping, after all, was a wheeze as old in Venice as the oldest profession itself. But then the affair began to take on an unfamiliar pattern. For the Lion had returned almost immediately with his client when, as de Benedetti had pointed out, the usual practice was to leave the chicken for plucking. Then on the quayside the man had written something on a piece of paper in his pocket, at the Lion's dictation. After that the two of them shook hands as though over a deal satisfactorily concluded.

It looked too involved for pimping and, in fact, the morals squad had no record of the Lion though, of course, that didn't prove anything one way or the other.

At this point in Peroni's thoughts, de Benedetti—who had gone to follow the man and find out all he could about him—returned looking pleased with himself.

'But there's a funny thing, *dottore*,' he said, the pleased expression giving way to puzzlement, 'I've seen him somewhere before.'

'Who, the Lion?'

'No, the tourist. And yet it's not very likely because he's Spanish, but still . . .' He concentrated for a second and then shook the thought away from him.

'I daresay it'll come back to me,' he said, 'but in the meantime, *dottore*, I've had a bit of luck. I followed him back to his hotel and when he went in, I saw the desk clerk give him a telegram. So I went in, too—he couldn't have recognised me before because there was too much crowd and he was too busy looking at his own reflection in the shop windows. Anyway, he read the telegram, looked a bit put out, crumpled it up and threw it into the waste-paper basket. Then he asked the desk clerk to contact a travel agency and book him onto the first possible flight to Barcelona. He'd just started towards the stairs to go and pack when he remembered something. He took the piece of paper out of his pocket—the one he'd written on here. He looked at it, shrugged and threw it after the telegram. So as soon as he'd gone upstairs I was able to get them both.'

He handed them over to Peroni. The piece of paper was an

envelope and on the back of it was written '*Campo Melone, 17 23.00.*'

'An appointment,' said Peroni.

'But for what? Gondoliering pimping isn't as organised as that.' He had an idea. 'Why not ask him?'

'If it's anything likely to interest us,' said Peroni, 'he's certainly not going to say. This envelope's not much to go on, and you have to be careful with foreigners. Who is he, by the way?'

'He's a Spaniard called Cristofor Rubio y Ors. An actor, according to his passport.'

'Here by himself?'

'That's right. He came for the Goldoni festival.'

Peroni looked at the telegram. It was in Spanish, but Spanish is sufficiently similar to Italian for him to get the gist. Shooting on some film project had been brought forward and the presence of Rubio y Ors was urgently required.

'What time's he flying out?'

'Twenty past seven this evening from the Marco Polo Airport.'

'Well, we certainly haven't got enough to hold him here against his will, and anyway I can't see it doing the slightest good.'

There was a pause and then de Benedetti said, 'I wish I could remember where I've seen him before.'

'If he's an actor, probably in a film,' suggested Peroni.

'Perhaps,' said de Benedetti, but he didn't look convinced.

TEN

The Lion's mysterious doings, thought Peroni as he flipped his motor boat dexterously off the Grand Canal, might or might not be the answer. But if they were, how did the ransacking of *avv.* Bixi's office fit into it?

The motor boat bee-hummed over the foul, romantic water and Peroni reflected that he had become a dab hand at navigation. It was all a question of adjusting oneself to the new element of water on which distances were subtly different.

Could the lawyer have had some tangible evidence concerning the mysterious doings? And was his head staved in because of it?

Delicate manipulation, he felt, and/or a characteristic Peroni *coup* were going to be needed if they were to find the answer to these questions.

He bobbed neatly beneath a low, hump-backed bridge. An onlooker, he thought, would surely take him for a native.

He rounded a tight corner stylishly and saw a flat, blue barge ahead of him loaded with crates of mineral water. A few days before Peroni would have chugged meekly behind until they were in a broader canal, but now he decided that there was ample room to pass. He accelerated and moved out to overtake.

The next thing he knew there was a grinding jolt, the boat shook beneath him as though in an earthquake and then came to a shuddering halt. He was jammed between a barge full of mineral water and low steps leading up to a mooring stage which he had not observed.

A large, bovine man in overalls looked down impassively at him from the barge. 'Who gave you a licence?' he enquired.

There are moments in which even a commissario of police cannot command the respect due to his position. This was one of them.

'Try backing,' said the purveyor of mineral water after eyeing the situation laconically.

Peroni muddled his gears and the boat heaved impotently, wedging itself more thoroughly. The barge man watched with the resignation of an expert.

'We'll have to get the police,' he said.

A police officer from Naples rescued from a watery predicament of his own making by northern policemen. It would make the front pages. *Peroni Jammed.* His legend would look as ridiculous as a statue of Dante with a pigeon sitting on his hooked nose.

Another motor launch was arriving behind them. The audience was beginning to gather. In a few minutes the canal would be filled with craft of every kind to watch a scene which, with a few superficial changes, might have been written by Goldoni himself. How the vanity of the foolish Neapolitan Marquis di Peroni led to his downfall.

'Trouble, Commissario?'

To his overwhelming relief Peroni recognised the voice from

the second launch as that of Estrella Partecipazio. She cut out her engine and stopped centimetres behind them.

'*Buon giorno, Signorina,*' the sandwiched Peroni greeted her.

'You didn't see the steps,' she said, and Peroni nodded. 'Hang on a second,' she continued, 'and I'll see what I can do.'

She swarmed about with the agility of a water rat, and the two wedged boats seemed to respond to her treatment as if they were alive. Within minutes Peroni's boat was bobbing free again. And with no less skill she also handled the barge man. Under her influence he was content to chug off with docility and his mineral water.

'Anyway,' she said when he had gone, 'it would take a bomb to do any damage to those barges. But I'm afraid your boat's in a bit of a mess. Tell you what—there's a man just round the corner I know who'll have it as good as new for you by tomorrow if I ask him nicely. I'll get him to come and pick it up, and then I'll drop you off wherever you want to go. Unless—'

She stopped as if she'd gone too far.

'Unless?' prompted Peroni.

'No, it's a silly idea. It's just that I was on my way out to the Island and I thought you might like to see it.'

'The Island?'

'We call it the Island with a capital letter, but it's really one of hundreds out in the lagoon, and it's tiny. Some 18th century Partecipazio built a sort of shooting lodge on it. It's falling to pieces now. Like everything else.' A distant cuckoo call of melancholy sounded. 'But papa sometimes uses it for shooting,' she went on, 'and I just like going out there.'

It was, of course, out of the question. He couldn't possibly take valuable time off to go riding about the lagoon with a girl.

'There's nothing I should enjoy more,' said Peroni.

Policewoman Sofia Michelangelo had a lot of reports to type, and the last but one thing in the world that she wanted around was *dott.* de Benedetti. The last thing of all was *dott.* de Benedetti's jokes. But she was being subjected to both of them.

'There's nothing for it, Michelangelo, you'll just have to give us a hand. We're stuck.'

'If you don't mind, *dott.* de Benedetti, I've got a lot—'

'No, no, I mean it seriously. This might be just the moment when feminine intuition is needed. There's something puzzling going on at the gondola rank outside Harry's Bar.' He started to outline the story. 'That Spaniard!' he said. 'Just your type, Michelangelo!'

She sighed with exaggerated heaviness and ripped a sheet out of the typewriter as though she were ripping de Benedetti's tongue out of his throat.

'Seriously,' he continued the persecution, 'he had a white suit and a tie like a laser beam display. And the shoes, Michelangelo! Mediterranean beach colour and shining like spotlights. Horribly good looking of course. A sort of Rudolf Valentino—'

He suddenly broke off and fixed her with an appalling stare, so that she braced herself for another awful joke. But for once it wasn't a joke.

'Now it's come to me!' he said. 'I know where I've seen that Spaniard before!'

'Whoever's that?' Peroni asked.

He pointed to a cluster of craft following some way behind a single boat rowed by a gigantic figure which reared up against the lagoon in primeval might.

'The Bull,' said Estrella, 'practising.'

'Training,' corrected Peroni. 'Yes, I've heard of him.'

'I should hope so indeed,' said Estrella severely. 'Let's go and have a look.'

The boat accelerated as naturally as a horse breaking into a canter and they quickly reached the group of boats. In one of them was a bishop, perhaps a cardinal, and the scarlet of his robes seemed of surreal incongruity in the nautical scene. As they passed him, he raised his right hand in benediction; Estrella crossed herself quite spontaneously and Peroni followed her more awkwardly.

'I wonder what he's doing here.'

'Anybody may get regatta fever,' said Estrella.

'Fever? Over a boat race?'

'You may be the greatest when it comes to murder, Commissario, but you've got a long way to go when it comes to Venetian customs. People get more worked up in Venice over the Regatta than anything else. The training they have to do for it! For one thing they have to—' She flushed attractively, '—well, stay away from women. That's fatal for the regatta.'

'Impressive,' said Peroni. 'It's next Sunday, isn't it?'

'That's right. We—that's to say the Partecipazios, because it's one of those old family traditions papa so dotes on—we always watch it from a gondola. Not from the canal bank or somebody else's balcony like the riff raff. You must join us this year, Commissario.'

'I'd like that.'

For a moment they stood watching the titanic figure of the greatest regatta champion of all time slowly dwindle in the distance, and then Estrella turned back in their former direction.

After a while they began to dawdle very slowly along in the desolate lagoon with nothing in sight except a couple of sandy banks, just emerging from the surface like the humps of underwater camels with seagulls perched on them.

'Why are you going so slowly?' asked Peroni.

'Can't go any faster here,' she said, 'or we'd run aground on a mud bank. It's very easy to do here. You have to hug the *bricole*.'

'The *bricole*?' queried Peroni, correctly assuming it was Venetian dialect.

'Those stakes sunk into the lagoon. They say there are 20,000 of them altogether—I've never counted. But if you even go a few inches off course—slurp!—there you are in the mud as likely as not.'

As they went in silence and Peroni observed Estrella's April-sky face, his thoughts began to get out of hand. They were coasting a forlorn stretch of marsh towards its point which, as they rounded it, unexpectedly revealed a tiny island on which stood a low, single storey building, neglected now, yet still retaining traces of an ancient elegance.

'The Island,' announced Estrella. She swung round it and then moored in a little harbour behind the house.

'Do you come here to paint?' asked Peroni, climbing out after her.

'Oh, no!' she said firmly. 'For painting I like scenes which are full of life. But all life abandoned this Island years ago. Papa used to come here during the war to hide from the Germans. Let's go and wake up the house.'

They walked round it to the front where she unlocked the door and they went in. The place smelled musty and was unexpectedly cold after the sun outside. Like a tomb, thought Peroni and shivered as his usually overheated Neapolitan blood went momentarily chill.

Estrella was going about opening wooden shutters, and at each one a new wave of light underscored the abandoned nature of the room: the sparse, broken furniture; the dust which lay thick on all surfaces and, newly aroused, swirled in a ray of sun; the patches of damp creating mysterious continents on the walls and ceilings.

Peroni watched lecherously as she leaned out to fix a shutter, her delightfully feminine bottom enticingly high-lighted by the tautened jeans. Naples was running amok in him now, and as he moved towards her his right hand was cupped ready for the time-old tribute of the Neapolitan male to bottoms such as this.

'Penny for 'em, commissario?' she said turning towards him.

In the very nick of time, thought the appalled commissario. 'I was wondering what that line of land is that you can just make out in the distance over there,' he lied.

And then he had a sudden intuition of an entire new world that was waiting for him and Estrella. Too late he realised that they'd been standing on the very frontier of it, and that Estrella was as anxious to explore it as he was. But the frontier seemed to be magic and its movements capricious; it had gone as unpredictably as it had come, and the two of them were left unequivocally on a small island in the Venetian lagoon.

'Pellestrina,' she said, 'I'll get us a drink, shall I?' But her smile seemed to indicate that she knew. And regretted the irremediable gesture had not been made? He couldn't tell.

'Coke or beer?' she said.

They took the cans outside and sat on the grass watching the water.

'What turned you into a policeman?' Estrella asked.

'A priest.'

'What?' Her eyes went very wide.

'When I was little, I was one of the *scugnizzi*, the gutter urchins of Naples who pick up a living any way they can provided it's on the wrong side of the law.'

'Ah,' she said, 'that sounds more like you, commissario! Don't misunderstand me,' she went on quickly. 'What I mean is you haven't got a very policemanly character. But go on—the priest.'

'He was called don Pietro. He took us in one day—me and my sister—and gave us food and drink and warmth. And freedom. That was the tricky bit. He let us come and go as we wanted. If he'd tried to institutionalise us we'd have been out just as soon as we'd pocketed all we could lay our hands on, and today I'd probably be all one piece, instead of being a commissario with a Neapolitan gutter kid inside.'

'But you wouldn't be any good as a commissario if you hadn't got a Neapolitan gutter kid inside.'

'I'd never thought of that,' said Peroni.

'The story.'

'That's all there is to it, really. Don Pietro just had a knack of discovering what people were good at and he had friends in the right places. So one day a kid would find himself discovering he had a talent for journalism, and a couple of days later the editor of the *Corriere della Sera* would happen to drop in for lunch. When don Pietro told me I ought to be a policeman, I told him that what he needed was a strait-jacket, but even as I said it I knew he was right, that I had an irresistible urge to get at the truth, as he put it. Shortly after that, the police chief of Naples paid us an unexpected visit. And that was the beginning. Or the end, whichever way you care to put it.'

When he had finished her silence lasted so long that he looked up to see what was the matter. She turned quickly away from him, but not before he had seen large tears following a crooked course down her cheeks.

'What's the matter, Signorina?'

'Nothing, Commissario, nothing! It's just that stories like that always make me cry!' She scrambled to her feet. 'Come on,' she said, 'I'll take you back to Venice. You've got a murder hunt on your hands, or had you forgotten? Just give me a second to close up the house . . .'

She was all movement now, and within a couple of minutes they were back in her motorboat heading away from the Island.

As Peroni looked back at it, he seemed to see that unexplored new world hovering over it like a mirage, and he wondered with pulsing insistence whether they would come to its frontier again.

ELEVEN

'You're not serious, *dottore*?'

'I suppose it is rather a crazy idea,' admitted de Benedetti looking shame-faced, 'It just occurred to me that it might . . .' He let the sentence trail awkwardly away.

They were in Peroni's office where he had just arrived following his wanton flight into the lagoon for which this proposal was plainly a retributory thunderbolt. But the gods were careless in their aim, for this one could be dodged. Or so he hoped.

'I couldn't possibly look so much like him as to fool the Lion,' he said.

'I assure you, *dottore*, when I finally realised *why* he looked so familiar to me, I was amazed at the similarity. If it wasn't for the enormous black moustache and the clothes you could be his double.'

Every so often in Peroni's career, fate peremptorily demanded that he improvise such an outrageous and possibly dangerous scene as this. He wriggled like all the eels in Comacchio to get out of it, only to be inexorably tilted in at the end; and each time he played the preposterous scene through, vowing solemnly that it was to be the last. And so it was until the next one came.

But there was still a little room for wriggling. 'Surely a conventional raid would be more sensible?'

'Without the customer?'

Peroni had to admit the truth of that. 'But there's something else,' he objected. 'The note says 23.00 all right, but how do we know it's tonight?'

'He put the time, so it's reasonable to assume he'd also have put the date if it wasn't today, don't you think, *dottore*?'

'And suppose it isn't what we think it is? I shan't have the knowledge to play it through.'

'But by the time you'd found that out, *dottore*, you'd also have discovered what it *is* all about.'

That was fairly inescapable. And when they knew that, they just might know why *avv*. Bixi had been killed. Perhaps even by whom. And what would the media make of it? It was of stuff such as this that the Peroni legend was made. '*Disguised Peroni Routs, Unmasks, Traces*—Routs, unmasks, traces what?'

The idea was quite out of the question.

The Hooker shuffled along the Riva degli Schiavoni, apparently oblivious to the looks he received. He was a sort of mobile tourist attraction, but appeared totally unaware of it. A large American woman with a pink trouser suit slashed with white lined him up in the view-finder of her movie camera.

The camera whirred and the Hooker shuffled on, scratching himself. The Riva itself was broad and offered abundant room, even for the huge crowd of tourists that moved along it. But on the bridges the crowd was squashed tightly together like grains of sand in the neck of an egg-timer, and you could see people pulling towards the parapets so as not to come into physical contact with him. Mothers clutched their children tightly away from him. If he noticed this revulsion for his person he gave no sign of it.

Where was he going? His movements were a mystery even to the gondoliers. But not to everybody. One person knew that it was not by sheer chance the Hooker was at the Zattere on one particular morning, at the Rialto in the afternoon and at the Fondamenta Nuova in the evening.

The Hooker was on his way to keep an appointment with that person now.

Peroni was not entirely displeased with his reflection in the mirror, outrageous though de Benedetti had created it. In the normal line of duty such clothes would have been unthinkable, but under the circumstances there was no avoiding them so he allowed his vanity cautious rein. He gave a practise twirl to the luxuriant false moustache and wondered what Estrella Partecipazio would have made of him.

Then with some reluctance he tore himself away from his

reflection and went downstairs where de Benedetti was waiting for him. It was half past ten.

'We may as well start,' he said. And then suddenly, no longer buoyed up by the sight of his own appearance, he felt the full ludicrousness of the project, and the sight of de Benedetti's freckled, homely, Venetian face gave him a kick of inner fury. But it was too late to go back.

'It really is extraordinary, *dottore*,' said de Benedetti, 'you just *are* him!'

Peroni could only hope he was right.

They went out to a waiting police launch, and as they got into it the driver started the engine and they throbbed over the black, night waters towards the Zattere.

'The English writer John Ruskin stayed there,' said de Benedetti indicating a *pensione* on their right. 'There's a plaque outside.'

Peroni grunted and reflected sourly that if the Lion had suddenly burst upon them with a blazing machine-gun, de Benedetti would still not neglect to point out the tourist attractions.

The launch stopped near the church of Santa Maria del Rosario which was as near as the water would take them to the address Rubio y Ors had scribbled down. It was 10.45.

Peroni lit an English cigarette and felt the bulk of the gun against his body and the miniature walkie-talkie with which he would be able to summon de Benedetti's aid. Finally he flicked the cigarette into the water and got up.

'I'll go now.'

'Good luck, *dottore*.'

De Benedetti offered his hand and, much though he would have liked to, Peroni could not refuse it. The solemnity of the gesture made the whole business appear yet more ridiculous.

He got out of the launch and went into a narrow *calle* running down beside the church. This led into a tiny square with a well in the centre. And on the other side of this square, as Peroni had seen from the wall map at the *Questura*, was the address at which the appointment had been fixed.

He crossed this deserted square, listening in vain for some sign of life and, an overgrown qualm in the pit of his stomach, pushed the doorbell. He heard a distant jangling as though from the bottom of a very deep well, then silence. A lifting breeze from the lagoon stirred the leaves of the nearby trees and, in the circumstances, this created an eerie whispering effect.

For a long time there continued to be no answer, and Peroni began to hope against hope that none would come. And then, suddenly, he knew he was being observed. It was a long, searching observation and he had to force himself not to look for its source.

Then the door was opened by remote control with a dull, metallic click and he knew he had passed the preliminary test. He stepped into the darkness within, feeling as though he were walking over a cliff's edge in Dante's Hell without knowing which particular form of torment awaited him below.

But it wasn't completely dark. A single candle was burning on a low chest, and by its light he was able to make out that he was in a bare hallway with a flight of stone stairs ahead of him.

What was he meant to do now? Rubio y Ors had presumably received instructions; Peroni would have to improvise. He went up the stairs. At the head of them, on the left, was a door, and as he approached it he could hear from the room inside the sound of a single flute weaving slow, languid patterns on the air. He tried the door and found that it opened.

With a murmured invocation to St Janarius he went in.

'A good mother is a man's best friend,' agreed the Undertaker unctuously, but with a perceptible slur, his eyes rolling squintily ceilingwards.

The reply to this which came from the deep shadows about the bed showed no signs of mollification.

'A glass or two,' he corrected, 'no more. Under the circumstances permissible, if you will allow me to say so, mamma.'

This time the reply was brief and sharp.

'Unkind, mamma, unkind,' said the Undertaker. 'You wound me. You forget that I am under considerable strain.'

This statement aroused no sympathy either, perhaps because it was accompanied by a cadenza of shuddering hiccoughs.

'If you will allow me to speak, mamma,' said the Undertaker with oily politeness when he had recovered, 'that is just what I'm trying to tell you. The reason that I am under strain is that the police are making enquiries about me.' He listened for the reaction. 'Yes, I thought that would startle you, mamma,' he said, and then listened again. 'Oh, nothing obvious,' he said, 'but one like myself who has worked in the legal profession is more readily aware than a layman would be when enquiries are being made about him. That is the point, mamma,' said the Undertaker. 'In what direction are these enquiries? The past or the present? If it's for the present, they can't possibly know about what we've done.' He stopped for an interruption, and then continued somewhat huffily, 'Very well, then, mamma, if you prefer it, what I've done—on your advice. They can't know about that, can they? You and I are the only people who know.'

He paused a moment and then looked sideways at the bed with a funereal ghost of a smile. 'And you're not likely to tell anyone, are you, mamma?'

The only lighting came from the candles at the foot of a coffin. And beside the coffin stood the Lion. That it was the Lion there was no question, but he was strangely transformed. Gone were the black trousers and striped shirt and red-banded straw hat, and in their place was a long, midnight blue robe with zodiacal and cabalistic symbols in gold upon it. Whether it was this robe or the surroundings or some inner magnetism it was impossible to say, but the Lion's daytime appearance was transcended and he gave an impression of supernatural mastery.

Peroni's eyes flicked like lizards about him. Apart from the door, the room seemed to have none of the usual features or apertures; no windows, fireplaces, pictures, shelves; just a uniform darkness, soft underfoot; a starless night.

Whatever the Lion was about, he was in no hurry to proceed. He stood at the head of the coffin, one hand raised in the air, staring at Peroni with mesmeric eyes. The candle-light made his wizened, monkey face curiously mobile.

Now he'll spot me, thought Peroni, but instead the Lion beckoned very slowly with his raised hand and Peroni, sunk in his conception of Rubio y Ors, went forward.

With an imperious gesture the Lion indicated the open coffin and, looking down into it, Peroni saw to his violent horror that it contained a body. Or rather the very decomposed remains of a body. The skull had caved in at one side and the remaining eye gaped at him balefully. The rest was little more than a heap of disjointed bones and dust lying in approximately human form.

'Rosina Medebac.' The Lion now spoke for the first time, and his voice was a solemn ritual chant. 'Stabbed to death in a brawl at the age of twenty-five in the year 1760. Formerly inscribed in the register of Venetian courtesans. This is the woman I have undertaken to recall to life for your pleasure tonight.'

Mad, thought Peroni inside Rubio y Ors. But he corrected himself even as he thought it. Casanova, he remembered, and other great adventurers of the 18th century were always rigging up apparently supernatural spectacles for the fleecing of rich foreigners. It was as much a Venetian speciality as fish risotto.

Time now for the Commissario to step out of the Spanish actor, put an end to the macabre farce and take the Lion off to the *Questura*. But Peroni was curious to see what was going to happen next, and so he decided to let things go forward just a few minutes more.

There was silence again beneath the haunting tracery of the flute and he caught himself trying to put flesh onto the dead bones. The Venetian courtesans of the 18th century were world famous for their skill and grace, and Peroni was trying to envisage what this Rosina Medebac could have been like, assuming she had existed. Small and slim with long black hair and—yes, green eyes; a sullenly pretty face with a beauty spot on the right cheek-bone and long fingers which looked as though they were adept at clawing as well as stroking.

Suddenly the Commissario realised what was going on and checked these thoughts in shocked outrage. But at the same time Peroni had the odd impression that he was being willed to see the girl like that, and in spite of himself the image persisted and grew clearer. It was plainly time to halt the charade.

'Have you brought the money?'

Peroni nodded, relieved that his hand was now to be forced. No money, no show. But then the Lion didn't ask to see the money, and the moment somehow passed. Peroni decided he would just wait to see how the trick was going to be played.

The flute continued to weave its hypnotic patterns. Not snake-charming, thought Peroni, but man-charming, sucker-charming.

And the Lion lifted a thurible that was beside the coffin and began to sway it rhythmically over the macabre contents while dense clouds of incense billowed out, filling the room with a heavy, bitter-sweet aroma.

Absurd, thought Peroni. Who in their right senses could be taken in by such a grotesque fraud?

As he swung the censer, the Lion murmured incantations which were not in Italian or any other language Peroni could recognise. They swayed like the music, rose to loud crescendoes and then sank again to a murmur, liquid sounding and flowing with sibilation.

And what with the music and the incense and the rising and falling incantations, above all what with the image of Rosina Medebac which continued to haunt him, Peroni found himself, not exactly believing in the fraud, but playing along with it. La Medebac seemed to have an objective existence somewhere outside his mind. Outside even the mind of the Lion. In some world or other she had her own being.

Peroni groped for reality. It was a conjuring trick. The sure sign of a conjuring trick is that you can't see at the crucial moment. That was what the incense was for. There were clouds of it like banks of mist on the *autostrada*, and through them you could just make out the sinister coffin shape and the compulsive gondoliering sorcerer beside it, his rising and falling incantations sounding as though they were heading towards some magical junction.

The coffin obviously had a false bottom and, under cover of all that incense, music and spell weaving, a 20th century Venetian courtesan in suitable costume would climb through, having removed the macabre remains.

But then Peroni remembered having seen underneath the table before the incense had been lit. So where would she come from? That was where the conjuring trick came in, he told himself with exasperated patience.

And yet ancestral Neapolitan voices, whose owners had all believed in the supernatural far more than the natural, whispered within him how much more interesting it would be if it were true. How banal a conjuring trick would be! How much more consonant the supernatural is with the real nature of things!

What a glowing existence Rosina Medebac had beyond the frontier of the possible!

The mercenary soldier from Turin had come to her as a client a week before, his pockets spilling forth money earned in some foreign war. There was something un-Venetian about his turbulent, violent nature which perversely attracted her and when, after the first time, he had proposed that she move in with him she had, against all her normal custom, agreed. At least—she added the tacit provisory clause for herself—until she had helped him spend the money from—Poland? Russia? England? Outside Venice all place names were one to her.

For a few days everything went well. They rode the crest of the Venetian wave at Carnival time, playing at the Ridotto, weaving masked through a sea of masks, dancing and drinking. But always returning to the room at the Golden Cock Inn which was the scene of all their stormy rides—except for one which had taken place in the back of a box during master Goldoni's latest comedy, *The Impresario from Smyrna*.

And then the money ran out, and she was ready to go back to the life she had led since the age of twelve.

The last thing that she had expected was that he would be jealous, but he was, savagely and possessively. She knew how to handle jealous lovers though; in her time she had handled more of them than she could remember. And so it was that she only realised in the last few seconds, when it was already too late, that he was different from the others.

There, in the room at the Golden Cock, he had railed at her and she had taunted him with her liberty to do as she pleased, there he had threatened to kill her and she had dared him to do it. She had even pulled open her dress, laughing at him, laying her breasts bare to onslaught.

Then she saw madness lighten in his eyes and a dagger in his hand. It seared into her belly, letting in an icy tidal wave which raced, mounting towards her heart; and in that moment Rosina Medebac understood why she had been drawn to him in the first place.

He carried the one gift she had longed for all her life.

They were reaching a climax. The Lion's incantations were wilder. The room eddied with a mystical fog of incense. The piping music had ceased to weave and was surging towards a shrill orgasm of sound.

Now the modern Venetian whore had climbed into her gruesome bed, ready to pop out. And yet in Peroni's mind something still insisted on showing him the disjointed bones and the dust coming together, putting on flesh and hair, eyeballs, nails.

Then suddenly everything stopped. The music cut short in mid-phrase, the Lion was silent, motionless as a statue with one hand stretched towards the coffin in a gesture of command. The silence was so absolute that you could almost hear the swirl of the incense.

Within the coffin something stirred.

Still in silence a head appeared, shoulders, breasts swelling beneath a low-cut neck-line. In the dim light and fog-like incense it was difficult to make out anything clearly, but Peroni was shocked, and at the same time perversely excited, to see that she was in fact small and slim with long black hair. Yet what was so surprising about that? It was a common enough Venetian type. But when she had climbed out of her coffin, when she had started to walk towards Peroni as though still not fully roused from a centuries long sleep, he was appalled to see that she also had a beauty spot on her right cheek bone.

And at the same time he began to wish that he were indeed Rubio y Ors. She exercised a powerful below-the-belt attraction, and there was something vaguely Neapolitan about her which always increased a girl's attraction for Peroni.

She stood before him, her eyes—were they green?—sensually half closed in sleep. Now was the moment to break the erotic spell. Now was the brink of the weir.

Rosina Medebac's arms snaked up to entwine Peroni's neck, pulling his mouth down towards hers.

Now! howled the Commissario a long way off. And it seemed to Peroni that he had become Rubio y Ors.

Rosina Medebac's lips crushed into those of the Spanish actor and enveloped them, while her tongue tickled a demand for admission and her long nails clawed his neck, just as he had imagined they would.

De Benedetti was waiting for a radio summons.

De Benedetti would continue to wait for a radio summons.

'*Questura.*'

Peroni could not believe that it was his own voice. But Rubio y Ors had been snatched from the arms of Rosina Medebac, and in his place was standing—panting a little, a little dishevelled—Commissario Peroni of the Venetian *Questura*.

And the Commissario was flipping a switch of his miniature walkie-talkie to establish radio contact with de Benedetti.

TWELVE

When Rosina Medebac was escorted into Peroni's office the morning after her near triumph over his virtue she looked more haggard than she had done in the scented room at the house off the Zattere. But still desirable enough for Peroni to be glad of the presence of Policewoman Sofia Michelangelo.

The tail end of the previous night had been confused and protracted. With the entrance of de Benedetti, reality had poured into the room like water into a torpedoed submarine. Amid screams, protests and insults it had emerged that Rosina Medebac was indeed a call-girl from Mestre, known to de Benedetti in his line of business, though not hers.

The conjuring trick, too, was depressingly banal. As Peroni had imagined, the coffin had a false bottom, and what had seemed like empty space under the table was an effect created by a mirror slotted at an angle between table and floor. The erotic windings of the flute had come from a tape recorder, and beneath his wizard's robe the Lion wore black gondolier's trousers and striped shirt.

And now it was all to be sorted out.

'Document,' snapped Peroni in his irritable functionary manner, trying not to look at her lips.

She took it out of an enormous shiny red handbag which sorted ill with the 18th century costume she was still wearing and handed it over to Peroni with the practised flip of one accustomed to showing her documents to the police.

Repubblica Italiana, said the front of the card, TESSERA N. 2873319. Did this mean that when it was issued there were only 2873319 identity card holders in Italy? Peroni determined to enquire about this one day. FORLANI Erica n. SMALTI, went on the card, adding that its owner was married and *operaia*.

'Where did you work?' asked Peroni.

'Ferraldi clothing factory.'

He contemplated asking her when she had passed to the un-clothing factory, but decided it would be in bad taste and might shock Policewoman Michelangelo. 'When did you start in the game?' he asked instead.

'Four years ago when my husband left me,' she said indifferently.

'And how long have you been with the Lion?'

'Just over a year.'

'And how long's the coffin business been going on?'

'Three weeks. He thought it up for the Goldoni festival.'

'The Lion?'

She nodded.

'How many times have you done it?'

'Eight. Nine including you.'

'Does he do it with other women?'

'No, I'm the only one.'

'And how much do you get out of it?'

'Fifty thousand a time.'

Perhaps ten per cent of what the Lion got, Peroni reckoned, perhaps less. He decided there was no point in detaining her, and told her to keep herself at the disposal of the police.

'I always am,' she said with a monstrous wink which evoked their relationship the previous evening.

Peroni pretended not to see.

Italian advertising men like to boast of mechanical products that they are endowed with German efficiency and Italian elegance, it being an accepted fact that each country is as rich in one as it is poor in the other. But if the Vivaldi Hotel in Venice were to need anything as vulgar as advertising it could go a great deal further than that. It could claim American opulence, French style,

English courtesy, Swiss discretion and Dutch solidity.

All of this made the chambermaid Marta's project seem the more outrageous. The security measures taken by the Vivaldi when assuming personnel are unimpeachable, but there are some things which nobody can foresee.

The office responsible for screening Marta had discovered that she came of an excellent family, her father being the sacristan in one of Venice's innumerable churches and her mother a self-employed seamstress. Having finished junior school, Marta had been employed by the family of a wealthy industrialist where she had acquired the domestic skills rarely demanded or even imagined in an age of automation and democracy, but still required by the Vivaldi where Marta had taken employment when the industrialist's family had departed for Switzerland, leaving her with impeccable references.

But nobody could predict love and the effects it might have. And so it was that Marta was planning how she might steal from one of the hotel guests, a prospect as horrifying as the murder of a patient on the operating table.

The guest in question wasn't even on one of the floors where she normally worked which meant that she would not easily come under suspicion if the theft were successfully completed. But it also meant that the operation was that much more difficult to carry through without being seen.

And now was the moment to set it on foot. Marta crossed herself and started off.

A fly was sitting on Peroni's desk. It was a fly of wily aspect, and its tiny eyes flicked between the Commissario and the monkey-faced gondolier, who had just been escorted in for interrogation, as though it were umpiring between them.

'Where did you get the skull?'

'Antique shop. One of those skulls old monks look at in pictures.'

'*Memento mori.*'

Peroni recognised to his embarrassment a note of complicity in the way he said this, as though there were a secret understanding between him and the Lion. And he realised the cause of it. The eternal Neapolitan con-man within him had recognised a brother in this Venetian con-man and was trying to signal to him.

'And the house?'

'Belongs to a friend of mine—working in Turin now. He gave me the keys to look after it. You know how it is.'

The Venetian con-man was clearly waving back. Being careful to give no sign of recognition, Peroni continued with the secondary point of the house and the friend who owned it. The fly seemed to lose interest and flew off to explore the crucifix above Peroni's shoulders.

After some minutes of toing and froing about the house, Peroni slotted in another question without any change of rhythm or emphasis. 'One day last week you were observed near Harry's Bar in conversation with *avv.* Bixi. What were you talking about?'

If the Lion was taken aback, he didn't show it. The fly, on the other hand, zoomed back from the crucifix and landed on the desk again, half way between the two men, perfectly still except for an almost imperceptible twitching of the two front legs. Not umpire, thought Peroni, but lawyer—the Lion's defending lawyer.

'*Avv.* Bixi?' said the Lion. 'The one who got himself killed?'

Peroni assented with rather too flashy Neapolitan courtesy.

'Can't say I recall him *specifically*,' said the Lion after what looked like deep pondering.

'Am I expected to take that seriously?'

'He might have been arranging for a gondola ride.'

The fly beat its wings and was instantly airborne and heading for the Lion whom it circled twice as though in tribute to his astuteness.

Not so fast, fly, Peroni said inwardly as he rose to his feet. 'Last Monday,' he announced aloud, '*Avv.* Bixi was murdered in Calle dei Assassini. Just a week before his death, his office diary carried a reference to Harry's Bar—where you work at the gondola station. On the same day, or perhaps the day after you were seen talking with him outside Harry's Bar. We now know that you were running a pimping racket with the macabre necrophiliac speciality of raising an 18th century courtesan from the dead for the entertainment of rich foreigners. It doesn't take a great deal of imagination to piece things together now, does it? *Avv*. Bixi found out about this profitable side-line of yours, duly noted your gondolier rank in his diary and went to see you. He threatened to denounce you if he wasn't cut in on the takings. You temporised, maybe agreed to go along with him. Then on Monday night you waited for him round a corner on his route between office and home, and when he passed—' Peroni flicked his right middle finger significantly against his thumb, leaving the words suspended.

The fly buzzed furiously about Peroni's head, indignant at this outrageous accusation against his client. The Lion took it more calmly, but the reasoning seemed to have had some effect on him just the same. Peroni waited to see what it was.

'Oh, I wouldn't have done that, Commissario,' said the Lion after a second, and the Venetian con-man's monkey face gave way to a grin like a nut ceding to the nutcrackers.

'Against your principles?'

Principles? The Lion's expression seemed to say. Between you and me? Come off it, Commissario! Out loud he said, 'There's more to it than that.'

'Oh?'

The Lion looked at the fly as though soliciting its advice, then back at Peroni.

'*Avv*. Bixi organised the whole thing,' he said.

Carrying a laundry bag with sheets and pillow cases which Olympic Vivaldi standards considered soiled, Marta went down a back staircase from the fourth to the third floor. Then, edging open a swing door, she peeped out right and left. Number 127 was just down the corridor on the right overlooking the lagoon, and the first part of her plan was to get unseen into number 125 which was next door to it and which she knew had been vacated earlier that morning.

Nobody was about, so she tip-toed down the corridor in a soundless run, found the door unlocked, opened it and went in. When she had closed it behind her she breathed deeply for a second. Then she crossed the room and looked carefully out through the balcony windows to the balcony of 127. It was empty of guests, though strewn with the remains of breakfast and a copy

102

of the *Gazzettino*. Making sure no one was watching her, she stepped further out onto the balcony till she could see into 127. It was empty and clothes were laid out on the chair. So far her timing was accurate.

Marta went back into the room and opened the door into the bathroom which backed onto the bathroom of 127. There was a small grating in the wall between the two, and she climbed up onto the bath to put her ear to it.

At first she could make out no sounds—no pouring of water, gargling or purring of electric razor. But then she distinguished something even better—the gentle, relaxed splashing sound of someone in the bath. That should give her at least three minutes, if not more.

As she looked out into the corridor she checked in horror. There was the famous actress, Maddalena Spinelli, walking towards the lift. But then Marta relaxed. Maddalena Spinelli hadn't seen her; it was well known among the staff that Maddalena Spinelli, who had a suite on this floor, didn't see anybody it didn't suit her to see.

When the actress had got into the lift, the corridor was empty. Marta slipped to the door of 127 and noiselessly tried the handle. There was always the possibility that he might have locked himself in while bathing. But no, the door opened.

Now she was in the deadliest circle of danger.

'*Avv*. Bixi organised the whole thing?' Peroni repeated.

Policewoman Sofia Michelangelo was following the interrogation with the attention of Moses on Sinai. She had read in a magazine article somewhere that Commissario Peroni had a chameleon quality which enabled him to change personality according to the person he was interviewing. She had scarcely believed it at the time, but it was true. He had somehow become more Neapolitan, and at the same time acquired the persuasive power of the man on television who always made her want to buy washing machines.

And within minutes of the interrogation starting he had elicited the startling admission that the murdered *Avv*. Bixi had organised the whole peculiar affair of the woman in the coffin. (The things some men liked never ceased to astonish her.) *Dott*.

Peroni was a genius, she thought, her tummy turning to treacle.

' . . . the whole thing,' she finished shorthanding in her note-book.

'That's right,' said the gondolier so improbably known as the Lion, 'it was his idea.'

'When did you first meet Bixi?' asked the Commissario.

'In the spring last year. He had somehow got onto the fact that I was introducing occasional customers to Signora Forlani and a couple of other young ladies of my acquaintance for their mutual advantage.'

'Pimping,' suggested Peroni.

The Lion made a liquid Venetian gesture which implied that if a gentleman from Naples cared to employ such a rudimentary word for a charitable service towards one's fellow creatures, he was at liberty to do so.

'Go on.'

'Well, the *avvocato* came to see me and said that if I didn't—how shall I put it . . .'

'Cut him in?' offered the Commissario.

An expression on the Lion's wrinkled, quizzical face seemed to say that even Venetian euphony couldn't find a kinder way of putting it.

'As you say, Commissario,' he confirmed, 'if I didn't cut him in, he would denounce me.'

'And you accepted? You didn't react?'

'React how, Commissario? By murdering him? But I suppose you're right—if I were going to murder him at all, *that* would have been when I'd have done it.'

The fly which had been buzzing about the office ever since the interview started, now for some reason zoomed three times very fast around Commissario Peroni and the Lion. The Commissario seemed to find it particularly irritating, and Michel-angelo wondered whether she ought to go and get some fly-killer, but didn't like to cause an interruption.

The radio fitted into the bedhead was playing classical music softly. Marta looked wildly about her. Expensive, newly pur-chased clothing, a glass zebra which must have cost a small fortune, a crocodile skin wallet with at least one 100,000 lire note peeping out of it and a plastic container with a book of traveller's cheques, but Marta wasn't a thief. What she was looking for was altogether different, and there was no sign of it.

A pall of misery enveloped her fear like fog over ice. Had she risked so much for nothing? And time was passing. She dared not stay there much longer.

She pulled drawers silently open, but without luck. And then she thought of the desk. It was an expensive piece of furniture by the window with a flap-top covering the writing surface which contained a blotting pad (changed daily), Vivaldi writing paper and envelopes.

She went noiselessly over to it and opened the flap, and there, on top of the blotting pad, was beyond any doubt what she was looking for. She scooped it quickly into the laundry bag and went out of the room, pulling the door gently behind her.

Luck held and she got out of the corridor without being seen. Once safely through the swing door she made her way to the service lift which she took down to the ground floor. She then went to the little room at the back of the hotel where soiled laundry was kept prior to being picked up by trolley and taken to the laundry.

'*Ciao*, Marta!' came a voice behind her. 'What are you looking so furtive about?'

When two con-men play each other, thought Peroni, the truth becomes as hard to find as a virgin at an orgy. That the Lion would have murdered Bixi at the *beginning* of their partnership if at all was indisputable. But to Peroni the story of Bixi's previous involvement in the pimping sounded just perceptibly false. If he was already in partnership with the Lion, why should he bother to write down Harry's Bar in his diary? For the moment, however, it would have to be accepted on trial and, although he knew that the three-card trick atmosphere the interview had taken on would inevitably become denser, he had no choice but to continue.

'And how much of a cut did he get out of it?'

'Fifty-fifty.'

'You must have come to know him pretty well—working as partners for over a year?'

'Oh, I wouldn't really say that. Not well. It was a business relationship.'

'You must have formed some idea of his character. What sort of man was he?'

The Lion considered it with pursed lips. 'Well, close I'd say. And clever. Not a man you'd like to be on the wrong side of.'

There was a pause. The fly buzzed irritably. If you've no further questions to put to my client . . . ?

'Was he involved in any other activities with gondoliers?'

'I couldn't say,' said the Lion, a look of infinite cunning passing over his monkey face. 'He didn't let his right hand know what his left hand was doing, if you take my meaning. Only—'

'Only?'

'It's just an impression, Commissario, but when he came to see me, I always had the impression that he'd come from somebody and that he was going on to somebody else. That he was doing his rounds.'

Which card was the truth hidden under now? thought Peroni.

It was a girl from Murano called Cinzia who was pleasant enough in her way, but a busybody.

'Furtive?' said Marta. 'Me? It must be the light.'

'And what are you bringing your laundry down now for?'

Mind your own business! thought Marta. Aloud she said, 'I prefer to do it in two stages—it breaks the morning up. D'you mind?'

'No, no! But don't let them catch you at it—it's *inefficient*!' Smiling, she underlined the word which was one of the more cutting terms of reproach used by the Vivaldi hierarchy. '*Ciao*!'

'*Ciao*, Cinzia!'

Marta went into the little laundry room and closed the door behind her. That could have been awkward.

The last phase of the operation. She crossed the room, put the laundry bag on a little table and opened the window which looked out onto a clammy-stoned *calle* at the back of the hotel.

'Marta—'

He was there, and the mere sight of him made Marta's entrails heave with love.

'Got it?'

'Here it is.'

She took it from the laundry bag and passed it through the window to him.

'Good girl! See you when it's all settled.'

He mouthed a kiss at her and she mouthed him one back.

'What's your impression, Michelangelo?'

Miss a chance like this, she told herself, and you'll be kicking yourself for the rest of your life. She martialled her thoughts carefully.

Two things emerged from the interview. One, the Lion couldn't very well be their murderer. When *dott*. Peroni had questioned him about his movements on Monday night he admitted having spent the relevant time between eleven p.m. and one a.m. in the company of the Forlani woman and a customer whom he described as an English milord. That more or less had to be the truth because it could be too easily disproved on checking.

And two, it seemed that the lawyer, instead of being killed for his knowledge of whoever was behind the various gondoliering malpractices, had been killed because he *was* that person.

She was about to express these thoughts when the Commissario started to beat the air about him with his hands. It was that fly again.

'Shall I get some fly killer, Commissario?'

'Please, Michelangelo.'

She got up and went to the door, but she had only just stepped into the corridor when he called after her, 'It's gone out with you, Michelangelo!'

He seemed surprisingly put out by this, almost as though the fly had heard their plans for it and deliberately escaped. But he must be on edge, she decided going back into the office, after his brilliant operation of the previous evening.

'You were about to say, Michelangelo?'

His dark southern eyes were entirely taken up with her. She sat down and prepared herself once again for a display of lucid, but feminine cogency. Her lips were parted to shape the first word of it when the door burst open and de Benedetti erupted into the office like a wild boar into an arbour. She closed her eyes for a moment of concentrated inner venom.

'I've got something on the Undertaker at last, *dottore*,' he said.

'Ah!' said Peroni, his attention now entirely focussed on de Benedetti.

'What are you looking so disapproving for, Michelangelo?' said the appalling Venetian detective. 'Have I got something undone? Yes,' he went on, sitting down, 'the Undertaker. I was making enquiries about Bixi's legal dealings on behalf of gondoliers. Nothing much there—small stuff. I'll prepare a report on it. But at the same time I got the true story of the Undertaker's change of job. He was blackmailing somebody!'

Even Michelangelo had to admit this was a find.

'I found out that he'd been involved with a man called Cappelli, a Venetian. So I got onto this Cappelli who told me that he'd been having an affair with a woman—shut your ears, Michelangelo—and the Undertaker had tried to blackmail him. It's all over and done with now, he said, but at the time he was getting a divorce and if this came out he'd have lost custody of the children who he was very keen on keeping. So what did he do? He went to a lawyer for help. And I bet you can't guess, Michelangelo, which lawyer he went to?'

She decided that the only possible reply was dignified silence.

'That's right!' went on de Benedetti. 'Golden Policewoman of the Year Award for Sofia Michelangelo! He went to *avv.* Bixi. And for a nice fat fee, *avv.* Bixi got the Undertaker off his back. So that's how it all started. The Undertaker wasn't ill at all. He was obviously threatened with a blackmail charge unless he put his talents and knowledge at the service of *avv.* Bixi.'

'It's time we had another word with the Undertaker,' said Peroni.

At that moment the telephone rang and Michelangelo picked up the receiver. '*Pronto*?' she said, '*Si*?'

She made notes as she listened, and an expression of such incredulous surprise came over her face that the two men abandoned their thoughts of the Undertaker and watched her. Eventually she put down the receiver with the look of a policewoman who knows she is going to cause a stir.

'Let me guess,' said de Benedetti. 'A gondolier trussed up in a sack and dropped by unknown hands from the Rialto Bridge? A

Soviet ship bearing machine tools spirited away from the lagoon by no less mysterious hands? Or the Madonna Nicopeia nicked from the Basilica of St Mark during the night when all the doors were locked from the inside?'

Michelangelo waited calmly. She knew she had the edge on de Benedetti this time. She waited until he had run out and then launched her announcement.

'An original Goldoni manuscript has been stolen from the room of an American staying at the Vivaldi Hotel.'

Part Three

THE HOOKER

This man whom you came across everywhere,
so well known and so much held in contempt . . .

Mémoires
Carlo Goldoni

THIRTEEN

The national patrimony being involved, the stolen Goldoni manuscript caused a considerable uproar. More than the murder, thought Peroni. Opinion was divided about fifty-fifty as to whether the manuscript was genuine.

'If there is even a one per cent chance of its being genuine,' *dott*. Amabile had ruled as though the honour of the school were at stake, 'we must treat it with the utmost seriousness. It would be the only Goldoni manuscript in existence and as such would be a priceless part of the Italian cultural inheritance. How did this American get hold of it in the first place?'

Nobody knew the answer to this.

'Well, if we recover it, he certainly can't retain it. *Santo cielo*, it would be like letting the da Vinci Last Supper out of Italy!'

Finally *Dott*. Muso went off to the Vivaldi Hotel to interview the American, and the murder hunt, now appearing somewhat anti-climactic, was resumed.

The first thing, decided Peroni back in his office, was to interview the Undertaker once again and this time mangle the truth out of him. He was ready to set off on this mission, but something held him back, an obscure dissatisfaction which at first he couldn't place.

Then he placed it and immediately tried to sweep it under a mental carpet as too disgraceful to be seen. But it wouldn't stay under the carpet and Peroni was forced to examine it.

He was publicity hungry.

Peroni was accustomed to a blaze of publicity. His investigations were usually accompanied by tele-cameras, press conferences, interviews. But the murder of *avv*. Bixi lacked the necessary appeal. The trouble was, he reflected bitterly, the Red Brigades had dulled the public appetite for violence to such an extent that you needed a holocaust to tickle it now.

113

Or, of course, the events of the previous evening. They had all the front page ingredients. But at the morning conference *dott.* Amabile had demanded the strictest discretion. *Dott.* Amabile was a great believer in strict discretion; Peroni believed it was something to do with his Friuli origins. So no press release on THE COURTESAN IN THE COFFIN.

But if somebody should leak the story? Amabile could hardly deny it. But who would be likely to leak it? Peroni eyed the telephone. The idea was, of course, unthinkable.

A moment later a male voice, speaking in a heavy Tuscan accent, was put through to a reporter at the *Gazzettino*.

'There was a sensational police operation,' it said, 'last night near the Zattere . . .'

Dott. Muso belonged to the fifty per cent which thought the manuscript was a fake, and consequently he was particularly exasperated when they had picked on him to interview the lunatic American at the Vivaldi Hotel. It had been done deliberately to spite him, he felt.

'*Il Signor* Cornelius Ruskin?' he said, making the unfamiliar syllables sound like the mouthings of somebody being submitted to severe torture.

The Vivaldi desk clerk, who had all the dignity of a pontifical legate at a diplomatic *soirée*, didn't even have time to raise an eyebrow before a wild-eyed and dishevelled American, who had been pacing the marbled entrance hall, had pounced on Muso.

'*Polizia*?' said the American.

'*Si*,' said Muso.

'Ruskin,' said the American gripping his hand as though he were a drowning man and it a rope, 'Cornelius Ruskin. We can talk over here.'

He dragged Muso over to the deep crimson leather armchairs which the Vivaldi Hotel had grouped about low glass tables for the convenience and comfort of its patrons.

'Perhaps you'd tell me the whole story, Signore,' he said when they were seated.

'I was in the bath maybe an hour ago,' said Ruskin in his scholarly Italian, 'and when I came out this manuscript, which I'd put in the desk, had disappeared.'

'What manuscript precisely?'

'The manuscript of a play by Carlo Goldoni—a lost play by Carlo Goldoni!' wailed Ruskin almost in tears.

'Genuine?' said Muso sceptically.

'Of course it was genuine!'

'How can you be so sure?'

'I am—considered an authority on the subject. Goldoni and his period have been my exclusive study since university. I've written various books on the subject.'

Muso felt a trifle less sceptical; the greatest experts on all things Italian were, in fact, always American. 'How did you come by the manuscript?' he asked.

For the first time the American's desperate urgency slackened He looked sheepish and fiddled with an enormous pipe. 'Well, it's a somewhat odd story,' he said. Muso continued to look at him with those flat eyes which are the characteristic of certain policemen. 'The day before yesterday,' Ruskin went on awkwardly, 'I received a telephone call from somebody calling himself Rossi. He said he had come into possession of the manuscript of a Goldoni play which he was prepared to sell me for a million lire.'

'Did he say how he'd come by it?'

'No.'

The probability that it had been stolen hung heavily between them and Muso did nothing to make it seem less unpleasant. 'Go on,' he said.

Ruskin described the instructions given him and the scene in the post office.

'How were you able to ascertain the genuineness of the manuscript in five minutes?'

'It was easy. For one thing I knew of the play's existence— Goldoni mentions it in his *Mémoires*, but nobody has ever seen it from then till now. And the ink, the paper were both clearly of the 18th century. The handwriting was Goldoni's, and plainly written in feverish haste—as he always wrote. And the style— nobody could have imitated Goldoni's style! It was unique, unmistakable, sublime!'

'How much would you say it was worth?' said Muso, unimpressed by Ruskin's flight of anguished lyricism.

'It was *priceless*!' he shouted, causing the Vivaldi desk clerk to look up with an almost imperceptible and instantly smoothed wrinkle in his urbanity. People did not raise their voices in the Vivaldi Hotel.

'You gave a million for it,' Muso pointed out unpleasantly, 'not an excessive sum these days.'

'But you can't reckon it in terms of money!' Ruskin blustered, 'A million, a billion, a thousand—there's no difference in such a context as this! From the point of view of calculable value, the manuscript is worth nothing. As a lost play from the peak period of Goldoni's genius the whole contents of the Bank of Italy would be nothing beside it!'

If Peroni had been present, he would have reflected that the contents of the Bank of Italy were not all that much to juggle with anyway. Muso, more submissive when it came to the establishment, merely calculated that, contrary to all expectations, he had perhaps stumbled on something big at last.

'If you don't mind, Signore,' he said pulling himself heavily out of the crimson leather armchair, 'I'd like to have a look at your room. And then I'll have a word with the management here.' Then a thought struck him. 'What was this play called?'

'*The Maidservant of Quality*,' said Cornelius Ruskin.

Reasonably confident now that his doings would no longer be ignored, Peroni was at liberty to deal with the Undertaker. But for some reason he delayed, fiddling with a pen, smoking one of his black market English cigarettes, throwing away the waste paper on his desk.

The internal telephone rang and Peroni picked it up.

'*Pronto*?'

'*Dottore*?' He recognised *dott*. Amabile's didactic courtesy of tone. 'I have just been notified that another body has been found in Corte Balbi. In exactly the same position as that of *avv*. Bixi.'

The news had arrived with a semi-coherent telephone call and Amabile could add nothing else. Peroni contacted de Benedetti and they ran down to the police boat waiting outside.

Their journey had the curious air of being a replay of the same journey they had made three days before. They even met a gondola as they turned off the Grand Canal, and Peroni half

116

expected to hear himself enquiring how they made such tight turns with such long boats, and de Benedetti replying that it was quite a skill, *dottore*.

But when they got out near the Fenice Theatre, the impression of a jump back in time was dispelled, for the crowd, which had then just spilled out of the archway into the courtyard, was already evident here, pressing, urgent with drama, towards the death.

It took Peroni and de Benedetti and the men with them ten minutes to push their way to the focal point, so dense was the crowd. As they pushed Peroni reflected that there would no longer be any need for artificial stimulation of the media.

The late inhabitant of the body, when finally they reached it, was revealed to be the last person Peroni would have suspected.

The manager of the Vivaldi Hotel made you think of an admiral-in-chief in civilian clothes, though at the present moment an admiral-in-chief whose flag ship has been torpedoed.

'You suggest,' he said to Muso, 'that one of the staff of this hotel is responsible for the theft?'

'Or one of the guests,' said Muso who didn't, as they say in Italian, have any hairs on his tongue.

It was hard to tell from the manager's expression whether this was better or worse than the previous suggestion. He sighed gently and rose from his swivel chair. He and Muso were extreme physical contrasts, the one small, fat, sweaty and crumpled, the other large, but perfectly built, cool and immaculate.

'This office', said the manager, 'will be at your disposal. I will see that the staff are sent to you one by one. I must only ask you to observe the utmost discretion.'

'Of course,' said Muso, recognising something in the manager's expression which said that he had acquaintances among the very highest ranking members of the police hierarchy who would know how to act if the smallest whisper about misdoings at the Vivaldi were to be made public.

Muso sat down with relief when the manager had withdrawn. Three minutes later came a knock at the office door which then opened to admit a chambermaid named Elena Turriddu who was looking very frightened indeed.

Lingering on in death, the Hooker's pungent and characteristic odour had provided him with a sort of temporary guard of honour which had kept the crowd at a respectful distance until the arrival of the police.

'Who found him?'

This time it turned out to be a group of children who had come into the courtyard to play. The body had been entirely concealed under the same piece of tarpaulin which had been used to cover Bixi's body, and the reason why it had been found so comparatively late in the morning—it was past eleven o'clock—was that nobody had been into the courtyard that morning until the children arrived and an enterprising little boy, whose curiosity had been aroused by the smell, had peeped beneath the tarpaulin.

'Same place, but not the same cause of death,' said Peroni, having ascertained that the back of the head was intact.

'And no sign of a wound,' said de Benedetti.

'There's some bruising just below the jaw line,' said Peroni, 'Hard to make out because of the stubble, but it's there.'

'Why him of all people?' said de Benedetti, squatting back on his haunches away from the smell.

'If we knew that,' said Peroni, 'we'd be a great deal further forward with everything.' Privately he thought that the Hooker's death was the greatest stroke of luck—for the police if not for the Hooker himself—since the finding of Bixi's body. Whatever the motive for it, it was bound to move things, and when things moved you had a chance to glimpse the truth beneath. Unless, of course, they merely stirred up mud.

The police doctor arrived and set to work, having shaken hands all round and made a couple of medical quips about the smell.

'*Mirabile dictu* indeed!' Unperceived by the police, *dott.* Tron had waved his high, grey top through the crowd and was now extending his branches for shaking.

'*Pallida mors aequo pulsat pede*,' he went on when he had learned the identity of the deceased, 'Pale death indeed knocks with an impartial foot. First a lawyer and now the Hooker. But what possible connection can there be between them?'

'The gondola,' said Peroni. 'They were both involved in the

world of the gondola.' His reflections waved like tentacles and clutched a hypothesis. 'And maybe something else,' he went on. 'What's the one thing we know for sure about the Hooker? That you might come across him anywhere in Venice. Like the water. He could turn up in any place at any time and nobody would be surprised. A person who can do that is singularly equipped for collecting secrets. And that gives us another possible link with Bixi—he was a picker up of secrets, too.'

'But the Hooker was retarded,' objected de Benedetti.

'How do we know?' said Peroni. 'It's easy for a rumour like that to spread about somebody. And the very fact that everybody *thought* he was retarded would make it all the easier for him to see and hear things that would be hidden away from anybody else.'

'And the dumbness?' said de Benedetti.

'It wouldn't stop him hearing. Or over-hearing. And as for communication, he could write or use sign language.'

'Where does this lead us, *dottore*?'

'Nowhere perhaps. It's just an idea. But if the Hooker was a specialist in secrets, then maybe he found out one secret too many. Maybe even the secret of who killed *avv*. Bixi.'

The doctor joined them, lighting a gnarled Tuscan cigar. 'I'll need to look at him properly,' he said, 'but I can advance you a little information with reasonable certainty. He was struck violently on the jaw and received another blow on the back of the head. And he was brought here after death.'

'Like Bixi . . .'

'*Si-i*,' the doctor let the affirmative trickle slowly out of his mouth mingled with cigar smoke, 'I'll be able to tell you more when I've examined him thoroughly.'

'And what do you propose now, *dottore*?' Tron asked Peroni.

'I suggest', said Peroni, flattered because the initiative at this point should strictly come from the magistrature, 'that we concentrate everything on finding out all we can about the Hooker. Background and movements.'

'*Optimum*!' said Tron, his uppermost foliage waving in approval. 'And perhaps it would be convenient for us to have a conference some time this afternoon? We should all be better informed then.'

It was decided that this should be held in *dott*. Amabile's office at 4 o'clock.

Shortly after this, the police photographer having got his snaps, *dott*. Tron gave formal authorisation for the removal of the finally hooked Hooker and uprooted himself for temporary replanting elsewhere.

There was a pause when he had gone during which Peroni brooded over the mortal remains as they were lifted onto a stretcher to be taken to a waiting ambulance launch.

'Don Amos and the Lion,' he said at last.

'I beg your pardon?' said de Benedetti looking surprised.

'I want to know about them, too. Not only the Hooker. Top priority for all three, *dottore*. Somewhere, somehow in their lives there's material to piece together the answer. A priest, a pimp and the last hooker in Venice.'

FOURTEEN

Muso was beginning to learn a lot about the workings of a great hotel, but nothing whatsoever about the theft of a Goldoni manuscript. A dozen polite and respectful girls had appeared before him, but in spite of his naturally dyspeptic nature Muso did not believe that any of them were responsible for the theft or had any knowledge concerning it.

A thirteenth knock came at the door. Barbara Melanzi from Padua. Engaged at Vivaldi a year before. Working on the fifth floor, two above Cornelius Ruskin. Mostly with Elisabetta Ferrari. And that interview checked exactly with this. Another blank.

'Can you think of anything the least unusual that occurred during the morning?'

For the first time that morning, Muso had some satisfaction. Instead of the polite look which denied the possibility of the unusual at the Vivaldi, Barbara Melanzi coloured and made a half-hearted attempt to shake her head in the negative.

Muso jumped on her like a starved dog on a wounded mouse. 'Come along now,' he snapped. 'It's no good trying to lie with me. I can tell! What was it?'

'But it's not—'

'I'll judge what it is and what it isn't! Out with it!'

'Well,' she began with trembling reluctance, 'I went into the toilettes on the fifth floor—' They were always called toilettes at the Vivaldi. '—and I pushed open one of the doors to change the—roll. I realised too late that there was someone in there. It was—'

'Well?'

'Susanna Bosi.'

One of the girls he'd already interviewed. 'And what was she doing?' he asked, too hot on the chase to realise how silly the question sounded.

'She was—smoking a cigarette,' stammered Barbara Melanzi.

Peroni was lost. A not infrequent state of affairs in Venice, but irritating nevertheless. De Benedetti, having had something to eat, had returned to relieve Peroni so that he, too, might eat. Pizza being the quickest thing available, he had headed for a *pizzeria* he liked. And somehow missed a turning. Or taken one too many. Whichever it was, he was in a part of Venice that was unfamiliar to him.

Rounding a corner and spotting a newspaper kiosk ahead, he decided to ask its inhabitant the way, but was deflected from this course when he saw a copy of *La Notte* with the headline GONDOLIER RAISES 18th CENTURY COURTESAN FROM DEAD and below, in smaller type, *Monstrous fraud uncovered in brilliant operation by Achille Peroni, the wizard of Naples.*

Momentarily oblivious of everything except the success of his reprehensible scheme, he bought a paper and walked away reading it. The hours preceding publication had been uneventful (the Hooker murder had not broken by then) and they had blown up the story like a multi-coloured aerostat to transport the readers' dreams into a glittering other world of intrigue, sorcery and forbidden delights. They even had a box on the front page about the Neapolitan wizard's career. PERONI THE INFALLIBLE! it was headed and went on to outline some of his more sensational exploits.

Well pleased with the result, though deploring the means by

which it had been achieved, he looked up from the paper and saw that he had come back to familiar ground, though precisely where he wasn't sure. And then he heard a voice.

'Hunting murderers round here, Commissario? You'd better come up and have some lunch. I've got a fish risotto all bubbling and ready for the table.'

It came from above his head and was instantly recognisable as the voice of Estrella Partecipazio.

Cinzia Murari was not looking forward to the ordeal. Nobody even knew why the police had been called in, though the wildest rumours were racing each other up and down the corridors of the Vivaldi. And the questions the policeman asked didn't make things any clearer; he just wanted to know where everybody had been that morning. And they said he wasn't particularly nice about it, either. Still the others had all come out alive, and it had to be gone through. She raised her hand and knocked at the office door.

'*Avanti*!'

She went in. The policeman was blotting his neck with a handkerchief and looked furious.

'Sit down!'

She sat and waited submissively for him to start. Name, date of birth, address, marital status. Where had she been that morning? Who with? Had they stayed there the whole time? Where had she gone? Had she seen anyone on the way there or back?

Suddenly the rhythm of the questioning checked and they both realised they had come to something crucial.

'Who?'

Marta *had* been looking furtive and it hadn't been her time for being down in the laundry room. But it was probably quite innocent, and anyway why should she tell on a friend to this unpleasant policeman?

'Who?' The fat man spat the monosyllable at her as though it were a gobbet of poison.

'Nobody!'

'Very well. I shall tell the manager you're withholding information.'

That did it. All the staff of the Vivaldi went in mortal dread of the manager, an almost supernatural being who seemed to wield powers of life and death. And Muso could see instantly that he'd won.

'Who?' It was a whisper this time.

'Marta.'

'I can't, Signorina. Somebody else has been killed and—'

'Who?'

'The Hooker.'

'Oh, no! But why should anybody want to kill him?'

'That's why I can't come up, Signorina—I've got to find out.'

'But have you had lunch?'

She was leaning out of a second floor window, her April face framed by geraniums. Peroni was bound to admit he hadn't had lunch.

'In that case you might just as well eat here,' she said. 'There's nothing quicker than what's already cooked.'

'I can't flaw that reasoning.'

'The front door's open. You know the way.'

As he walked round to the front of the palace, Peroni told himself that it must be a floating edifice that drifted about Venice, coming to rest where and when its fancy took it, but the truth was, and well he knew it, that the dubiously moralled inner Peroni, with the complicity of the maze-like Venetian geography, had deliberately led him here in the hope of just such an encounter as this.

When he was once more on the sweeping circular staircase of the Partecipazio palace, he saw Estrella's father bowling down it towards him like a human cannon-ball. And the cannon ball was a prey to two conflicting emotions which each took him over alternately, ousting the other.

'My dear Commissario! Such an honour! Such a delight! But what news you bring! How could I have expected when I awoke this morning that the great Commissario Peroni would be under my roof once more! The Hooker of all people! Poor, poor fellow! But why did you not telephone, Commissario? I would have come to fetch you by gondola! We could have prepared something a trifle more worthy of such an honoured guest! What a tragedy! Murdered you say, Commissario? How can such things be?'

Once again Peroni went into the high-ceilinged room overlooking the canal. This time Estrella was at the table where she was laying an extra place.

'All bubbly and ready for the fork,' she said, 'just as I promised. You sit down and I'll bring it in.'

Peroni and Partecipazio both sat down and Partecipazio poured wine for them.

'Your health, my dear Commissario!' he said.

'Yours,' said Peroni. 'You knew the Hooker, of course, didn't you?'

'Poor fellow, indeed I did.'

'How did you communicate with him?'

'I can't say I did communicate with him that frequently, but when I did it was by means of signs such as one would use in a foreign country to make oneself understood.'

'Last time we talked about him you implied that he was simpleminded. Are you convinced that was true?'

'It was generally assumed to be so.'

'But that's not necessarily the same thing, is it? Would you have called him an idiot?'

'No, no, probably not an idiot . . .'

'Considerably below normal?'

'Possibly . . .'

'Very slightly below normal?'

'It's hard to assess a man's intelligence, Commissario, when he's dumb.'

'That's exactly what I thought,' said Peroni.

Then Estrella came in with the risotto and they started to eat. Once again Partecipazio entertained Peroni with stories of the Venetian nobility, but as the meal drew towards its close, the stories became more fitful as though Partecipazio's mind were no longer dedicated to them. Then they ceased altogether and his eyes started flickering towards the clock over the fireplace. He drew his antique snuff box from his pocket, not to take snuff, but to open and shut the lid and restlessly to feel it with his thumb. Then, when Estrella announced she was going to get coffee, he stood up as though he could no longer bear to remain seated.

'Not for me,' he said, 'not for me. Alas, I am obliged to leave you, Commissario,' he went on turning to Peroni, 'I have to visit an old friend who is sick and who waits for my visit every afternoon. It grieves me to deprive myself of your company which I value beyond all things, but friendship demands the sacrifice. But we shall see you again, Commissario—you must consider this house as your own!'

Bowing and effusing he backed towards the door and then, with a final flourish of admiration and devotion, disappeared through it. The room seemed strangely quiet without him.

'You must go, too. I'll get the coffee,' said Estrella and then, with an expression Peroni couldn't interpret, went out.

'Help yourself to brandy,' she called from the kitchen. 'There's a bottle of Courvoisier in the cupboard in the corner—papa always says Italian brandy's disgusting. There are glasses there, too.'

It was the wrong moment for brandy and Peroni knew it, but it is always difficult to refuse from a distance, so he helped himself.

'Your father's very full of good works,' he said when she arrived with the coffee. 'Gondoliers in trouble, and now visiting the sick as well.'

'Nobody's sick!' she said disgustedly. 'Or if they are, Papa's not visiting them. He's gone gambling. He must have got hold of some money this morning and now he's gone to throw it away.'

'But the casino's not open at this hour.'

'Papa doesn't need a casino to gamble any more than an alcoholic needs a bar to drink. And as there are a lot of other people in Venice like him, they ruin each other by mutual agreement so to speak. Gambling is the great Venetian vice, Commissario, and papa is nothing if not Venetian. Besides, it's in his blood. Gambling is what you might call the Downfall of the House of Partecipazio.'

She said it as a joke, but Peroni could hear the distant siren call of melancholy which was never silent for long in Estrella's conversation. 'And you?' he asked.

She pursed her lips. 'Me gambling? No, I don't gamble. At least not with cards.'

'With what then?' Even as he said it he knew it was an imprudent question to ask, liable—if not downright designed—to steer

125

the conversation into dangerous waters.

'Oh, life in general,' she said. 'Like you, Commissario. Or like that Neapolitan gutter kid inside you.'

From experience Peroni knew that when a woman had learned of the existence of that Neapolitan gutter kid, the Commissario was in serious trouble. It was time to go before things got altogether out of hand.

'Help yourself to some more brandy,' said Estrella.

It was as though the bottle of Courvoisier were lifted by the hand of an ancient enemy. While he was drinking it she went over to one of the high windows over the canal and stood beside it looking out.

'Commissario,' she said after a minute.

'Yes, Signorina?'

'Come over here a minute.'

He went, wondering what she could possibly have seen; he was, therefore, the more surprised when she took his face into her hands and kissed him. The pull of duty slackened obligingly. But something else suddenly niggled irritatingly in his mind, preventing him from fully enjoying the kiss that was moulding his mouth so delightfully.

And then he knew what it was. He resented the fact that she had taken the initiative, and so skilfully at that. All the years away from Naples, all the experience he had had with women from other places had not cured him of the dreadful pride of the Neapolitan male which expects the right to the first step.

Forget it, he told himself, just enjoy the gift.

But it was as though his stubborn and unwanted reaction was passing insidiously with the kiss into her mind, and he felt her stiffen in his arms and a moment later break away.

'It shouldn't have been me who started, should it?' she said, and there was a mist of sadness over the anger in her voice.

'It's not true, Signorina—'

'You find it shocking, don't you Commissario, that a woman should show she wants a man before he asks her?'

'No, Signorina—'

'There's nothing to protest about, Commissario. You're a man. A man of the south. And there's nothing wrong with that. It's what makes you what you are—it's what makes you desirable. But it's also what makes you think the way you think.'

'Signorina', said Peroni, 'can't we just forget all this and start from the beginning again?'

She shook her head with slow regret. 'You'll call me a hypocrite,' she said, 'or something worse. I'm not sure I don't call myself both those things. But the moment's gone that was here before, and I believe it's wrong when the moment isn't there.'

'May the moment come again, Signorina?' Peroni sounded uncharacteristically humble.

'I hope so, Commissario.' She paused, and then went on with a smile that wasn't of amusement. 'Go on,' she said, 'you've got to find out who murdered the Hooker.'

Only when he was downstairs on the canal bank did Peroni realise that the unexplored world of the shifting frontiers which he had first glimpsed on the Island had drifted up to them again, inviting entry.

And he had pushed it away back onto the tide again.

FIFTEEN

A visit to the laundry room was enough for Muso to establish what *dott.* Tron would have called the *modus operandi*. Marta could have gone there with the manuscript hidden in a laundry bag and then passed it out to an accomplice through the window.

That was easy enough to deduce. But to get the girl to admit it might well be another matter. When she appeared before him, Muso studied her with a hostile expression that was only partly simulated. She was a dark girl of about twenty with the peculiarly Venetian prettiness which even the severe uniform of a chambermaid at the Vivaldi could not douse. Muso let her stand by the door for a full minute, his piggy eyes observing her flatly.

'Sit down,' he said at last, using the second person singular as though she were already a convicted thief. She sat and Muso waited again, carefully aiming his interrogative missile. 'What do you know,' he asked at length, 'about Goldoni?'

The question was shrewdly judged to break her in one, for

nobody except the manager had been told of the object of the interrogations, but as far as he could see her expression showed no more than surprise at the unexpectedness of the question.

'Luca Goldoni, Signore?'

Without knowing precisely how, Muso felt as though he had misplayed his ace of trumps and the black wave of irritation that had been massing in him ever since he had been sent to the Vivaldi now swept towards her. 'Don't try that with me!'

'Try what, Signore?' She spoke with the restrained politeness of a Vivaldi maid facing a blustering, ill-mannered tourist who has put himself irremediably in the wrong.

'You're not going to tell me that a girl like you, hearing the name Goldoni thinks of the journalist, Luca Goldoni, and not the dramatist, Carlo Goldoni!'

'I'm sure you're absolutely right, Signore,' she said. 'It's just that Luca Goldoni was a guest in the hotel last week.'

Muso felt the interview slipping out of his control which set goblin hammers throbbing painfully in his stomach. 'Describe your movements this morning,' he snapped, trying to re-establish his mastery with a crescendo of surliness.

'My what, Signore?'

He couldn't make out whether she had really failed to understand the question or whether she was playing on the double meaning of the word which had hitherto never occurred to him.

'Where you went this morning,' he said, 'everything you did!'

'Yes, Signore.'

She frowned in an effort of concentration, and then started to go through her morning in detail, not omitting her clandestine visit to the laundry room.

'Why did you take it down then?' Muso jumped at her. 'Shouldn't you have taken it half an hour later?'

His last hope of disconcerting her was disappointed. 'Exactly, Signore,' she said. 'The laundry on my floor should go down at half past ten. But there was such a lot of it this morning, you see, and I do that every so often when there's a great deal—take it in two goes, I mean. Besides, it's not really against the law.'

Once again he couldn't make out whether the double meaning was intended. He continued to question her, but without learning anything. It was as though he had glimpsed the truth,

128

pounced upon it and grabbed, only to find himself with a fist full of nothing. Peroni could have told him you should never try and grab at the truth.

In disgust he let her go. It was only when she was out of the room that he remembered the title of the stolen comedy.

The Maidservant of Quality.

On his way back to the *Questura*, Peroni stopped off to pick up his motor boat which was ready and waiting. He paid for the repair work and climbed in and started the engine. But he hadn't gone for more than a few minutes when it began to be uncomfortably hot in the cabin so he slipped open the roof and felt the welcome touch of canal cooled air.

His mind, deliberately eschewing the painful scene with Estrella, began to mull over the Bixi-Hooker killings. The situation presented itself to him like one of those double photographs which present two different pictures to you as you shift your position. In one picture *avv.* Bixi was what Peroni's niece, Anna Maria, would probably have described as the Mr Big behind the various gondoliering misdeeds. In the other he was merely himself trying to find out who Mr Big was. In both pictures he finished up dead.

He turned into a very narrow canal with, just ahead, one of those impossibly small bridges which look as though they were specially built, like the chapel in the Gonzago palace at Mantua, for dwarfs.

In the second picture Bixi is killed by Mr Big. And in the first presumably by a rival aquatic mobster. And in either case the Hooker had known or discovered the identity of the slayer. It was neat enough; there was just the problem of discovering which of the two pictures corresponded to reality.

The bridge ahead had seemed too low for Peroni's boat to pass beneath it, but it slipped through as neatly as a mouse into a mousehole and nosed its way out the other side. And then, just as it was re-emerging from the brief, tomb-like darkness, Peroni had a sudden acute sense of danger being imminent, and some instinct honed in the alleys of Naples made him dive to his left.

He wasn't a micro-instant too late. Even as he went something of about the same weight as St Mark's campanile crashed past his right shoulder where his head should have been, and as he reached the floor of the boat a large piece of rock splintered into it beside him.

Although he managed simultaneously to get up, spin round and pull out his gun, he could see nobody on the bridge. Not surprising. Whoever-it-was had had more than ample time to crouch behind the parapet or jump into the protection of one of the buildings at either foot of the bridge.

Blank walls on each side of the canal allowed no landing. The quickest thing would have been to back underneath the bridge and hoist himself up onto it, but that would have left him entirely at the mercy of Whoever-it-was while he scrambled, not having a third hand in which to hold the gun. He preferred to go forward until the wall on one side gave way to a quay-side walk.

But by the time he had got there, landed and doubled round back to the bridge, Whoever-it-was had vanished. The only people anywhere near the bridge were a couple, but they were so besotted with each other that they wouldn't have noticed if King Kong had gone by, though the girl thought she had heard running footsteps.

Back in the boat, Peroni discovered that a small but extremely active demon of terror had taken up residence in his stomach. Somebody who had already murdered two people had just tried and most narrowly failed to eliminate him as well.

And, as the demon pointed out, Whoever-it-was would probably try again.

Policewoman Sofia Michelangelo was concerned about *dott*. Peroni. He had not been seen since lunchtime, and the conference with *dott*. Tron, *dott*. Amabile and all the people involved in the Bixi-Hooker killings had started five minutes ago. He was not particularly punctual, it was true, but he wouldn't be late for a conference like this. *Dott*. de Benedetti, who had put himself beside her so as to torment her while she took notes, had gone so far as to suggest that he was off somewhere enjoying himself, but she was worried that something might have happened to him. After all, a murderer was roaming Venice and *dott*. Peroni was hunting him down. One forgot these things could be dangerous.

Then, to her relief, he arrived.

'I apologise for being late,' he said, 'but somebody threw a rock at me while I was coming under the Bridge of the New Wine.'

Michelangelo shuddered. So she had been right to worry. But how brave *dott*. Peroni was, she thought. Anyone else would have gone all to pieces, but not him. He just flicks the news off like—like an 18th century dandy flicking a piece of fluff off his lace cuff. She couldn't help darting an I-told-you-so look at *dott*. de Benedetti. Enjoying himself indeed! When all the time he'd been out risking his life! With enthralled horror she listened as he told the story.

'I made immediate enquiries myself,' he concluded, 'but with no success. Now I've got two men onto questioning people in the vicinity of the bridge. That's why I'm late.'

'Perhaps it might be wise,' suggested *dott*. Amabile from his smoke wreathed heights, 'to give you police protection—just until this business is cleared up.'

Once again Michelangelo had cause for admiration. An expression passed over Peroni's face which she could only interpret as anger at the very idea of police protection. He seemed to battle for a second to suppress the emotion, then he said, 'Thank you, *dottore*, but no. A policeman who needs other policemen to protect him is no policeman, as my chief in Naples used to say. Besides, I've always believed that a man's moment comes when it will come, and all the police protection in the world won't stop it.'

She couldn't restrain a murmur of approval, and she was pleased to hear that she was not the only one.

The demon of terror had dozed off when Peroni had reached the relative safety of the *Questura*, but had stirred violently in his sleep when Peroni, after a mute civil war, had forced himself at mental gun-point to refuse police protection. Nothing could be more comforting than the idea of an armed guard, but it just didn't fit with the Peroni image.

That settled for better or worse, there was a sound like leaves crackling and the wind playing through branches caused by *dott*. Tron clearing his throat and searching through his brief-case.

'There is one point I'd like to raise, *dottore*, before we continue,' he said to *dott*. Amabile.

To his horror, Peroni saw the branch-like arms holding out a copy of *La Notte* with the 18th century courtesan story in it.

'I am curious about this,' said Tron. 'You assured me that no statement would be made to the press from the *Questura*, and equally no statement was issued from my office. I wonder how they got the information.'

'I asked the same question,' said *dott*. Amabile, 'when they telephoned me for confirmation—which I could hardly deny, but naturally they said their source was anonymous.'

Peroni felt heads turning towards him interrogatively. 'Probably a gondolier,' he said. 'They always know everything.'

'I only mention it,' said *dott*. Tron, 'because I believe it may partly explain the attack on *dott*. Peroni.' Peroni looked at him in concealed but appalled surmise. 'For one thing,' continued Tron, 'if the assassin is responsible for these various illicit activities his animosity is likely to have been aroused against *dott*. Peroni on learning that he was responsible for the arrest of the Lion. And for another, whoever he is, he will be extremely alarmed by this eulogistic, albeit deserved, report of *dott*. Peroni's infallibility. However, *nescit vox missa reverti*, as Horace puts it. A word published cannot be recalled.'

Peroni hadn't thought of this; it was appalling, but, as Horace had known a good many years before, irretrievable. He should have studied classics.

'The Hooker,' announced *dott*. Amabile as though it were the subject of a lesson. 'I haven't had the full medical report yet, but I telephoned the doctor half an hour ago and he told me that the bruising is consistent with the man having been struck heavily on the jaw and then, while falling, striking something else with the back of his head. It was this that killed him and not the blow on the jaw. He died about fourteen or fifteen hours before the body was discovered and he was taken to Corte Balbi.'

'A replica of the Bixi murder,' said de Benedetti.

'Not quite,' corrected Amabile. 'There are two divergencies. First, the blow was struck from in front and not from behind and was not the direct cause of death which might indicate that there was no intention to kill. Second, the killing took place earlier, around eight or nine o'clock in the evening. And that suggests it was more likely to have happened indoors, for a scene of that nature out of doors would be likely to attract attention.'

'And yet there remains a similarity,' said Tron, 'underlined by the fact that in this age of mechanical violence two murders have been committed, and', he went on looking at Peroni, 'a third has been attempted *with bare hands*.'

'And gondoliers', said *dott*. Amabile expressing what everybody was thinking, 'are all men with exceptionally strong hands which they are traditionally accustomed to rely on for everything.'

De Benedetti cleared his throat to test whether *dott*. Amabile had finished making his point. 'I've been enquiring about the Hooker,' he said. 'He lived in a sort of basement apartment behind the Frari church. The old woman who let it to him didn't seem to know much about him and obviously avoided him as much as possible, like everybody else in the house. But she did say that the apartment had been taken for him in the first place by a rich Venetian gentleman.'

'I know about that,' said Peroni, 'A man called Partecipazio— a sort of gondoliers' friend. He told me about it himself. But he's not rich—he just talks as if he were.'

'Oh,' said de Benedetti, disappointed. 'But there's something else,' he went on, 'I asked about the rent. Seventy five thousand lire a month. Paid for him regularly every month by a gondolier who, from his description, couldn't have been anybody but the Lion. So I went to see him and he confirmed that this was so. Said he made the payment on behalf of *avv*. Bixi.'

'So,' said *dott*. Amabile, 'it begins to look more and more as though *avv*. Bixi was the man behind these gondoliering activities.'

'If it's true that the Lion paid the rent on his behalf,' put in Peroni, remembering the Venetian con-man's clever, quick eyes.

'Have you any reason to believe he's lying, *dottore*?' asked Amabile.

'I think he's one of those people who are constitutionally incapable of doing anything else.'

'*Falsus in uno, falsus in omnibus.*'

'But why should he lie about this? Why *pretend* that *avv*. Bixi was involved if he wasn't? After all, it's not as though it lessened his own culpability.'

'I don't know,' said Peroni, 'I don't know.'

'Did he know why Bixi should have been paying the Hooker's rent?' Amabile asked de Benedetti.

'He said he had no idea.'

'Ha!' said Peroni.

'One man pays another man's rent,' said Tron, 'and they both meet violent deaths within a week of each other.'

'Things would be clearer,' suggested *dott*. Amabile, 'if we could establish that there was some contact between *avv*. Bixi and the Hooker, independently of that witnessed by the Lion.' He turned towards Michelangelo. 'Make a note to have that enquired into, Signorina.'

'One more thing,' said de Benedetti, 'I've been trying to check on the Hooker's movements which isn't easy because he was all over the place without apparent rhyme or reason. But one thing does emerge—he's been hanging about the Bull a lot recently.'

In his mind's eye Peroni saw the huge figure hacked out against the lagoon and the unexpected scarlet ecclesiastic giving a benediction.

'It was almost as though he were watching the Bull,' said de Benedetti.

'The start of all this in a manner of speaking,' said *dott*. Tron musingly, 'was when *dott*. Peroni uncovered a gambling ring for the Historical Regatta. *Primus*. *Avv*. Bixi was trying to coerce Tonino who is a regatta competitor. *Secundus*. And now—*tertius* —another principal figure in these confusing events also appears to have been taking an interest in the Regatta. *Hominus est errare*, and it may be just a coincidence, but passions in Venice run higher over the Regatta than anything else. Could it in some way have influenced—be influencing—the events which concern us?'

Peroni wasn't sure whether this was altogether too wild a sweeping of the net or whether it was a brilliant idea which he ought to have had himself. Either way, it went into Michelangelo's notebook along with everything else, and when it had done so *dott*. Amabile asked her to telephone the Trattoria alla

Conchiglia for drinks and coffee. Then the conference began to break up into scattered pockets of conversation.

'One last point,' *dott.* Amabile dominated the confusion as though he were quelling a class, 'no less than two ministers have been onto me about this stolen Goldoni manuscript. They are taking it with the utmost seriousness and I'm instructed to use every means available to recover it. How did you get on at the Vivaldi today, *dottore*?' he asked, turning to Muso.

They listened to the adventures of Muso among the maid-servants. When he had finished there was a silence. Although Muso had told the story his way, it was clear that either the girl, Marta, was innocent or she had filleted him as neatly as anything ever caught in the Adriatic.

'One thing needs doing immediately,' said Amabile, 'The American must be shown photographs of everyone involved in the Bixi-Hooker side. He just might recognise somebody he saw in the post office. That way we might find out where the manu-script *came* from and if there's any possibility of a link between Goldoni and gondolas so to speak.' He underlined his academic little joke with two rapid puffs of pipe smoke.

At this point there was an excuse-me sort of cough from the only person at the conference who had not so far spoken. Every-body looked at Policewoman Sofia Michelangelo and she flushed doge scarlet.

'*Si, Signorina*?' said *dott.* Amabile politely.

'It just occurred to me,' she said, 'that if this girl, Marta, did steal it, she'd hardly have done so for herself. Chambermaids don't steal rare manuscripts. She must have stolen it for some-body else. Somebody she was in love with.'

The room of men looked at her in awe.

'I've said all along,' de Benedetti whispered to her, 'that what we need round here is feminine intuition.'

'An excellent idea, Signorina,' said *dott.* Amabile. 'But if she stole it for a man, their relationship is likely to be clandestine in view of her respectable family and position at the Vivaldi. And if, moreover, she realises that she's under suspicion now, they won't be seeing anything of each other for a while. So how are we to find out who he is?'

At that moment one of the telephones on *dott.* Amabile's desk rang and he picked up the receiver. He made notes as he talked and then, putting down the receiver, looked up with the expression of a headmaster who has some particularly brilliant examination results to communicate.

'That was the scientific squad,' he announced. 'They've been examining the Hooker's clothing and they found some flakes of varnish on his boots. It is a varnish which is concocted exclusively in the gondola boat yards. So we can be fairly sure that the Hooker's body was transported by gondola.'

SIXTEEN

Marta had worked late, staying on till after dinner, and it was dark when she came out by the staff door which led into that same *calle* where earlier that day. . . . She shivered inwardly, but retained the expression of modest innocence she had forced herself to wear all day. The danger had been terrible, thanks to that interfering busybody, Cinzia, but she felt fairly certain she'd passed the worst of it.

It had been a very near thing when the fat policeman had asked her point blank what she knew about Goldoni. But luckily she'd managed not to give anything away, and after that it had just been a question of handling the policeman without him knowing it, and her experience with guests at the Vivaldi had given her imperceptible but considerable expertise at this. He might suspect her, but now nobody could ever prove anything.

She had the next day off, luckily, which would give her time to get over it. She planned to have a long lie in bed the next morning and then—? *He'd* said they'd better not meet until he'd been able to go to Switzerland and sell it which would need a bit of organising. Perhaps she might go to the Lido. Or see a film . . .

It was a twenty minute walk from the Vivaldi to her home, but she preferred doing the journey on foot. The water buses were crowded and often kept you waiting so long that it was quicker to walk.

She weaved her way through the network of *calles*, the dense crowds around her thinning out as she moved towards the

Fondamenta Nuova, thinning and thinning until she could hear the sound of her own footsteps alone.

No, not quite alone. There was another pair of footsteps some way behind her, heavier and moving somewhat faster than she was. She felt a temptation to look round, but resisted it, at the same time slightly quickening her own step.

But as she did so the other footsteps also accelerated.

Suddenly she felt frightened. She was in a deserted part of Venice where cries for help were likely to go unheard. Or ignored.

She tried telling herself to be calm. Whoever it was, he was probably just in a hurry. His speed was nothing to do with her. If she could only slow down he would overtake her in a few seconds. Slow down, she told herself.

But her body wouldn't obey her; her legs, despite the order, took her into a run. And in the same instant the footsteps behind began to run.

And as she ran the thought of the murders suddenly flashed like a red emergency in her mind. They said there'd been another murder the night before. And the murderer was still at large in the streets of Venice.

Running behind her.

And in blind panic she realised he was going to get her. She wasn't accustomed to running and he was pounding hard, close behind her. She opened her mouth to scream, but before the sound came out he had hurtled upon her shoulders bringing her crashing to the ground.

She struggled wildly, but it was a losing battle, for he was a big man with ten times her strength. Again she tried to scream, but his hand, hot, hairy and enormous, clamped down over her mouth, crushing it painfully. With his other hand he started to rip at her clothes and Marta, knowing that she had no hope and no defence, went limp before the onslaught, her eyes closed.

And at that moment she felt the man's body being blasted off her as though he had been sucked up in a tornado. She opened her eyes and saw him apparently flying through the air and then crashing into the front of a house.

And then she saw the tornado. It was a girl of about her own age, wearing trousers and a shirt and apparently no more robustly built than she was herself. In the confusion of the scene, that was all Marta was able to make out about her.

For now the man was moving towards the female tornado to attack, grunting with rage. She didn't stand a chance, thought Marta, he was twice as big as she was.

And then, just as his huge fist was about to smash into her face, she flicked out a leg and an arm with the lightning rapidity of an ant-eater's tongue and the man was once more air-borne, crashing this time towards the opposite side of the *calle*.

When the man straightened himself up again he seemed less aggressive, and it was the girl this time who moved in on him. There was another flick of her arms and the man's back arched like a snapping twig as he toppled onto the pavement.

With all that he had left of strength he skewered round onto his knees, helped himself to scramble up with his hands and ran staggering off in the direction from which he had come.

The girl knelt beside Marta. 'Hurt?'

'N-no,' said Marta feeling herself uncertainly. 'And thank you—you were wonderful. If you hadn't been coming by just then—' It didn't bear thinking about. 'But how did you do it?' She looked at the girl with awe.

'Simple. My hobbies are judo and karate. They make a change from sitting in an office all day, and they can come in very handy. You need something to drink. Let's go and find a bar.'

As they went Marta began to take in something more of this super-girl. She had a friendly, open face, lightly freckled about the nose, brownish shoulder length hair and a grin. She was pretty without being what those magazines called sexy. The sort of person you could trust.

'Brandy?' she said when they got to the bar.

'Oh, no!' said Marta who didn't drink.

'It'll do you good,' said the girl. 'We'll both have one.' Then when they were sitting down she asked, 'Any idea who it was that attacked you?'

'None.'

'Too many people like that about these days. You on holiday?'

'No, I live here. Are you?'

The girl used her grin. 'No, I *work* here. I come from Vicenza.'

'Are you all by yourself?'

'Uhuh.'

'That must be awfully lonely!'

'It is at times. But it's worth it for the job—I'm with the Cattolica insurance.'

'What do you do at weekends?'

'Sometimes I go back to Vicenza, sometimes I just loaf around here.'

'And tomorrow?'

'I just loaf around here.'

'I suppose you wouldn't like to come to the cinema or something with me?' suggested Marta timidly, afraid she might be presuming.

'That would be fine,' said the girl, giving Marta a little surge of pleasure. 'Finish your brandy,' she went on, 'and I'll take you home. After an experience like that you ought to go to bed.'

Michelangelo didn't enjoy deception, and the need to deceive was the only thing about police work which galled her. But she couldn't deny that *dott.* Peroni's idea had been a brilliant one. If Marta had stolen the Goldoni manuscript for a man, she was going to keep that man very quiet indeed for a while. But a girl-friend who had so dramatically rescued her might just learn something about him.

Raising her wrist to look at her watch she could just feel a slight bruise which the young *carabiniere* had given her accidentally during their simulated fight. It was after eleven; *dott.* Peroni would be at the Rialto bar where she had agreed to report to him.

He was sitting at a table outside when she spotted him, drinking a glass of Chivas Regal whisky. He hadn't noticed her and as he stared at the waters of the Grand Canal, she thought that in solitude there was something tragic about him. What sort of a childhood had he had? She had read somewhere that he had been one of the gutter urchins of Naples which probably meant that he was an orphan, and that did terrible things to a person's character.

All of a sudden Michelangelo felt herself aflood with copious femininity. A mother, a sister, a wife and a mistress within her all clamoured to embrace and cradle the tragic Neapolitan orphan with their separate functions.

Then she felt a bruising certainty that tonight was the night for her to enter that bachelor apartment only a few minutes' walk away on the other side of the Rialto Bridge. True, the shops were closed, but she would find the ingredients for an intimate supper if she had to claw them out of thin air.

'*Buona sera, dottore.*'

He looked up with a violent start from Venice's great aquatic highway. What brooding thoughts had she interrupted? she wondered.

'*Buona sera*, Michelangelo,' he said standing. 'Sit down. Have a drink.'

Her brandy with Marta was quite enough, but she feared he would think her silly if she refused, so she asked for another brandy.

'Did it work?'

She told him the story, feverishly speculating at the same time how she could help him to issue the invitation, without his realising, of course, that he was being helped. He might be shy, but he was a man alone with all the ravenous hungers, spiritual and physical, which her overflowing cornucupia of feminity was waiting to satisfy.

'So,' she finished, 'I'll be seeing her tomorrow.'

'Who knows how many ministers will be grateful to you, Michelangelo.'

He fidgeted. Obviously he was trying to think of a device to invite her with him, but he couldn't. So it's up to you, Michelangelo, she told herself, go on! And then suddenly the idea was in her head, fully grown, shining and infallible.

'I'll walk home with you, *dottore*,' she said. 'I admired you very much this afternoon, the way you refused police protection, but it's late now and the *calles* will be dark and empty at the other side of the Rialto. I'll be delighted to come with you.'

It was going to work! She could see emotion heaving within him like a choppy sea. Twenty minutes and that intimate supper party would be a reality.

'No, thank you, Michelangelo,' he said. 'It's very kind of you, but as I said this afternoon, a man's moment comes when it will come. But thank you for the thought,' he went on, offering her his hand. 'Goodnight, Michelangelo.'

'Goodnight, *dottore*.'

Broken-hearted and a little drunk, Policewoman Sofia Michelangelo stumbled off into the dark.

The little demon of terror which had slept on Peroni's arrival at the *Questura* had re-awoken after the conference and, like the evangelical demon, had gone off to find seven of its friends, and now they were all holding a party inside him. Nothing would have delighted Peroni more than to have the company of Policewoman Sofia Michelangelo at least as far as his front door, but the Peroni legend would have none of it.

There were times, and this was one of them, when Peroni would gladly have throttled his legend, but to his resentment he knew that it was stronger than he.

He swallowed his Chivas Regal, paid and set off for the Rialto Bridge. It was illuminated and crowded. But once on the other side the *calles* were indeed dark and deserted.

He had to force himself off the bridge. The demon party was getting uproarious. He had a gun, of course, but he could hardly wave it about, and it would be of little use if he were jumped suddenly out of the dark by some gondoliering giant. Or giants.

And he thought of all the huge, powerful hands he had seen in the last few days. Hands that could brain or throttle as easily as most people can crumple a piece of paper. He remembered Tron's phrase 'Two murders have been committed and a third attempted with *bare hands*!'

He turned into the narrow *calle* with his palace at the end of it. It was almost completely dark and the demons had started breaking up the furniture. He forced himself not to run. Fifty paces to safety. Forty. Thirty. Twenty. Ten.

Then he was through the front door and up the stairs into his own apartment. He'd never liked it particularly, but at least it was safe.

The demons pitched into a bottomless, drunken sleep.

SEVENTEEN

There were three piles on Peroni's desk which, as information poured into the *Questura*, were starting to grow with the weird anarchical growth of certain cacti left unpruned. The pile nearest the window was that of don Amos as though, being a messenger of spiritual light, he were entitled to have his place nearest to the physical light. The pile nearest to the door was dedicated to the Lion, apparently poised for a hasty exit if the going got rough, while in between them, mute and variously scattered as he had been in life, was the Hooker.

And Peroni, his demons temporarily cast out with the new day, started to sort through the piles. He learned various items of interest about the priest, the pimp and the hooker. He learned that don Amos had, at one stage, been attached to the entourage of Pope John XXIII when he was Cardinal Patriarch of Venice, that he kept pigeons, drank rather more than he should have done and had a sacristan who had once been in prison for receiving but was now considered to be reformed.

He learned that the Lion's real name was Enzo Scandolo, that he was the illegitimate child of a Burano lace-maker and an itinerant artist-cum-poet who sold an elixir of life (which explained a lot, but was of no immediate help), that he had himself roamed Europe before getting a gondolier's licence, that he ate live crabs when he had drunk more than usual and that, in spite of his multifarious exploits in the field of cash n' carry eroticism, he had once had a fairly steady mistress whose identity had not yet been established.

He learned that the salient facts of the Hooker's life, as outlined by Partecipazio, were correct and that various other charitable people had collaborated with Partecipazio in helping him when he had been left alone in the world. He would do anything for hard drink, so one of the main difficulties had been to see that he never got aid in the form of money—a fact of which *avv.* Bixi had obviously been aware (if it was indeed on behalf of *avv.* Bixi that the Lion paid his rent).

There was something else about the Hooker which Peroni did not so much learn as sense from the formal data before him. When asked to form a considered opinion on the Hooker's mentality, Partecipazio had been hesitant. But there was no hesitancy in the opinions expressed in the early part of the Hooker's life; he had been officially and universally considered an idiot. And yet the doings in the last year or so of his life seemed to have a certain logic about them. It was almost as though his intelligence quotient had imperceptibly risen towards the end of his life.

All this Peroni gleaned from the three piles. But the crucial fact or facts he had hoped to find were not there. Or perhaps they were, and he just didn't have the code to interpret them.

There was a knock at the door and de Benedetti entered. 'Luck, *dottore,*' he said. 'I've been round to the Vivaldi to show the American photographs of the various characters in the Bixi-Hooker affair and he recognised one as having been in the post office when he picked up the Goldoni manuscript.'

'Which one?'

'The Undertaker.'

'It's time', said Peroni, 'for that one to talk. We should have seen him yesterday, but he got postponed by the Hooker killing. Have him in, *dottore.*'

'Immediately, *dottore.*'

One of Peroni's telephones rang. '*Pronto?*' He listened with gathering attention, finally said '*Grazie*' and put the receiver back.

'Revelation upon revelation,' he said to de Benedetti who was still at the door. 'There's just been a report in from the lady you spoke to at the bar opposite Bixi's office. She's seen the Hooker's picture in the *Gazzettino* and she says that he was in Bixi's office last Sunday morning.'

'How does she know?'

'Bixi telephoned down to her for a bottle of whisky and two glasses. She took the order up to him and saw the Hooker there.'

'Vanilla strawberry lemon pineapple banana chocolate pistachio malaga stracciatella?' said the waiter.

'What about you?' Michelangelo asked Marta.

'Strawberry, please,' said Marta.

'A strawberry and a malaga,' said Michelangelo and then resumed her description of an imaginary boy friend in Vicenza, making him as unlike *dott.* Peroni as she possibly could. 'He works for the *municipio*,' she improvised. 'Births and deaths, you know, putting roneo plates in the files for people when they're born and taking them out when they die.'

'Has he got any hobbies?' asked Marta who seemed avid for information about him.

'Trains,' said Michelangelo, nearly taken by surprise. 'When he was a little boy he used to collect train numbers. He knows train timetables for the whole of Italy off by heart. And he makes trains as well—you know, models.'

'Does he live alone?'

'Oh no—with his parents. He can't tear himself away from his mother and father.'

I couldn't spend five minutes with a man like that, thought Michelangelo, let alone a lifetime.

'You're lucky to have a boy friend with a steady job,' said Marta enviously.

'Why?' asked Michelangelo.

'Because mine hasn't got one—and that can cause a lot of worry.'

'What is yours then?'

'He's a gondolier.'

'Little by little Italy has been stripped of the material advantages which other countries enjoy more or less abundantly.' Peroni's tone was bland, amiable, remote; he was a Neapolitan university lecturer delivering an address to postgraduate students. 'The Italian economy', he went on, 'is a joke, the armed forces would be as effective as a peashooter in the event of nuclear conflict, the parliamentary system, to put it at its mildest, is a chaotic political fruit salad. But one thing we do still possess, and that is an artistic heritage unique in the world which is, in its turn, the motive force behind the country's largest industry, namely tourism. For this reason, better late than never, laws are being made to safeguard this heritage. The only reason your sale of an original Goldoni manuscript to what amounts to a foreign power does not entail the death sentence is that the death sentence hasn't yet been reintroduced, but it will certainly bring you a life sentence unless you collaborate with me unreservedly.'

The Undertaker had not followed it all, but sufficient to appreciate the position he was in.

'To start with,' Peroni went on, 'what did *avv*. Bixi employ you for?'

'For carrying legal documents and—'

'What else?' said Peroni with a life sentence peering out of the phrase.

'My late employer,' the Undertaker went on hastily, 'was anxious to learn certain items of information circulating in gondoliering circles.'

'For blackmail?'

The Undertaker joined his hands as though in prayer and lowered his head in a gesture which Peroni took for assent.

'And you told him about the Lion's pimping business?'

The head rose and fell as though he were giving silent assent to an underling for the removal of a coffin from a hearse.

'And about the betting on the Historical Regatta?'

Another necrological affirmative.

'Did you know who was behind that betting?'

'I was endeavouring to establish that when my late employer was called to his final rest.'

The Neapolitan lecturer was forming an intricate question for an examination candidate. 'I have been given to understand,' he said slowly, 'that *avv*. Bixi was behind the Lion's pimping business and various other gondoliering activities. Is that true?'

The Undertaker gave a doleful but unmistakable negative shake of his head.

Peroni sighed with satisfaction. In one go that mute negative cleared a mountain of untidy rubbish and debris away from the scene. Now the issue was clearly visible and stark.

'Who is behind it all?'

'I don't know.'

It was the first time Peroni had heard the Undertaker deliver an uncomplicated, monosyllabic phrase; and it wasn't difficult to see why he displayed such unwonted simplicity.

He was afraid.

The assignment was proving trickier than expected. Having revealed that her boy friend was a gondolier, Marta was not being as voluble about him as she was about other subjects. Indeed, she was as tight shut as a mussel.

And then Michelangelo had a piece of luck. They were walking back from the cinema towards St Mark's Square and when they arrived at the Fondamenta Orseolo where dozens of gondolas lie moored in long lines together she felt Marta stiffen almost imperceptibly. She was looking across the water, and, following the direction of her eyes, Michelangelo saw a gondolier bringing his craft in and, though she was certain that recognition had flashed between him and Marta, they made no attempt to greet each other.

'Was that him?' asked Michelangelo as they went into the little passage that led into St Mark's.

'Who?' said Marta, obviously flustered.

'That gondolier—is he the boy friend you were talking about?'

'I didn't notice any particular gondolier,' said Marta.

She's lying, thought Michelangelo. Now change the subject quickly, she told herself. 'Shall we have another ice cream?' she said.

As they came out into the largest drawing room in Europe, a cloud of pigeons suddenly took off and circled towards the glowing mosaic facade of the basilica.

Beneath the funeral parlour trappings with which the Undertaker dressed it, the truth—but not yet the Truth—was unequivocal. The Undertaker did not know the identity of the gondoliering Mr Big, but avv. Bixi must have done, though he had let no clue of it slip.

'My late employer did not rely exclusively on my services,' he said. 'He pursued his own lines of enquiry and did not acquaint me with the results.' His eyes rolled once again in pursuit of the electric light. 'May God have mercy on his soul, he was a close man!'

'Last Sunday morning,' said Peroni, 'the Hooker was seen in *avv*. Bixi's office.' An air of genuine surprise flickered over the Undertaker's face as though a jack-in-the-box had popped out of a coffin.

'Did you know of any contact between them?'

'None,' whispered the Undertaker.

'To the best of your knowledge they'd never met?'

'Never.'

If this were true, and Peroni saw no reason to doubt it, two questions jutted craggily. One: why did the Lion say he was paying the Hooker's rent on behalf of Bixi? Two: what was the Hooker doing with Bixi on Sunday morning?

To the first question Peroni was fairly certain he knew the answer. The Lion had involved Bixi in this for the same reason he had tried to involve him in the pimping before—to draw Peroni's attention away from the real organiser.

At the second question Peroni could still only guess, but he felt that his guess was a shrewd one.

'Now,' he said, 'we pass to your trading in national heirlooms.' The Undertaker breathed one of his windy sighs and assumed an expression of patient martyrdom. 'Where did you get it from?'

'My late employer,' he said, 'utilised a metal container for the safe keeping of documents and valuables when the banks were closed. This container he lowered by means of a chain onto the bed of the canal behind his office. When he passed to his final rest, I felt that he would have wished me to have anything it contained as, during the period of my employ, God forgive him, he remunerated my services in the sparsest possible manner. So I gained possession of the said container, but found that there was only a manuscript by one Carlo Goldoni within. I thought it was worthless, but my m–' he drew himself up short. 'A close relative advised me to sell it. Perceiving in the *Gazzettino* that a famous American expert on the late Carlo Goldoni was in residence in the city, I took the liberty of offering it to him and he was kind enough to accept it.'

'For a million lire,' Peroni reminded him.

The Undertaker washed his hands and smiled. It was the first time Peroni had seen his smile and the sight was a horrible one, with large yellow teeth like tombstones bared in a funereal parody of amusement. 'I took the money for religious motives,' said the Undertaker. 'I felt that a small posthumous recognition of my services would reduce my late employer's sojourn in Purgatory.'

'This relative who suggested you sell the manuscript,' said Peroni, 'did he or she know you sold it to the American?'

'She has been bed-ridden for many years and is not always very clear in her mind. I didn't bother her with such details.'

'Who did know?'

'Nobody.'

'You mentioned it to no one?'

The Undertaker paused, and then a broken expression appeared on his face. 'To one person.'

'And who is that?'

'A gondolier,' he tolled, 'a gondolier known as Smiler.'

'Description?'

'About one metre seventy-five, and sixty-five kilos. Long, powerful arms and big hands. Mid-twenties, I should say. Sandy hair, darkish eyes. And a smile.'

Peroni focussed hard on her. 'We've all got smiles, Michelangelo,' he said.

'Not like his, *dottore*. It's one of those smiles that's stamped on the face—that goes on all the time.'

'Well, in that case—*Pronto*?' he went on to the telephone which, in that moment, had rung. '*Si, dottore*?' he said. '*Si. Si. Si* . . .' He looked across and made a note. '*Si, dottore*,' he concluded, '*buon giorno, dottore*.'

'That was *dott*. Amabile,' he said. '*Dott*. Tron has been onto him about the Regatta tomorrow—he wants us to listen in to the preparations. Apparently there's a big crowd over on Burano where the Bull is training. I really can't believe,' he added with irritation, 'that anyone could get so excited over a boat race as to commit two murders, but he insists. I'll go over and have a look.'

Michelangelo's face, he noticed, was clouded with alarm. 'You mustn't worry about me,' he said, correctly interpreting her expression. 'If I can't go over to Burano on a Saturday morning, I might as well take up work as a baby-sitter straightaway.'

And, indeed, with the sun pouring in through the windows of

the *Questura*, he even felt confident himself. The demons were not in residence.

As for Michelangelo, she felt silly for having let the worry show, and sillier still because it wouldn't go away, but continued to grow within her, an unwanted but unabortable foetus of anxiety.

'As I was going to say,' continued Peroni, 'your smiling gondolier clinches it. The Undertaker made a drunken confession of his sale of the mansucript to a gondolier nicknamed Smiler because he's got a permanent, involuntary grin. That's one thing. But there's something else, too. The Undertaker stole *The Maidservant of Quality* from Bixi's underwater safe deposit. That makes it look very probable that whoever ransacked Bixi's office— whoever killed him—was looking for the manuscript.'

Two gondoliers were leaning against a rail smoking and waiting for work. They looked at Muso and then quickly away, obviously rejecting him as a potential customer. This didn't improve his temper.

'Smiler,' he snapped at them, 'the gondolier known as Smiler.'

'Smiler!' one of them called without even bothering to look at Muso.

'*Si?*'

The voice came from somewhere below their feet and, looking down, Muso saw that there was a third gondolier polishing the woodwork of a gondola moored there.

'Gentleman to see you.' There was an ironic ring to that 'gentleman'; Muso could hear it as strident as a violin going flat during the Grand Canal serenade.

The gondolier in the craft down below looked up at Muso. If he read policeman his face didn't show it, and the genial smile didn't even flicker. He climbed up onto the quay, rubbing his hands on his trousers.

'Can I help you?'

'*Questura.*'

Maybe that did shake him, but you couldn't tell because of that smile.

'We have reason to believe,' said Muso moving down the quay

until they were out of earshot of the other two, 'that you are acquainted with a young woman by the name of Garzoni, Marta.'

A pause. Short, but perceptible. 'That's right.'

'We have further reason to believe that you received a package from her some time after ten o'clock yesterday morning in the vicinity of the Vivaldi Hotel.'

Smiler seemed to give jocular consideration to this. 'No,' he said, shaking his head, 'no, you must be misinformed.'

'In that case,' said Muso, 'I must ask you to accompany me to your place of domicile for purposes of verification.'

What happened next was entirely unexpected. Smiler's powerful arms suddenly shot out towards Muso's chest. Too late the policeman realised he was standing on the edge of the quay. He toppled backwards helplessly. The last thing he saw before the murky waters closed over his head was the gondolier's radiant, benevolent smile.

Carrying the bundle under his arm he walked rapidly away from Piazzale Roma till he came to the 1800 which he parked near there during the summer for occasional excursions onto the mainland. He unlocked it, put the bundle under the driver's seat, climbed in and drove off.

Just as he got onto the causeway he heard the wail of a siren behind him, and his palms on the steering wheel prickled with sweat. He looked in the driving mirror and saw that it was a police car. If they had spotted him, he didn't stand a chance for the 1800 could no more race with a police car than a gondola could with a speed-boat. The whole scheme would be over and he would have plotted for nothing.

Then the police car stopped. Two uniformed men got out of it and one, pulling a disc out of his boot, moved into the flow of traffic to stop a car. An 1800 like his. It was a road block for him and the bundle, and he had missed it by seconds.

Wiping his hands one after the other on his trousers, Smiler drove on towards Mestre.

Part Four

THE BULL

'Oh Heaven, what a destiny! How many vicissitudes!
How many overthrows!'

Mémoires
Carlo Goldoni

EIGHTEEN

The church tower of Burano tilts, if anything, slightly more than
the leaning tower of Pisa, giving the island a curiously lop-sided
air. As Peroni made his way among the multi-coloured houses
this tower seemed to be playing hide-and-seek with him. It kept
disappearing from view, but always popped up playfully again
within a minute or so, leaning alarmingly over a new prospect.

Everywhere he went women were sitting outdoors, heads bent
over the lacework which was their and their island's principal
source of income.

Peroni liked Burano, perhaps because the washing hanging
everywhere, the front doors open to reveal kitchen-cum-living
rooms and the women cooking in the streets reminded him of
Naples. Perhaps he liked it, too, because he didn't feel afraid
there; the island seemed too benevolent for murder. He just
wished that Estrella were with him.

It didn't take him long to find out where the Bull was training
for the crowd of local supporters and tourists was indeed impressive.

The Bull was some way out on the lagoon surrounded by other
craft and, as on the previous occasion he had seen him, Peroni
experienced a sense of awe at the sheer size and seemingly
super-human strength of the man. It was as though the Greek
Olympus had unexpectedly revived and Jupiter had come to
earth, half-bull half-man, for the love of some human woman.
But on those occasions didn't the goddesses wreak havoc in
human affairs? Peroni wondered what *dott*. Amabile would
make of that as an explanation of the double murder.

Then he started to look about him for anything *dott*. Tron
might consider significant. But everybody in the crowd seemed
entirely taken up by the timeless drama of the vast man scudding

across the horizon in a boat which seemed to be powered by invisible wings.

And at that moment he saw the woman. She was sitting at the water's edge and wore a long white dress and an enormous hat with a rim as big as a hoop which entirely hid her face from him. He couldn't have explained even to himself how he deduced it, but he was certain she was English. And something in her bearing suggested nobility. An English aristocrat.

Very gently, so that she shouldn't notice, he began to edge towards her.

The Bull felt at the very height of his power as the sun and the eyes of the adoring crowd illuminated his massive glory. No power on earth could stop him winning the Historical Regatta tomorrow for the tenth year in succession.

'You're the greatest of all time!' he told himself. 'That's what all the papers say.' Not that he actually read the papers himself. He could read as well as the next man of course; it was just that some of the words those journalists used didn't make sense. But he had them read to him, and the cuttings were framed in the restaurant in Burano where they kept his trophies. It was even named after him and was a sort of temple to his Regatta might.

The Bull only lived for the Regatta season. When it was over, he went about his ordinary gondoliering, ate, drank and slept, but everything except these functions went into hibernation until the time should come to start training for the next season.

Only one other thing in the world existed as far as he was concerned.

Her face was still hidden by the hoop-like rim of the hat, but Peroni could see the most magnificent flaxen hair streaming down her back, and as she looked out over the lagoon she toyed with a parasol.

To see her face directly, in her present position, he would have to jump into the water. His glances were blocked at one side, like arrows fired against the buttress of a castle, by the hat and on the other by a brick wall, for she was sitting at the extreme end of the quay.

He had tried to will her to look round, an exercise at which he was proficient, but for once it just didn't work. He contemplated a direct approach. How do you do? I believe you're English. But at this point the Commissario stepped in. He had not come to the island to pick up foreign tourists; *dott*. Tron would be expecting a report. Reluctantly, Peroni set himself once more to observing the crowd. It still seemed innocuous and entirely taken up with the mighty Bull.

He shifted position to get a different viewpoint, and as he did so his leg brushed accidentally against the woman.

'Oh, I am very sorry,' he felt obliged to apologise, and then added, 'How do you do? I believe you're English.'

The Bull turned his boat in towards the quay and obediently all the courtier craft moved their prows in towards the shore. He had trained enough for the morning; now the mighty machine needed feeding.

He put on a last burst of speed, rather like a pianist flicking off a seemingly impossible encore, and then stepped out of his boat to a burst of applause from the crowd which surged all about him, clapping his monstrous shoulders, darting about him like tadpoles round a whale. Somebody pushed an autograph album at him, but he brushed it aside with a hand like an outsize boxing glove. It wasn't that he couldn't write, but he never carried a pen with him.

He raised his clenched hands over his head as he'd seen boxing champions do on television and beamed his great, slow smile. The crowd roared.

'They love you,' he told himself. 'They all love you because you're a great champion. You're a god to them. The Bull god.'

With his immediate entourage about him he set off, and the crowd came behind him. Across Corte Novello they went, over the bridge to the Fondamenta Pescheria and then up Calle della Provvidenza. An uninformed onlooker might well have taken it for a pagan religious procession.

Giulio, the proprietor of the Bull Trattoria, gave a quick all embracing look around his waiters, rather as a conductor checks the entire orchestra before raising his baton. They were all there, napkins draped over forearms, as strategically placed as fielders in a test match, for any minute now the Bull would come in with his following and there wouldn't be a chair free in the place.

The restaurant had been founded by his grandfather and named *da Gigi* after him, there being no Bull around at the time. But it had always had a regatta flavour about it, and Giulio had changed its name to that of the greatest regatta hero of all time in exchange for his exclusive custom when in Burano. It had been an astute move and the place was invariably thronged. Giulio, whose sport was football, couldn't really understand this regatta fever, but he was grateful for it.

The door was pushed open and the Bull's huge frame loomed into the restaurant. Giulio and three waiters were instantly about him, escorting him to the table of honour, the Bull god's temple stall. Here Giulio himself celebrated the ritual, serving raw eggs which the Bull gulped down as an orang-outang would consume peanuts, and pouring out glass after glass of red wine for which the Bull had a capacity legendary even among gondoliers.

When the eggs were done, leaving behind a mountainous desolation of egg-shells, Giulio saw to the preparation and serving of a Florentine T-bone steak almost raw and large enough to play ping-pong on. This would keep the Bull going for a while, and Giulio went off to inspect elsewhere.

As he went he assessed the takings with a rapid computer calculation in his head. He was never more than a few thousand lire out one way or the other with these calculations.

And then he spotted the couple in the corner. They were an extremely handsome couple, she nordic, perhaps English, and he southern. The sort of people who habitually ate in expensive restaurants, and the sort of custom that Giulio would have chosen if restaurateurs could have afforded to be choosers—cultured, intellectual, polished, witty.

He edged nearer to see if he could hear something of their conversation. At first he was only able to make out that it was in English, which he could understand well enough, without distinguishing any particular phrase.

He moved a little nearer still and managed to catch a single phrase spoken by the woman, but she realised that he was eavesdropping and gave him a look of such fiery ice that he moved rapidly off in confusion.

But confused though he was at being caught, he was no less astounded at the single phrase he had heard her utter.

'Must we,' she had asked her southern companion in a tone of heart smothering melancholy, 'Must we die?'

'As a matter of fact I am.'

The face, still partly veiled by the enormous hat and the flaxen hair, had at last been revealed. It lived up to all Peroni's expectations. Cool, with the famous English rose-like beauty, and a self-possessed expression of aristocratic hauteur. The voice, too, was impeccably English of the sort Peroni imagined the Queen would speak. It left him, uncharacteristically, at a loss for words.

But only for a moment, and then the Neapolitan magician was, to the indignation of the Commissario, in full control of the situation. Weaving his improbable English like an incantation he issued an invitation to lunch within two minutes flat, and was not at all surprised when it was accepted.

He would have preferred to take her to a more intimate restaurant than the Bull Trattoria, but she insisted, so, having gained his main point, he pandered to her tourist whim.

'You are come to Burano,' he said when they were seated over vodka and Campari aperitifs, 'for to see the Bull?'

'The Bull?' she said in the sort of tone in which he imagined the Queen of England might have said, 'Spaghetti?'

From where they were sitting the Bull was out of sight, so Peroni swelled himself up like a toad and made rowing motions. 'He of the gondola,' he said.

Her laugh rippled like a fountain in an English garden. 'No, no,' she said (how could the English pronounce such bell-shaped vowels?), 'I have come to pay homage to Baldassare Galuppi.'

Peroni was taken aback. He had heard the name, but wasn't quite sure whether it belonged to a minor inventor or a henchman of Garibaldi's. 'Baldassare Galuppi?' he echoed.

'You haven't heard of him?' asked the milady, as Peroni mentally considered her.

'Yes and no,' he said truthfully.

'The street outside and the square at the end are named after him. Baldassare Galuppi is the most famous of the sons of Burano.'

'Famous because?' asked Peroni.

'Famous for his music. He was a musician in the 18th century—a most superb musician and a contemporary of Goldoni. Oh Galuppi, Baldassare,' she unexpectedly proclaimed, having downed her vodka and Campari in a surprisingly un-milady-like gulp, 'this is very sad to find! I can hardly misconceive you; it would prove me deaf and blind; but although I take your meaning, 'tis with such a heavy mind!'

'Will you please repeat more slowly?' said Peroni, dredging up complete one of the first phrases he had learned in English.

'It's a poem,' she said.

They ordered fish hors d'oeuvres, and Peroni noticed that a man in a neat blue suit and tie, who looked like the owner, was edging towards them.

'What?' continued his companion, musically nostalgic in spite of a mouthful of prawns. 'Those lesser thirds so plaintive, sixths diminished, sigh on sigh, told them something? Those suspensions, those solutions—"Must we die?"'

She paused to look up at the owner who then moved off very rapidly.

'Those commiserating sevenths,' she concluded, 'Life might last! We can but try!'

At the table of honour, the Bull had now consumed an unspecified number of raw eggs, the T-bone steak, a mixed salad of the dimensions of a fair-sized garden, a hunk of Parmesan cheese as big as a rock and five litres of red wine. His entourage, having partaken of considerably less, had grown comatose, incoherent or slurringly jocular, but the Bull, whose capacities for food and drink had no known limits, was still in full possession of his mighty faculties.

He squinted intently at his watch. He was good at telling the time and only occasionally had to make a special effort of concentration over the difference between the long and the short hands; he experienced a little confusion over this now, but had it sorted out and the exact time registered in less than fifteen seconds. When this information had been fed back to the appropriate centre of his brain, he uttered a series of grunts which those of his following still sufficiently alive to events about them were able to interpret as an announcement that he would be back presently.

He then loomed to his feet and made his way out of the restaurant to the scattered applause of the fans which he acknowledged with an absent wave of his paw.

Outside, Via Baldassare Galuppi was semi-deserted in the early afternoon sun. He went to the top and turned off into Rio Terrà Pizzo, looking back to make sure that he was not followed.

Having reassured himself about this, he continued on his way until he came to an attractive, two-storey pink house with geraniums exploding at its windows. He looked round once more to make sure he was unobserved and then knocked at the door, twice slowly and twice more rapidly.

The promptness with which the door was opened suggested that somebody had been waiting inside. The interior was pitch dark, but the Bull, with the stride of a three-league boot, stepped confidently in and the door closed behind him.

Peroni had a theory about the amount of time women spent in the toilette when they were at a restaurant with a man. Less than five minutes indicated that something was wrong. From five to ten minutes suggested that she was in love with her partner, spending the necessary minimum to make herself appealing, but getting back to him as quickly as possible. If she was away for longer than ten minutes, but less than quarter of an hour she was more interested in herself than the man accompanying her. But if she was gone for more than quarter of an hour, things became complex; she was trying to goad him into apprehension, to tingle his emotions.

The English milady had been gone for twenty-five minutes.

Peroni ordered another grappa.

Half an hour.

A murderer, possibly a maniac, was stalking the streets of Venice, killing people and leaving their bodies in a little courtyard off Killers' Way. And Peroni was sitting in a restaurant on Burano waiting to take up dalliance with an English milady.

Forty-five minutes and the restaurant was beginning to empty. He went to the toilette which was unisex and presided over by one of the rare ladies of Burano not engaged in making lace. And apart from her it was deserted.

Peroni questioned her closely, but she was unyielding. Nobody even remotely resembling the English milady had ever been in the toilette.

In twenty minutes Peroni had scoured the whole of Burano on foot without finding any trace of her. As improbably as she had appeared, she had vanished.

NINETEEN

Lucino, who worked at the Mont Blanc Hotel just outside Aosta, was one of those waiters who have the world at their finger-tips. Whatever a guest might want, like transport during a taxi strike or other less openly avowed objects, he could obtain it. At a price.

He came of a gondoliering family, but hadn't gone in for the family trade which he considered a mug's game. But waitering was another thing altogether. And the joy of it was that there were so many waiters who couldn't eat spaghetti and scratch their ear at the same time which meant that the way was open for those like Lucino who brought to the job the independence of an alpine guide, the persuasiveness of a super-salesman, the charm of an expensive dental nurse and the wiliness of—well, a gondolier.

He had just come from the room of an Australian canning corporation's widow who had only been in Aosta for a few hours and had already found many of her problems solved by Lucino who would probably be able to solve one or two more before she left for Capri the next morning.

Coming downstairs into the lobby, he was surprised to see his brother sitting in one of the hotel's plush armchairs.

'*Ciao*,' he said. 'What are you doing here?'

'*Ciao*,' said his brother. 'I've got something to dispose of in Switzerland which could bring in enough money to buy half a dozen hotels like this, but I'm going to need your help.'

'Tell me all,' said Lucino enthralled.

After looking round to make sure that nobody could overhear him, Smiler started to talk in a low voice.

The English milady had been unusual, but not what *dott.* Tron had had in mind. Fortunately Peroni came across something else for him. The betting on the Regatta, he found, was continuing unabated, and in spite of low odds a lot of money was being placed on the Bull. Back in Venice that afternoon he had ascertained that the organisation had passed quite simply from don Amos to his sacristan, the one who had been in prison for receiving and had subsequently reformed.

Fresh action at this stage seemed pointless, so Peroni drew up a cautious report for *dott.* Tron and then checked once more through the piles of information on his desk. The only new facts were that the Lion had once acted in a film and don Amos was reported to have miraculously cured a gondolier's mother of hay fever. He brooded over this for a moment and decided it didn't get him any further forward.

Goldoni. The name jumped uninvited into his head. So nearly an anagram of gondola, it had continued to appear here and there like an eccentrically dressed stranger you keep running into by accident. And now it was beginning to look as though a Goldoni manuscript might have had something to do with Bixi's death.

Peroni felt a prickling of curiosity about the 18th century Venetian dramatist and, on an impulse, walked round to a bookshop which was still open and bought a copy of the Goldoni *Mémoires* which he took back to his office and started to read.

He soon found himself following the varied and often disastrous adventures with sympathy: the escape from a Jesuit college when he was fourteen in a ship full of *actors and actresses, a prompter, a stage manager, a watchman, eight servants, four maidservants, two nurses, children of every age, dogs, cats, monkeys, parrots, birds, pigeons, a lamb,* and the encounter on the same ship with the girl who played the maidservants' parts and gave him a most singular feeling when he observed her closely.

The theme of these maidservants ran throughout his life,

reappearing time and again in his plays and his life—two worlds which constantly merged and imitated each other. *I have always*, he said, *had a sort of preference for the actresses who played these parts*. And Peroni of the questing right hand felt a bond of fellowship over the centuries with the plump and lecherous Venetian playwright.

Of these actresses Goldoni wrote and Peroni read with delight. Antonia Ferramonti who died so tragically in childbirth; Elisabetta Passalacqua of the green eyes, the dagger and the Venetian alley-cat morals; Teodora Veronese for whom, he said, he had written *The Maidservant of Quality* to tempt her back to the theatre after she had broken his heart (for a couple of days) by marrying into the Venetian nobility; Anna Baccherini, *a pretty and cheerful Florentine girl, most vivacious with a plump little figure, a clear complexion and black eyes*, who died suddenly when she was twenty-three and before she could act in *The Well-Mannered Lady* which he wrote for her; Maddalena Marliani, *so swift of wit that all the actresses feared her*, who drove the leading lady literally insane with jealousy and inspired and interpreted *La Locandiera* . . . The list was endless and enthralling.

And then, finally, following a vicious wave of persecution the move to France where Goldoni eventually died as good humouredly as he had lived. Peroni liked the characteristically allegorical way he had marked his departure from Venice, writing a play about it in which the real-life events were described in theatrical disguise. *One of the Last Evenings of Carnival*, it was called, and in it Goldoni presented himself as a pattern designer, tempted away by an offer from Moscow.

The book was a long one, but Peroni became so involved in it that he was surprised to find it was after midnight when he got to the end. He took a police launch to the Rialto and, lulled perhaps by his voyage along Goldoni's crowded life, managed to walk the rest of the way without looking over his shoulder.

Smiler's original plan had not included Lucino, but the haste with which he'd had to leave Venice had rendered his brother's help indispensable. So now the two of them sat staring in silence at the cause of it all.

The paper was crinkly and yellowed, but well preserved and untorn. The pages had been bound in brown leather with a heavily ribbed spine so that it seemed from the outside a book rather than a manuscript. But when it was opened there could be no doubt. The pages were covered with wild handwriting which looped, hooked, soared and swooped forward as though the writer had been possessed.

'How did you get it?' asked Lucino at last.

Smiler told him the whole story beginning with the Undertaker's bulging wallet right through to the fat policeman's involuntary plunge and Smiler's own hairbreadth escape from Venice.

'But how can you be so sure you're going to get such a lot for it?'

'I once knew somebody,' said Smiler with a dream in his eyes, 'who got very rich very quickly indeed. He'd managed to get hold of some rare stamp collection—but really rare—and he sold it to a man in Switzerland. I saw some of the things he bought for himself with the proceeds, and I swear to you, Lucino, he must have got more out of it than most people who do the pools even know how to imagine. He told me at the time that if ever I got onto something similar he'd put me in touch with one of this man's agents.'

'Then why not go to him?'

'I did. He's dead.'

'Oh. Well, in that case how are you going to go about it?'

'He told me one thing. He told me that the stamp deal was done in Geneva. So I go to Geneva and put this in a safe deposit—I don't want anybody taking cheap short cuts to it, do I?—and then put out the word through some of the Italians working there— in the hotels, the casinos, the expensive night clubs and restaurants—that I've got something special to sell. This man's got agents everywhere. Within a week the whole thing should be tied up.'

'It might work . . .'

'It's got to work, Lucino!'

'OK, so how do we do it?'

'I've thought it all out. The only tricky thing is getting over the border where they'll be watching for me. So I need to change my appearance a bit and I'll want a false identity card. And new number plates.'

'Lunchtime tomorrow.'

'So quick?'

'Being near Switzerland we have to be efficient here. I can probably get you Milan or Florence number plates—which'll it be?'

'Florence,' said Smiler for no better reason than he'd once been there on a school outing.

If Smiler's teacher, twelve years before, had chosen Mantua, for example, instead of Florence, the entire course of her pupil's life might have been different.

Peroni was not accustomed to waking in the middle of the night. When he did so the cause was usually indigestion so, waking now, his mind groped sleepily after what he'd eaten the previous evening. A cold toasted sandwich and a beer. That wouldn't give a sparrow indigestion. He tried to think of other possible causes, shifting over to switch on the bedside light.

But before he reached it a blow, apparently delivered by a gigantic hammer, crashed into the pillow where his head had been a split second before.

All the fears that had been rising and falling within him now massed into a single tidal wave of terror which swept away the remaining wisps of sleep and propelled him almost physically out of bed onto the narrow strip of floor by the wall. What would the lethal Other do now?

There could only be one answer to that, and pyjama-ed as he was, horizontal and gunless (he had never conceived attack in his own apartment, and the gun was in the living room—*cretino*!), Peroni was in no state to face another onslaught.

Without a conscious decision, he found himself rolling under the bed, and only when he was there, the wire springs beneath the mattress pressed against his face, did he realise it was the most prudent thing to do. It gave him temporary shelter and a few seconds' respite.

It also gave him the possibility, he realised, if he rolled and squirmed silently enough, to catch the Other's ankle and topple him which would at least make the combat a little more equal. He manoeuvered himself to the other extremity of the sheltering bed and groped in the blackness where he calculated the ankles should be. If the Other had not moved.

But he had. Perhaps he had guessed Peroni's intention, perhaps he had feared him in his new position of precarious safety. But an almost imperceptible whisper of footsteps indicated that he was moving. In what direction? It seemed towards the living room.

But why? That wasn't so easy to answer. Was he making for the front door, having abandoned his murderous project? With all the force of his Neapolitan soul, Peroni hoped it might be so. He waited with his breath held for the sound of the front door. But it didn't come.

Instead, with rending unexpectedness, the telephone rang in the next room. It gave Peroni a momentary lift of hope. It meant help. But the hope was throttled in the process of birth. Any move towards the telephone would pinpoint his position for the other man.

Twice the long drawn out drrring sounded in the blackness. Three times. Peroni and his would be murderer listened to it in silence, neither of them moving. Ten times it rang. An anonymous outsider making a temporary interval in the tragedy for two players. Fifteen times. Whoever it was was persistent. Go on ringing, Peroni silently urged. Seventeen times. And then it stopped. Now the drama could be taken up again.

The silence after the clamorous screaming of the telephone was terrifyingly absolute. And the whole apartment was pitch black—it was dark enough by day with the cupboard-wide *calles* outside the windows, but by night it was as remorselessly black as a priest's soutane in a cellar.

Peroni listened for the sound of fumbling, calculating that as soon as the Other had found the front door and got through it, there would be time to move into the living room, collect the gun and get to the downstairs front door before the Other had reached the end of the *calle* outside.

PERONI TRAPS DOUBLE KILLER. But the light which illuminated the headline in his mind went out as fast as a candle without air. The Other wasn't trying to find the front door. He wasn't fumbling in the darkness. He was standing quite still. Waiting.

'*Pronto*?'

'*Dott*. de Benedetti?'

'Michelangelo! This is so sudden!'

'*Dottore*, you're going to think me crazy—'

'I wouldn't dare!'

'—but I just can't get rid of the idea that *dott*. Peroni is in danger. Now!'

'Aren't you stretching your feminine instinct a bit far?'

'I know it must sound like that, but I've got this certainty—'

'Then why don't you telephone him?'

'That's just it—I have done and there's no answer!'

'Well, you know *dott*. Peroni—maybe he's not alone.'

'He told me he was tired and wanted to go to bed hours ago!'

'Then maybe he's sleeping at the *Questura*.'

'I've tried there, too. He's not.'

'What d'you want me to do about it then?'

'Go round to his place. I'll come too. We'll make sure.'

'No. I've got a great respect for your instinct, Michelangelo, but it's like grappa—fine in small doses, but dangerous if you take too much. Look, why don't you make yourself some camomile tea, get a good book and read yourself to sleep? Hello, Michelangelo, are you still there?'

'Yes, I'm here. I was just thinking. Maybe you're right. I'll try. Sorry to have disturbed you, *dottore*.'

'Don't mention it, Michelangelo. Goodnight.'

Peroni contemplated turning on the bedside lamp, but decided against it. It would only illuminate him and put the Other in the darkness of the living room at an advantage.

What was he waiting for? Peroni tried to assess the motives behind the shift of position and the total silence next door. Was he waiting for Peroni to follow him into the living room? Waiting in ambush?

But if that were the case, the advantage was all Peroni's, for he knew where the light switch was immediately inside the living room entrance on the left. Barefoot, he could reach it without alerting the Other to his movement, switch it on and dive for his gun which was in a desk-drawer on the other side of the room.

He wriggled silently from under the bed and stood up. The silence was like an impenetrable sonic fog hiding some over-riding advantage of the Other's which Peroni had yet to discover. This just wasn't logic, but logic didn't thrive in the circumstances.

He started to cross the bedroom floor. Silence pitted against silence, his in motion was as total as the Other's in repose.

Half a footstep away from the opening between the bedroom and the living room, Peroni stopped. His hand touched the plastered side of the opening, then slithered round it to the light switch. His index finger smoothed down to where the switch jutted out from the frame. The half centimetre which it must move inwards to flood the room with light was a plastic crag, stark between the abysses of life and death.

He pressed it. In the fog of silence between himself and the Other, the click sounded like a crack of thunder.

But no light came.

'I am dead, too.'

'Dead? Then what are you doing at the window there?'

'I am waiting for the coffin to come and take me away.'

Policewoman Sofia Michelangelo was a constant reader of Pinocchio. The book with the original Mussino illustrations had followed her from childhood into maturity. It still had some of the power of an old teddy bear or blanket to lull and bring peace. But for once it didn't seem to be working.

'He felt himself seized by the throat and the same terrible voices muttered threateningly at him, "Now you won't get away again!"'

Dott. de Benedetti was right—she was stretching her feminine instinct too far.

'And drawing out two hideous long knives, as sharp as razors, zaff—they slashed him twice in the kidneys.'

'Well, you know *dott.* Peroni—maybe he's not alone.' The thought cut her as much as the knives cut Pinocchio.

'Now I understand,' said one of them. 'We'll have to hang him. Let's string him up!' No sooner said than done, they tied his wrists behind his back and putting the noose round his neck, they hoisted him dangling to the branches of a large tree known as the Great Oak.'

'Fine in small doses, but dangerous if you take too much.' That was her trouble—she'd taken too much instinct.

'Little by little, his eyes dimmed, and although he could feel death approaching, yet he still hoped that from one moment to the next some pitiful soul would arrive to help him . . .'

Pinocchio, not Peroni!

'He closed his eyes, opened his mouth, stretched his legs and, after one convulsive heave, hung there, stiff and motionless.'

Oh, go to sleep, Michelangelo!

It was no time for closely reasoned calculation as to why the light had not come, but Peroni knew that either a malign fate had decreed this moment of all moments for a power cut, or the double killer had pressed the button of the fuse box in the cellar below. This cellar was reached by a ramp from the *calle*. It contained a series of garage-like booths which were rented for storing purposes by firms. These were kept locked, but the main body of the cellar, in which there was nothing but the fuse boxes for the various apartments, was open.

The thought of the other apartments set Peroni contemplating a yell for help, but it would only the more clearly indicate his position for the Other, and anyway nobody would answer. You were as effectively alone in an apartment surrounded by other apartments as if you were on a desert island.

The first thing was to move away from the immediate area of the light switch where the Other knew him to be, and this Peroni did, treading silently, using his only advantage which was a detailed knowledge of the room's complicated geography.

Having reached the cemeterial cupboard, he stopped in its shelter and listened. Silence. Not even the sound of breathing. He had the impression that the Other had moved in time with him, stopping when he stopped.

And now, first the gun or first the door? Instinct said the door. Reason said that the Other would get him at the door, so he would need the gun.

He hesitated for an instant, and his hesitation was invaded by the second alien voice to sound since the man-hunt had begun.

'Ma—ma Ma—ma'

The Other could not have been prepared for this and Peroni heard a jolt of shock somewhere near the door.

'Ma—ma Ma—ma'

There was something hostile in the very impersonality of the mad one-eyed doll's voice.

'Ma—ma Ma—'

As meaninglessly as it had started the doll ceased. I have spoken, it seemed to imply, now let the murderous game continue.

Peroni started to edge towards the desk, once more having the distinct impression that the Other was again moving at the same time. This was confirmed by a soft thud of collision somewhere near the light switch.

Peroni sensed that he had an advantage now. He was near the desk, the desk was near the door and the Other was at the far side of the room. Unless either of them abandoned a more or less wall-hugging technique, the distance was reassuring.

He touched the edge of the desk and experienced a little swell of relief. Escape was now feasible. He found the drawer and edged it open. It made a dry, wooden noise, but when he had the gun, he could afford to concede that advantage. He put his hand inside and felt for the gun.

It wasn't there.

For a second it occurred to him that the Other had somehow managed to spirit it away, but then he realised there was a simpler explanation. In the darkness he had gone to the wrong drawer. In hurricane panic, he fumbled for the right one, the one above, found its handle and started to pull it open.

But as he did so, a pair of hands grabbed at him from behind and pulled him away. Peroni knew enough mean tricks of in-fighting to maim a gang of Mafia thugs, but even these were rendered largely useless when two large and murderous hands, powered with giant strength, jerked you off balance unexpectedly in the pitch dark. He aimed kicks that should have been deadly, but missed their mark. And the hands were around his neck.

Gondolier's hands.

The thought bubbled like marsh mud in the darkling slough of his mind as he made futile and increasingly feeble jerks to free himself from the world-strangling fingers. Which gondolier did they belong to? The question seemed a more and more distant and academic one as even the marsh light dimmed.

In the last flicker of consciousness left to him, Peroni remembered St Janarius, the patron saint of Naples who never says no to Neapolitans, good or bad. And with the lungs of his soul he howled an anguished yell of supplication. But for the first time St Janarius made no answer, and Peroni saw the end bearing its leaden, cosmic palms down upon the tiny corner of heaving mud that was left to him of life.

And then the palms obliterated even that.

The room in which Peroni found himself was a strange mixture of familiarity and unfamiliarity and, though he had no idea how he'd got there, he knew that the journey had been long and dangerous.

Knew, too, that he was waiting for somebody, though he couldn't for the life of him think who. Was it somebody who would expect to meet Commissario Peroni, or was it one of the small group of people who knew the truth? Man or woman?

This amnesia was unusual; he didn't normally suffer such total blanks. He would just have to wait for his memory to return. In the meantime he turned his head to look towards the door in the hope that it might give him some clue as to the person who was to come through it. But it was one of those doors which give nothing away.

Then as he looked at it he sensed rather than saw a glimmer of light above him. He raised his head and understood that he had been wrong about the door. This caller was coming through the ceiling, and the ceiling was opening to admit him.

Wrong again. It wasn't a him, but a her. An oddly simplified sort of her, sitting upon a cloud with the right hand raised, the index finger pointing. And on her lips was a fixed, peaceful, painted smile.

And then Peroni realised who she was—the unorthodox St Angela of don Amos's church. But why? Somewhere a long way off a memory was waving to be recognised. Peroni couldn't make it out clearly, but it had something to do with St Janarius. That was it—he must have been on to St Janarius for help, and this not being his territory the Neapolitan bishop had stepped aside for St Angela as a matter of professional etiquette.

That was logical enough, but her smile sorted strangely with the agitated tone of her voice.

'*Dottore*!' she was saying, '*Dottor* Peroni! Are you all right, *dottore*?'

Peroni closed his eyes to try and work this out, and when he opened them again St Angela had gone, and in her place was Policewoman Sofia Michelangelo.

TWENTY

Like a child's scrawly capital S written backwards, the Grand Canal snakes through the conglomeration of patched together islands that is Venice. It is an old stretch of water and there is little it has not seen, but this morning, decked with flags and banners for the Historical Regatta, it sparkled and rippled in the early September sun with all the vivacity of a young river gathering strength from its source.

It was still morning and the Regatta was not till the afternoon, but the banks were already beginning to be crowded while miscellaneous craft bobbed, darted and chugged between them. One of these was a police launch containing de Benedetti and Policewoman Sofia Michelangelo who had been called in as part of the security measures the *Questura* always take for this occasion.

Even a double murder loses some of its urgency on the day of the Historical Regatta.

'How did you do it, Michelangelo?' said de Benedetti for at least the twentieth time that morning. 'How could you *know* something was going to happen? Many more tricks like that and you're going to make all your colleagues redundant!'

Michelangelo was a heroine. Last night, against all the dictates of reason and de Benedetti, she had left the little apartment she rented from a piano tuner's widow and rushed across the Rialto Bridge to the palace where *dott.* Peroni lived. Banging the bells of all the apartments simultaneously, she had got the front door opened for her, and then had run up the stairs until she had located and knocked at his door.

No answer. But listening carefully, she had caught sounds of movement and heavy breathing.

'You know *dott*. Peroni,' she had heard de Benedetti's voice inside her, 'maybe he's not alone.'

That had almost sent her home again. But although Michelangelo's experience of love was not encyclopaedic, the movement and the breathing didn't sound right, and the shrill cry of alarm within her was more strident than ever.

She set to work on the lock and, though she didn't have the right instruments with her, it was soon audibly evident that it was giving way.

When she had burst into the flat with a torch, she had thought at first it was too late. *Dott*. Peroni was lying on the floor apparently dead. Then by the light of her torch she saw the shape of a man disappearing through the bedroom window.

She had to choose between pursuit and succour. Being a woman she chose succour, and so *dott*. Peroni revived, but his assailant, in spite of hastily summoned police reinforcements, escaped.

The outline had been easily pieced together. The building with the window opposite Peroni's bedroom window—just across one of the narrowest *calles* in Venice—was boarded up and due for demolition. Earlier the previous day somebody had broken into it and gone up to the second floor where the window, in which the pigeon had its own apartment, was less than a metre from Peroni's window.

While it was still light, and before Peroni came home the assailant had been able to study the lay out of both bedroom and part of the living room including the front door.

Then, when Peroni had returned and gone to bed (with his window open as he always kept it) the man had waited until his light had been out for long enough to guarantee sleep—although at that distance he could practically have heard his breathing—before going down to the cellar of Peroni's place and switching off the switches of the apartment.

He had then climbed to his former position, reached across the *calle* and climbed through Peroni's open window, taking with him the weapon—a massive spanner which he would have been able to carry tucked into his trousers.

This, abandoned on the bed, was all they had to go on. It bore no finger prints, but one of the few policemen who was not taken up with the Regatta was trying to trace where it came from.

When finally Michelangelo had returned to her own apartment and the copy of *Pinocchio*, still open where she had left it, she toppled into a sleep streaked with nightmares in which she found herself listening to heavy breathing from outside a door and then bursting in to find *dott*. Peroni dead on the floor in the arms of the prostitute from the Lion's coffin.

She had woken from this to a sensation of spiritual and physical numbness with dissatisfaction and irritation prickling at its edges. This persisted in spite of the inescapable air of high fiesta on the Grand Canal.

'If it had been him who'd rescued you,' said de Benedetti, 'we should have had a straightforward prince-princess routine, but as it's you that rescued him I don't quite know what the form is.'

Dott. de Benedetti did nothing to make things better.

Peroni sat staring at the piece of paper. It was a brief report which had been added to one of the three piles on his desk. Taken by itself, there was nothing unusual about this report which merely gave details concerning the woman who had been the Lion's regular mistress. But viewed alongside the inescapable inference you couldn't help drawing from it, it was about as usual as a sea monster suddenly appearing in the midst of the Historical Regatta.

This was at strident variance with the established facts. It was literally impossible.

It could only be a coincidence. And in that case no sea monster, no variance and everybody friends as before. Though, of course, now the possibility—or rather the impossibility—had reared its head in the Grand Canal of enquiries it could never be overlooked until definitely sunk.

Waking that morning in the *Questura*, bruised and sore, Peroni had contemplated convalescence. But a Commissario of police can hardly haunt the place in pyjamas in the middle of a double murder hunt and a Historical Regatta. So he had got ready. And then the sun and the sea air coming in across the lagoon, and coffee and croissants at the Trattoria alla Conchiglia had combined to make him feel himself again.

Besides he was to view the Regatta with Estrella in the Partecipazio gondola. And so he had gone to his office to see if anything had been added to the three piles on his desk. And this had.

He continued to stare at the paper. What action to take? First of all re-check the established facts; everything else was subject to that. He picked up the telephone, but as he did so there came a knock at the door.

'*Avanti!*'

Dott. Tron rustled into the office, his branches waving in sympathy.

'*Veritas odium parit*, as Terence put it,' he said. 'Truth begets hatred, so maybe this is an indication that you are near the truth.'

'But am I?' Why had *dott.* Tron arrived at just that moment when Peroni was gloating in incredulous surprise over the impossible? Strictly, this information should have been passed straight on to the magistrate, but Peroni felt invincible reluctance to do so; it would have been like giving away an unfinished creation of his own. Instead he put the paper at the bottom of the pile and imagined that he could feel the magistrate's eyes upon him as he did so.

He then gave a detailed verbal report of everything which had happened the previous day. *Dott.* Tron listened with silvan calm, though it seemed illogically to Peroni that a benevolent upward tilt at the corners of his mouth suggested that he knew something was being withheld. But what? Peroni asked himself in exasperation. An impossibility?

When the report was done and the magistrate had renewed his sympathies, he got up to go and gave Peroni his cracking twig fingers to shake.

'*Forsan et haec olim meminisse juvabit*,' he said at the door, 'Perhaps some day we shall like to remember even these things.'

When he had gone, and Peroni was certain he was out of earshot, he picked up the telephone to start re-checking.

'Always keep an eye open behind you—'

'Whatever happens you must be among the first into the Grand Canal—'

'It's behind that's dangerous—'

'Then edge in towards the centre—'

'Because in the first part they'll try and sneak up behind you and get themselves carried in your wake—'

'And when you turn round the pole keep your oar as close in as you can—'

The scene of the young gondolier preparing for the Regatta is a classical one, and it was now perfectly reconstructed in the front room of Tonino's house. In the centre of the group was Tonino himself, pallid, but handsome and immaculate in striped vest, white cotton trousers and flaring red sash. His mother, no less pale and unable to conceal her anxiety, fussed about him together with Gemma whose glass-like delicacy was suffused by a flush of excitement.

Seated at the table with glasses of wine two old gondoliers—both ex-Regatta competitors—kept up a running flow of advice from their own now faded and often inaccurate memories.

'You look fabulous, Tonino!' breathed Gemma.

'Are you quite sure you feel all right?' asked his mother.

Tonino nodded, and in spite of his pallor his eyes had the almost fanatical glitter of the gondolier who will sacrifice anything for Regatta glory.

'Keep an eye out for bumping and boring—'

'If you block somebody else with your oar, make sure the judges aren't looking—'

'And don't forget to cross yourself when you pass the Madonna della Salute,' said Gemma.

The preparation of the Bull was a ritual to which about a hundred initiates were admitted, and so it did not take place at his home, but at an *osteria* in Venice dedicated, like the restaurant on Burano, to his cult. No advice was offered here, for no one in the wide world could advise the Bull how to win a Regatta, but in its place there was a murmuring as of prayer and a libatory sluicing of wine.

The priests of the cult swarmed buzzing, alighting and zooming about the toweringly impassive Bull. You could see his fingers twitch as though impatient to curl themselves about the oar and send his boat surging to victory as it had already done for nine Historical Regattas.

He was utterly confident. Apart from his almost superhuman strength and inexhaustible capacity for committing the most damaging 'incorrectnesses' as they are euphemistically known, he had another unassailable quality.

Before a regatta he closed his mind, like a prehistoric stone fortification, against any possibility of defeat.

It had to be a coincidence. Peroni had checked, cross-checked and checked again. The thing was unshakable to such an extent that it was far easier to accept the coincidence than the conclusion to which it might seem to point.

And if enquiries should uncover another coincidence like that? Peroni eyed the three piles of documents, reports and photographs as though they were human and flexing themselves to produce one more impossible thing for him to believe before lunchtime.

For the hour of day, the *Questura* seemed strangely quiet, almost dead. Then he realised that it had transferred itself, almost to a man, to the Grand Canal.

It was time for him to join the Partecipazios.

Some 500 kilometres away in Aosta, Smiler had other things to worry about, but even so he couldn't help remembering the Regatta. He looked at his watch. 'They'll be off soon,' he said.

Un-Venetianised though he was, Lucino didn't have to ask who would be off. 'Tourist stuff,' he said.

'The Bull again, I suppose,' said Smiler.

'Bound to be,' said Lucino.

In spite of themselves, the two brothers stood for a second visualising the scene on the Grand Canal which they had seen so often and which, as boys, they had dreamed of playing a prominent part in.

'Time to be off,' said Smiler, taking his brother by the hand. '*Ciao*'.

'*Ciao*.'

'Thanks for all you've done.'

Lucino had done a lot. Not only did Smiler have a false but impeccable identity card and a new licence plate, but he also had a new appearance. A heavy, drooping moustache largely disguised his giveaway smile, and he had steel-rimmed spectacles, a black wart on his left cheek and a close cut hair cut. The frontier carabinieri would never recognise him.

'You're welcome,' said Lucino. 'A brother's a brother.' And a ten per cent cut on the sale of a priceless manuscript carried its weight, too.

Smiler climbed into the car, waved and drove off, following the green signs which said Mont Blanc. The bundle was under his seat once again and, although he couldn't see it, he could feel its presence.

It was like having another person in the car.

'Step in, Commissario—pray do me the honour!'

Peroni, as he stepped into the gondola, contemplated telling them of his near brush with death the night before, but then decided that as Estrella was bound to hear of it anyway, he would cut a more heroic figure if he didn't mention it himself.

'It's early yet for the Regatta,' said Partecipazio, 'but while we wait what pleasanter occupation could there be than floating in a gondola? You know what Count Volpi said of it? "The gondola is the most beautiful of God's creations!"'

'And,' said Estrella drily, 'since Count Volpi was responsible for the development at Porta Marghera which is rapidly strangling Venice, the causeway with Mestre *and* that appalling garage in Piazzale Roma, we can consider him a leading authority on beauty.'

'Let us not be ungenerous, Estrella!'

'Facts, papa, facts.'

Don Amos was a fanatical Regatta fan. Many years previously this had even caused his priestly vocation to hang in the balance. If he became a priest, he could never compete in the Regatta. Though less spectacular than some of the sacrifices that are made to follow a vocation, don Amos's was not without its heroism.

However, he watched the event every year from the balcony of a parishioner of his, an elderly bachelor who had devoted his mature years to a monumental, intricately detailed and still unfinished history of glass-blowing in Venice.

So now the two of them sat on the balcony with a bottle of the finest *amarone* between them watching the aquatic fancy dress parade which precedes the Regatta. It floated in heady magnificence beneath them, commemorating the lavish welcome bestowed by the Serenissima Queen of the Adriatic on Catherine Cornaro, Queen of Cyprus.

The doorbell rang and the literary cicerone of glass-blowing went to answer it. It was don Amos's sacristan who squinted and looked as pale and slippery as one of the candles he dealt in.

'The betting's just closed, *reverendo*,' he said, 'and in spite of the policeman, it's a record—more than three million on the Bull alone!'

Don Amos gave him his benediction.

'Caviare, Commissario, another glass of champagne!'

'You do things in style,' said Peroni.

'Papa always does.' The melancholy chimed in Estrella's voice.

The banks of the Grand Canal were packed now, and every balcony and window was so bulging with spectators that you expected them at any moment to be squeezed out and projected like pips into the water. Even the canal itself seemed to be so jammed with craft that it looked as though there wouldn't be room for the Regatta. But a place was reserved for the Partecipazio gondola ('One of papa's gambling friends,' Estrella told Peroni when her father wasn't listening).

In this place they now tied up between two majestic barber's poles of deep royal blue twirled with gold. Although no expert, Peroni realised that the position was a particularly favoured one. They were, in fact, at Ca' Foscari right opposite a monstrous floating raft which was both half way mark and finishing post, for the boats went down the Grand Canal as far as Santa Lucia, rounded a pole in the water and then returned to Ca' Foscari.

On the floating raft opposite the authorities had just taken up their places. They included the Cardinal Patriarch of Venice who added a magnificent splash of scarlet to an already riotously coloured picture.

'Here they come!' said Peroni, taken aback at such lack of enthusiasm for the arrival of the racing gondolas.

'No, no, no, Commissario,' said Estrella, 'there's time yet. It's a bit like boxing—you know, when there's a big heavyweight championship they have various preliminary bouts which nobody takes any notice of. It's the same here—there are two introductory races, this one for four-oared gondolas and another one for boats from Caorle.

'Hello,' she went on, looking up, 'd'you recognise that woman on the balcony? It's Maddalena Spinelli, the actress.'

The men looked up and, when Peroni had seen her, one face in the jigsaw puzzle fell into place.

Or to be strictly accurate three faces.

Not even his mother would have guessed at the struggle that had raged within the recently appointed head of the Venetian Municipal Tourist department. One of the many functions pertaining to his office was that of firing the starting pistol for the Historical Regatta. But as a result of a bottle of mineral water exploding in a restaurant which his mother had gone to during the later stage of her pregnancy, he had had a life-long terror of loud bangs, and the prospect of deliberately creating one himself in the immediate vicinity of his right ear filled him with horror. On the other hand to renounce the job was unthinkable; it was one of his glories.

So here he was now standing by the starting cord—the *spagheto*—at the Public Gardens with eighteen boats bucking and rearing before him, waiting for the starting signal. The *dodesona*—the boat rowed by twelve ex-champions to clear the way for the racing *gondolini*—had already set off. Nothing remained but for the pistol to be fired and the eighteen racing gondolas to make their leap forward to glory.

To make matters worse for the head of the Venetian Municipal Tourist Department, he had already been on the extreme verge of firing the pistol and getting it over with five times. But each time something had happened to stop him. Three times the Bull had nosed his craft over the starting cord and across the path of another competitor in the last split second. Twice other gondoliers had tried the same trick, though less deftly.

'Bang!' The appalling sound uttered by a little boy immediately behind him made the head of the Municipal Tourist Department jump as high as the gondolas bucking in the choppy water and lose every last vestige of civic dignity.

Sweating with panic, the pistol extended as high in the air as he could reach, he perceived the boats before him, the eighteen gondoliers looking towards him with impatient fury. They were as much in line now as ever they would be. He screwed up his eyes tight and pulled the trigger.

The explosion rocked him to the deepest shelter beneath the headquarters of his being. It also propelled the eighteen craft forward as precipitously as if they'd been exploded from the mouths of eighteen cannons.

The Historical Regatta was under way.

TWENTY-ONE

'Why is there a Carabiniere submarine corps?'

'I don't know—why is there a Carabiniere submarine corps?'

'Because deep down—I mean really deep down, as far down as you can get, the Carabinieri are very intelligent.'

That is the sort of joke people tell about the Carabinieri, and although there must be an historical motive for it, it has long ceased to hold objective truth. The Carbinieri branch of the Italian armed forces contains as much intelligence as any body of men in Europe.

The Carabiniere colonel in Genoa had certainly been intelligent enough to see that Lance-Corporal Lorenzo Simeoni would have to be transferred. Not that he was anxious to lose Simeoni, but after what had happened he judged it elementary prudence.

Simeoni's best friend had been another lance-corporal named Gervaso. One day these two had been cruising in a squad car near the docks when they had spotted a fat, plain child howling its head off. Lost presumably—a job for the urban police. But Gervaso didn't reason like that; when help was needed, he gave it without quibbling over whose job it was.

Simeoni, who was driving, stopped the car and Gervaso got out and walked towards the child. He never reached it. Before he had taken three steps a squall of bullets from a passing car chopped him down. They also raked the car in which Simeoni was sitting. He was almost miraculously untouched, but unable to give pursuit because the Carabiniere car had been put out of action by the shooting.

As a result of this Simeoni had become fanatical in his hatred of terrorists—and who would blame him? But such fanatical hatred can be dangerous in a place like Genoa which is one of the new centres of Red Brigade violence, so the colonel decided reluctantly to have Simeoni transferred; and in Rome they came up with the ideal posting—the Mont Blanc frontier station where Simeoni could look at passports and check for smuggled drugs, mineral water, cigarettes and chocolate.

So now Lance-Corporal Lorenzo Simeoni stood before a long queue of cars waiting to drive into the fourteen kilometre long tunnel which ran straight as a giant ruler through the bowels of Mont Blanc between Italy and Switzerland. He waved on one car full of children and a Mercedes with an elderly German couple in the front, his eye on the third car now partially visible behind the Mercedes. The driver was a single man, and Simeoni decided to stop it for a spot check.

But as the Mercedes moved forward, allowing him to see the one behind, his glance sharpened. A Fiat 1800 with a Florence number plate. And a Fiat 1800 with a Florence number plate had been reported as stolen by a hunted Red Brigade combatant.

Simeoni waved the car to a halt and leaned down to look inside the front window.

The gondolier nicknamed Abracadabra was rowing in the Historical Regatta for the first time and, although it had only been under way for a few minutes, he now fully understood why the Bull was hailed as the greatest of all time. Understood not so much with his head as with his guts, for rowing in the Regatta is not a question of brain power. The Bull seemed an elemental force of nature, sweeping his craft forward as though before a hurricane.

They were crossing the basin of St Mark's, moving towards the great dome of the Salute. The Bull was in the lead and the rest were straggling behind in three separate bunches of five *gondolini* apiece with two others bringing up the rear.

Abracadabra was in the second group of five, and out of the corner of his eye he could see Tonino rowing almost level with him. Abracadabra could have been in the first, but he was reserving his energy for a burst when they got past the Doge's Palace which would take him among the first into the Grand Canal.

Now they were passing the Vivaldi Hotel and Abracadabra prepared himself for the spurt; with any luck he hoped to finish among the first half dozen, maybe the first four.

The Bridge of Sighs flashed by unnoticed on their right and now they were coming up to the Doge's Palace. Abracadabra bent his back and accelerated the rhythm of his rowing. By the time they were level with the *piazzetta*, he was out of the second group and moving up towards the first with Tonino some way behind. When they got to Harry's Bar there were only four craft between him and the Bull.

But a lot could happen yet. Now it was time to relax the gruelling pace which had brought him into the Grand Canal.

Just a little.

Strictly speaking, Policewoman Michelangelo and *dott.* de Benedetti were there to see that the biggest tourist attraction of the year was not marred by the politico-criminal violence that threatened incessantly in the most politically tormented country of the west; their eyes were for the roof-tops, the balconies, the crowd. But the press of craft was so great that they found themselves, willy nilly, doing the urban police job of helping to clear a way for the *dodesona*—the boat rowed by twelve ex-champions—which in its turn was opening a path for the racing *gondolini*.

'Urban Policewoman Michelangelo,' commented de Benedetti, 'I'd like to see you in one of those fetching little caps they wear.'

At least if I were in the urban police there would be no *dott.* de Benedetti, she thought, but said nothing, merely swatting hard at a fly on her forearm and looking at him sideways as she did so.

'There's *dott*. Peroni,' said de Benedetti.

'Where?' The word had been spoken too quickly, she realised when it was out.

'There—in that gondola with the large, untidy man who looks as though he's falling to pieces and the pretty girl.'

Now Michelangelo saw him. And she saw something else which de Benedetti, being a man, didn't see. She saw that *dott*. Peroni was in love with the girl.

The sun continued to shine on the Grand Canal, but in Policewoman Sofia Michelangelo's heart it went out.

You're alone, said the voice inside the Bull, there's nobody else in the race. The Historical Regatta belongs to you. It is you and you are it.

They were coming up to the Accademia Bridge and the Bull god bestrode the Grand Canal making it appear a mere stream. With gigantic sweeps of the oar he took his boat under the bridge and into the beginning of the great curve which leads to Santa Lucia, the pole and the final stretch back to Ca' Foscari. The cruellest stretch of all.

The cheers of the huge, anonymous, shouting mass, packed upon either bank, came to the Bull like incense. They love you, said the voice, they're willing you to victory. The television cameras are all trained on you, the newspaper men are scribbling about you and the women are adoring you. The whole world is centred on you; nothing but your victory is any longer of interest to anybody.

Worship the Bull!

When Lance-Corporal Lorenzo Simeoni saw the driver, his heart seemed to halt. He had studied an identi-kit portrait of the hunted Brigader which had not been particularly indicative. But one or two points had emerged from it. The man had been in his mid- to late-twenties, had worn a heavy, drooping moustache with steel rimmed spectacles and had closely cropped hair.

All these particulars were applicable to the man now seated in the driving seat of a Fiat 1800 with a Florence number plate. Just like the stolen car.

'Do you mind stepping out of the car for a moment, *signore*?' said Simeoni, fighting to maintain a detached, polite tone.

Fear flashed unmistakable behind the steel-rimmed spectacles. Simeoni's hand moved towards his pistol and, as it did so, the 1800 jerked forward, at the same time swerving to overtake the German car.

'*Alt!*' shouted Simeoni.

But the driver had no intention of halting. The pistol seemed to leap into Simeoni's hand of its own accord. Two explosions barked at the gigantic serenity of Mont Blanc, and then the 1800 slewed across the road, smashed into the Mercedes and overturned.

In the collision, a bundle was catapulted from under the driving seat onto the road.

The heavy moustache had been ripped off in the crash so that when the Carabinieri came for the driver they were greeted by a sight none of them had ever seen before.

A dead man smiling.

Partecipazio's hectic and variegated body made it seem as though he were himself an entire crowd united by a common absorption in the bounding mass of little coloured boats that was sweeping towards them. The individuals that composed his face were all pale and oblivious of the large drops of sweat that were coursing among them.

'It's his bets,' explained Estrella. 'They're as complex as half-a-dozen computers, and he carries them all in his head.'

There was some arcane magic about the phalanx of boats that was about to pass them, the Bull way out in front threshing the water with his oar, and Peroni for the first time understood what Estrella had meant about Regatta fever. He wished he'd laid a few bets himself.

Now the Bull was level with the Partecipazio gondola and now he had flashed past it, and Peroni realised that the inchoate mass of the other seventeen *gondolini*, seen close to, was in fact divided into separate groups of five or six craft each.

He felt a surge of primitive excitement at the ruthlessness of the struggle, the physical power that was being so painfully spent to gain a few centimetres' advantage.

But the excitement didn't stop him observing something else. It was barely perceptible, but it created a solid buttress of confirmation.

They were just coming under the Rialto Bridge when Tonino started to overtake Abracadabra, the two of them lying roughly seventh and eighth. Abracadabra decided it was time for another burst of speed and so—for a period of time which could have been measured as just over two minutes from the banks, but which seemed timeless to the two warring gondoliers—the prows of their craft lay level in the water except for when, first one and then the other, they flicked forward gaining a centimetre's advantage.

It became a private combat between them, and the presence, even the existence, of the other gondoliers was forgotten by both of them. Only when Abracadabra emerged as the temporary victor, with half a length advantage, did they realise that in the process of duelling together they had unknowingly overtaken three other craft and were now lying with only two other *gondolini* between them and the Bull.

But Abracadabra knew that the gondoliers they had overtaken were by no means to be discounted. It was a well known strategy to drop slightly behind so that over-confident competitors should burn up their energy and so allow the craft in their wake to sweep forward again when they rounded the all-important pole at Santa Lucia which they were just coming up to now.

This was one of the most delicate moments of the whole Regatta. You had to take it as tightly as possible, flipping your gondola around as dexterously as if it were a ten lire piece, at the same time keeping a shrewd eye open to the boats nearest you, for this was the point at which bumping and boring were most likely to be attempted.

The Bull's head-on lead—he must have been at least three and a half gondola lengths in front of the nearest boat—meant that no such problems need worry him; there was nobody there to bump or bore.

Nevertheless, he made the turning with consummate skill in one compact sweep like a fish flicking round a rock. Now he was rowing up the Grand Canal while everybody else was still rowing down. In a few seconds he would cross with his nearest competitors.

In the instant when their boats met, Abracadabra looked up from the craft milling about him to observe the all-time Regatta immortal. With stunned incredulity, Abracadabra saw that the Bull's face was a mask of livid horror.

For the first time since he had started rowing in the Historical Regatta a spy of doubt had somehow crept its way into the prehistoric fortress of certainty which was the Bull's mind, and that spy had whispered that victory was not as inevitable as tomorrow's sun.

Just how the spy had penetrated the fortifications he didn't know. Maybe, as he rounded the pole, he had felt an almost imperceptible flagging in the huge machine of his body which said that it was not omnipotent.

And then, as though the spy had opened a breach for an arrow of ice to be shot through the bastions, he understood why this was so, and the very fact that there was a reason—for all that it had gone unconsidered until now—made his situation the more appalling.

The Bull god was toppling from his Olympus and no fall is so headlong as that of a god.

But then, with a lift of relief, he realised that the fall could be arrested; it was not inevitable. He glanced over his shoulder and saw that there were still three clear gondola lengths between himself and the nearest competitor. With a lead like that, they could never reach him, and the imperceptible draining of his strength need not bring disaster. He only had to call on the massive reserve still left to him.

Row, Bull, row!

At the pole Tonino was level with Abracadabra again, and it looked as though he might even get ahead when they started rowing up the Grand Canal. There was only one way to prevent this, Abracadabra realised, and that was to row in suddenly, colliding with the prow of the other boat and cutting off the water space between it and the pole. This would serve the double purpose of getting a helpful push forward himself and at the same time causing Tonino to halt and lose vital seconds getting on course again.

Abracadabra swerved in to the left and, at the same time, as though he had anticpated this move, Tonino made his boat leap forward to get through before the collision. They both rowed until it seemed as though the beech-wood of their oars must split under the strain.

As his *gondolino* moved in inexorably, Abracadabra saw with satisfaction that the space ahead of Tonino was narrowing rapidly; to get through it in time was now next to impossible.

Three seconds, Abracadabra calculated, and Tonino's burst of rowing would only mean a harder thrust forward for his own boat.

Two seconds. The water of the Grand Canal seemed to boil under the thrashing of their oars.

One second. Already the gap was too narrow.

But then, incredibly, Tonino was through it. Abracadabra's craft collided harmlessly with the stern of the other, making it veer slightly to the right. Then, as Abracadabra looked up from the demolition of his scheming, he saw that there was no other boat between Tonino and the Bull.

'They'll be back again in a minute. Just time for another quick glass of *amarone.*'

'*Salute!*'

'*Salute, reverendo!*'

'Here they are! Just coming under the Rialto Bridge!' the priest gasped as he choked over his drink.

'You shouldn't have swallowed so quickly, *reverendo*. Allow me to pat your back. There—is that better?'

'The Bull's still in front!'

'But isn't that someone coming up behind him?'

'Tonino! It's Tonino!'

'How can you tell at this distance? *I* can't see who it is.'

'St Angela—she gives me intuitions sometimes.'

'He'll never level with him!'

'Anything may happen!'

'Yes, now I can see him—it *is* Tonino!'

'David and Goliath—no less! Tonino!'

'Calm yourself, I beg you, *reverendo*—you'll fall into the Canal!'

The glass-like delicacy of Gemma's complexion was suffused with incredulous excitement. Tonino was rowing practically alongside the Bull. Tears of pride and joy streamed unnoticed down her cheeks.

But could he ever overtake the Bull? They were rowing neck and neck with about three hundred metres still to go and three other *gondolini* pressing them hard behind.

It seemed impossible that two boats could move through the water so fast while staying at the same time so motionless with regard to each other; it was as though an invisible bar held them together. One of them must drop behind. A draw was unheard of in the entire history of the Historical Regatta.

'He's fighting for his life,' she heard somebody saying behind her, and she realised they were talking about the Bull.

And then as the two boats drew exactly level with her she saw that the gleaming, silver-toothed bow-prong of Tonino's gondola was moving fractionally ahead of the Bull's. And, as she watched, it gained, centimetre by centimetre, until she could see the black bodywork draw out in front.

Suddenly the Bull's collapse was catastrophic, as though a main-spring had broken inside him. Within metres Tonino's gondola was out in front with an ever widening gap of water between him and the Bull.

After this, with the Bull's powerful spell of invulnerability at last broken, first one boat, rowed by Abracadabra, moved up on the once mighty Regatta champion, hovered alongside him for a few seconds and then overtook.

'He's finished,' Gemma heard the same voice behind her say, 'For good.' The tone was mournful as though the death of a great man were being announced and at the same time Gemma saw a woman cross herself. But she was incapable of sharing in the elegiac mood as she watched Tonino streak forward towards the finishing raft amid a Heaven-swelling roar of cheering which swept him to the greatest of all Regatta victories. And as he stepped out of his boat onto the platform and raised his arms in acknowledgement of the applause, she did not even notice that the Bull was rowing into fourth place: the place of the sucking pig. Her attention was skewered by something else. For the raised hands of Tonino were streaming with blood.

In the aftermath of a Historical Regatta, the Grand Canal is like a broad highway along which a coronation procession has just passed. The dense crowds of people and of craft break up and disperse; there is an unseemly drift of empty cans and food containers; the general attention, so uniquely focussed a few minutes before, is now divided among a thousand different objects, and the air is heavy with anti-climax. Only the cats and the pigeons of Venice are immune to it. For them life has always gone on just the same, unaltered by the clamorous and, in the long run, pointless doings of human beings in the Serenissima Republic.

This mist of aftermath had drifted its way into the police launch in which de Benedetti and Policewoman Sofia Michelangelo were riding towards the *Questura*. De Benedetti was affected by the atmosphere, thought Michelangelo; he hadn't made a bad joke for ten minutes. As for herself, the sight of *dott*. Peroni with the girl had left her feeling as though she had just undergone major surgery; not quite fully conscious, she was uncertain as to what sort of existence awaited her now.

About her the magnificent palaces of the Grand Canal loomed unobserved. Beside her de Benedetti broodingly steered the launch. Perversely, because he was silent for the first time since she had known him, she almost wished that he would make a bad joke.

And then suddenly the launch seemed to buck beneath her as though the Grand Canal had come alive and was trying to throw it off. She lost her balance and staggered helplessly while the wildest explanations jostled in her mind. Earthquake? Freak wave? Whirlwind?

But the true explanation was simpler. It was de Benedetti who had suddenly accelerated and, at the same time, jerked the boat off towards a side canal. She didn't have time to speculate on the reason for this seemingly lunatic behaviour before she was hurtled into his arms which somehow seemed to be waiting to receive her.

A carved lion of St Mark was the only spectator of the long embrace between a policewoman and a detective, both on duty in an official police launch, but as the lion in its time had seen even stranger sights, its only comment on this, as indeed on everything else, was *Pax tibi, Marco*.

'Have you gone crazy?' asked Policewoman Sofia Michelangelo with an unconvincing show of indignation when the embrace finally came to an end.

'On the contrary,' said de Benedetti, 'I have, as people say in old films, at last come to my senses. For too long now, whenever I wanted to kiss you, I made a bad joke instead. But whenever I want to kiss you from now on, I shall just do it. Is that understood?'

'*Si, dottore.*' He was, after all, her superior in rank so she could hardly disobey an order, and besides kissing was always better than bad jokes.

For a moment the vision of *dott.* Peroni floated before her, glowingly southern, but she gently shook it away; *dott.* Peroni was for dreaming about, not marrying.

And then she and de Benedetti returned to their bad joke substitute.

Part Five

THE IKON

'This business so well conducted and so happily terminated did me immense honour; but my star did not delay in making me feel its evil influence.'

Mémoires
Carlo Goldoni

TWENTY-TWO

Mirandolina, the *Locandiera*—variously translated at one time and another as the Mistress of the Hotel, Mine Hostess and the She-Inn-Keeper or the Landlady—had her back to Peroni when he went into her dressing-room after a special performance on the evening of Regatta day. But he could see from her reflection in the mirror that it was indeed she; the taunting smile, the quick eyes, the total femininity were all Mirandolina; and the carefully placed beauty spot, the bosom magnificently swelling behind the low cut dress, the black curls and the dimpled cheeks were all part of a unique incarnation of the most beguiling woman in Italian comedy.

She swivelled round on the dressing table stool with the smile that so helplessly enmeshed the misogynistic Cavalier of Ripafratta whom, in the play, she besieges, conquers and finally spurns; and Peroni found himself falling willy-nilly into the role.

'Commissario!' said Mirandolina. 'How incredible actually to see you in the flesh!'

'We have,' said Peroni, his tone as formal as the still unbewitched Cavalier, 'met before.'

She arched her eyebrows at him in feminine bewilderment and her perfume drifted headily in his nostrils. It was not going to be easy, he realised, to follow the path of duty without deviation.

'Those suspensions,' he quoted firmly, 'those solutions—Must we die?'

She looked at him quickly, Mirandolina caught cheating the bill. 'I was heartbroken to have to leave you, Commissario,' she said at last, 'but I suddenly felt that if I had stayed an instant longer the inevitable parting would have been too painful.'

'Was it that,' said Peroni, 'or was it that you had an appointment with somebody else?'

Her eyes flashed; Mirandolina in a dangerous mood. 'What makes you think that?'

'Because we met on another occasion,' said Peroni, 'on the lagoon. You blessed me.'

Her face lit with amusement for a second, then clouded with irritation.

'I saw you during the Regatta this afternoon,' Peroni went on, 'and I realised at once that you were the English milady on Burano—where the Bull was training—and that you were the unexpected prelate on the lagoon—where the Bull was also training. And if the natural conclusion I drew from that needed any confirmation, I got it when the Bull passed in the Regatta and looked up at the balcony where you were standing. The look that passed between you was what I can only describe as intimate.'

'What business is this of yours, Commissario?' Mirandolina was now a serpent about to strike.

'Business?' The Cavalier of Ripafratta was in control of the situation for the moment at any rate. 'I don't know. But speaking, not exactly as a policeman so much as a Neapolitan on the make, I can't help recognising it as the story of the century for the scandal magazines. *The Actress and the Gondolier—Why the Bull Lost his Tenth Successive Historical Regatta.* Or perhaps you didn't realise that amorous activity is the one thing which is absolutely fatal for a gondolier in Regatta training? The public appetite is already sated with political scandals which are as routine as spaghetti—this is just what it needs to stimulate it. And your fiancé, that column of the Roman Black aristocracy Prince Attilio Cattamini, I daresay he would be enthralled.'

He ducked just in time to miss the bottle of perfume which whistled past his head and crashed into the dressing room door, but he was not quick enough to miss the crystal powder bowl which exploded over him like a sweet-smelling bomb, enveloping him in its fall-out. He fought his way through it before anything else could be thrown and gripped the superb Spinelli wrist.

She writhed ferociously in his arms and just for a moment the Cavalier of Ripafratta thought wistfully of the other way in which she might be writhing now, but he manfully slammed the cupboard door of regret on the idea and continued with the business in hand.

'But if you co-operate with me, Signorina,' he said, 'I think I can guarantee that nobody need know about the Bull.'

Abruptly she stopped struggling and he let her go. Mirandolina and the Cavalier looked at each other, and in their glance like recognised like. An agreement, their eyes announced, could be reached.

Several hours earlier, after the first moments of swirling bedlam at Mont Blanc following on the death of the smiling terrorist, order and efficiency had quickly reasserted themselves and established that he wasn't a terrorist at all, but a gondolier whose description had also been radioed to the frontier that day.

The priceless national heirloom was recovered and, after contact had been established with the *Questura* in Venice, sent back home with a heavy police motor cycle escort to the bafflement of motorists on the *autostrada* who couldn't conceive what was being escorted.

Just before *The Maidservant of Quality* set out on her return journey to make the acquaintance of Achille Peroni, her existence was made known to the world at large for the first time in a press conference held by the Carabiniere Colonel at Mont Blanc.

So it was that, while Mirandolina and the Cavalier of Ripafratta were sizing each other up, a young sub in the *Gazzettino* office was thinking up a headline for the Mont Blanc story. Italian headlines are generally weighty affairs, three-tiered with a sort of trailer running along the top, the headline proper in the middle and various bursts of information below, so that by the time you've got through all that, the story itself is largely superfluous.

But the young sub was a subscriber to *Time* and dreamed of introducing *Time*-style headlines into Italian journalism. SMILER SLAIN, he envisaged, and below in smaller type: *The Maidservant Returns*.

Unfortunately, he knew, *Gazzettino* staidness would never allow it. With a sigh and a cigarette he set to composing a more acceptable headline.

Alarming Incident at Mont Blanc.

Missing Gondolier Mistaken for Terrorist and Killed by Carabiniere while Attempting to cross over to Switzerland.

Priceless Goldoni manuscript retrieved—Was being smuggled into Switzerland—Identified during Carabiniere enquiry—Sent back to Venice—Being examined by Commissario Achille Peroni.

The young sub did not know that he was playing his part in bringing about the final catastrophe.

The dialogue had gone a long way from the original script, and there was a pause while Mirandolina and the Cavalier of Ripafratta adjusted to the new situation.

'When did your relationship with the Bull start?'

'About a month ago while I was rehearsing.'

'Why the complicated disguises?'

'Not disguises, Commissario, *transformations*! I was *transformed* into those people!' The almost mystical tone with which she said this gave way to practical earthiness as she went on, 'Well, for one thing, Commissario, if I hadn't literally turned myself into other people Atillio would have been onto me like a mountain storm. And for another—' Again her expression changed, this time to almost childish glee. 'For another there is only one thing in the world that gives me such pure and undiluted joy as transforming myself into unlikely characters.'

Peroni did not need to ask what the other thing was. 'Even Cardinals?' he asked.

'Particularly Cardinals! Those glorious purple robes! The rings! The expression of *hauteur*!' Quickly she changed into a Cardinal again and blessed her reflection in the mirror.

'Who knew of your relationship with the Bull?' resumed Peroni when she had ceased being ecclesiastical.

'Nobody! Don't you appreciate, Commissario, my transformations are *total*! So it was never I who was with the Bull, but the person I was playing!'

'When you met for the first time—you can't have been transformed into anybody then. Was anybody present at your first meeting?'

Spinelli's expression was so mobile that Peroni could see the memory spring into her mind like a sudden mushroom. 'Well?' he said.

'There was *somebody*,' she said, 'somebody who, in a sense, introduced us. Somebody who observed us on various occasions afterwards. But a person of no possible significance.'

'*Who*?' Peroni insisted.

'An idiot. A dumb idiot with the word GANZER in gold letters on his cap.'

For an endless moment ideas whirled in Peroni's mind like a merry-go-round out of control, but when they settled he knew that he had had his second great intuition and that it chimed in perfect harmony with the first one which had come to him on learning the identity of the Lion's mistress. And yet the impossibility remained as solid and inescapable as Vesuvius. Vesuvius. The analogy hooked Peroni's attention.

Vesuvius erupts.

And if the impossibility should erupt? He had no more than the dimmest conception of how this might be, but he understood for the first time that it *could* be; and if it were to happen, then by the light of that eruption he would see the Truth.

'A dumb idiot,' he retraced the way they had come, 'you say that in a sense he introduced you. How was that?'

'I was coming out of the Vivaldi Hotel one morning,' she said, replaying the scene as she went, 'when before me on the lagoon I saw the most glorious, the most mountainous, the most *bull-ish* man in the world standing on the poop of a gondola and I knew at once that I *must* be rowed by him alone!' She gave the verb its full double meaning. 'But before I had said a word, there was this Ganzer person hailing him for me and hooking his gondola into the quay.'

'And then?'

'And then, Commissario, and then—have you any conception what it is like to be rowed through Venice by a bull in human form? No, perhaps the idea wouldn't appeal to you, but to me . . .' She registered the rapture. 'I just had to have him immediately, so we went back to the hotel. Oh, they're discretion itself at the Vivaldi so I had no fears on that account. When we got back to the hotel the same creature hooked in our gondola.'

'And saw you going in together?'

She nodded. 'And several times later when I met the Bull, he was about. He saw us. He gave no sign of recognition, but it occurred to me to wonder. I asked the Bull, but he said the man was an idiot and dumb into the bargain, so I thought no more about it.' Suddenly she looked alarmed. 'You're not suggesting—?'

'No,' said Peroni, 'I don't think you've got anything to worry about on that score. For one thing he's dead—murdered. You might have seen it in the paper.'

'I never read the paper,' she said looking relieved.

'And now?' said Peroni. 'I mean your relationship with the Bull?'

She shrugged. 'What would you? It was a *coup de foudre*, a *folie*, an episode—it is my duty to Attilio to put it behind me.'

'He lost the Regatta because of you.'

A smile hovered at the corners of her mouth as though she were relishing the thought of all that Regatta power being spilled out for her, as though a lover had committed suicide for her. As, in a sense, he had.

'Poor Bull,' she said. It was an epitaph.

'I've just read the manuscript of a Goldoni play called *The Maidservant of Quality* which has been lost for two centuries.' He told her on an instinct and immediately regretted it.

'Commissario!' She was awash with awe. 'You must let me be the first to present it! Across the centuries I can feel that it was written for me! But tell me—how did you get it?'

He gave her a brief, guarded account of the manuscript's peripatetics.

'So whoever murdered the lawyer person did so for the manuscript?'

'It's possible.'

'In that case you should certainly suspect me, Commissario.' Vintage Mirandolina again. 'Nobody in the whole of Italy would be prepared to go to such lengths as I would to get hold of an original Goldoni manuscript!'

'Your hands are wrong,' said Peroni looking at them with their long fingers and their scarlet nails which carried on such a passionate liaison with the surrounding air. 'Whoever did it had very powerful hands.' He could still feel them around his own throat.

'I could have procured somebody to do it for me. There must

198

be thousands of men who would be willing to kill for me, Commissario.'

'I believe it,' said Peroni sincerely.

'But the plot of this play,' she said, 'tell me the plot!'

'It's a very thin plot really—'

'All Goldoni's plots are!'

'And its really time I was going—'

'Commissario, I *beg* you on my knees!'

'Well . . .' He marshalled the characters. 'It takes place in Venice. Pantaloon is trying to arrange a marriage between his daughter, Rosaura, and the Marquis of Monteverde. They have a maidservant, Corallina—'

'My part! The maidservant of quality.'

'Exactly. She's always putting things to rights when they go wrong. Well, at a certain point a dressmaker, *Sior* Zulian, arrives to show Rosaura some stuff for new clothes. And during this scene Corallina and *Sior* Zulian flirt together in a series of asides . . .'

Without even noticing that he was doing so, Peroni brought his spontaneous Neapolitan histrionism into play and the Goldoni comedy which he had deciphered only a few hours earlier with the help of Cornelius Ruskin, sprang into life.

He played the arrival of the foolish Marquis of Monteverde who, on his arrival is received by Corallina and, mistaking her for Rosaura, falls in love with her. He threw himself into the scene when the truth comes out and Corallina, having been dismissed by Pantaloon, receives a formal proposal from the Marquis which she accepts.

He steered the story into act two, opening with the disastrous, childless marriage of the Marquis and Corallina, and told how Corallina tried unsuccessfully to re-establish her relationship with *Sior* Zulian by getting him to design some clothes for her.

Then, hands weaving and face as mobile as a teenage party, he launched into the big act three scene where, the Marquis having gone to stay with his sister, Corallina sends for *Sior* Zulian once more, this time receiving him as a maidservant in her act one costume, and they repeat part of the dialogue at their first meeting.

'When the Marquis returns from his sister,' he went on, 'he has

199

no cause to suspect her conduct in his absence because as the servant, Harlequin, points out "She couldn't have misbehaved because she ceased to exist". There was a maidservant, he says, who had an understanding with *Sior* Zulian. And in fact, even after the Marquis's return this maidservant doesn't disappear altogether. Occasionally Harlequin sees her going out or coming in through the back door, though he believes that the Marquis has never set eyes on her.

'And in the last scene of all, Corallina tells the audience that the time has come for the transformation to cease. Then she turns herself back into the Marchioness just in time to greet the Marquis to whom she announces that she is going to have the much desired heir to the Monteverde family. So everything ends happily.'

Even as he told the story Peroni had the odd impression that it was whispering something altogether different to him. But however hard he strained his inner ear he couldn't catch what it was.

TWENTY-THREE

Peroni was essentially an asymmetrical person, and he mistrusted symmetry in life. So he was disconcerted by the addition of two pieces of information to the piles on his desk, one to don Amos's pile and one to the Hooker's. That made one piece of information concerning each of the three men and all pointing at a brooding totem-pole of conclusion. You could hardly be more symmetrical than that.

And all this information was inescapable, even though the impossibility was still there and giving no premonitory rumbling which might prelude eruption. But in spite of the impossibility, active or extinct, the facts now clamoured for a decision.

Orthodox procedure called for detention and questioning, but this would bring them straight up against the impossibility and a claim that the facts were coincidental. Which just possibly they might be.

What was needed was something unexpected if he could only devise it.

What was needed was another Peroni *coup*.

Some things happen, especially in Italy, which, by the light of hindsight, never should have been allowed to happen. But by then, of course, they have happened, and it's too late. Such was the escape of the Lion.

He had been travelling by police launch, handcuffed and chained to a Carabiniere, to an interrogation with *dott.* Tron. A *Maresciallo* of the *Pubblica Sicurezza* was with them carrying a police file which contained a comprehensive report of all the police investigations into the Bixi-Hooker killings and the allied gondoliering malpractices, including Peroni's most recent calculations concerning the identity of the person behind it all.

Everything happened at once. It was still early and few people were about. The police launch was chugging gently along Rio Santa Maria Formosa, the escorting carabiniere was getting out a cigarette for the Lion and helping him light it, the *Maresciallo* was reading the *Corriere della Sera* when the Lion suddenly brought the heavy weight of chain down on the Carabiniere's neck. The Carabiniere crumpled. The *Maresciallo*, who had been doing domestic odds and ends about the *Questura* for more than a decade and was totally out of training for emergencies like this, dropped his newspaper and sprang up, but not in time to prevent the Lion from grabbing the police file and jumping onto some stone steps which were less than a couple of feet from the launch.

The Carabiniere revived and staggered to his feet, tugging a gun from his holster.

'Stop!' he called, and when the Lion didn't, he fired. The shot must have hit the Lion's arm for he grabbed in the direction of his right shoulder with his left hand, but did not stop running. A second later he had rounded a corner into a *calle*.

The policeman driving the launch moored it hastily and the Carabiniere and the Maresciallo jumped off in pursuit. But when they reached the *calle* into which the Lion had disappeared he was nowhere in sight. The spot had been well chosen, for there was a whole network of alleys here. The Carabiniere took one and the Maresciallo another, but the Lion was in neither. Ten minutes later they were obliged to admit that he had got clean away.

'*Fama nihil est celerius*,' said *dott*. Tron when *dott*. Amabile called him. 'Nothing is swifter than rumour. I have already been informed of the Lion's escape, *dottore*. How did he get the keys?'

'At the moment nobody seems to know.' The tone was scholastically guarded.

'An enquiry has already been opened.'

There was a stirring sound at the other end of the line as of branches lifted by the wind. 'On the face of it,' said *dott*. Tron, 'it would appear that one of your men was an accomplice.'

Dott. Amabile made the defensive throat-clearing noise of a headmaster when doubt is cast on the probity of the entire body scholastic. 'He was being escorted by the Carabinieri,' he pointed out. 'They had the keys.'

'A *Maresciallo* of yours was in the boat,' said Tron and, not for the first time, *dott*. Amabile wondered how the magistrate always managed to know certain things before anybody could possibly have told him.

'He's one of the most trustworthy men in the *Questura*,' *dott*. Amabile said, 'It seems more probable that the Lion got the keys from some other source altogether.'

'And the file?' said Tron. 'That would seem to be the motive for this elaborately organised escape. But how could the Lion have known that there was such vital information in the file?'

'Come to that,' said Amabile, 'how could he have even known that the file would be in the launch this morning?'

'*Felix qui potuit rerum cognoscere causas*—happy is he who can know the cause of things. But in the meantime it looks as though we have all the ingredients of yet another major national scandal.'

'I'm afraid you're right, *dottore*.'

'Well, let us keep it from the media as long as we possibly can, and of course I don't need to stress that all available means be used to recover both the Lion and the file. And let us meet in your office at midday to discuss progress.'

'Certainly, *dottore*.'

'*Speramus meliora*—let us hope for better things.'

But the Lion had by no means vanished into thin air. A gondolier rowing in the Rio Barcaroli with a honeymoon couple from

202

Vermont looked up from an envious study of his customers' dalliance to see a familiar figure limping along the canal side, holding his right arm. He could observe him neither well nor long, but the salient traits were clear: it was the Lion.

Soon after that a little girl, the daughter of a gondolier, was playing a Venetian version of hopscotch in Campo Sant'Angelo when she saw the Lion, who was a friend of her father's and an honorary uncle, just about to turn into a *calle*.

'*Zio!*' she called, but he can't have heard her, for he disappeared into the *calle* without looking round, and she went on with her hopscotch.

Then a waiter, carrying a tray of coffee and drinks to an accountant's office, saw him limping down Rio Tera Foscarini towards the Zattere. He wanted to pass the time of day with him, but was too laden to run, and by the time he got into Rio Foscarini himself, the Lion was out of sight.

But none of these sightings went unreported, and before long news of the Lion's escape and the route he was following was circulating along the centuries-old, aquatic grapevine of Venice which is one of the most efficient in the world.

And, of course, something as sensational as the seizure of the police file would have been impossible to keep quiet for long. So very soon, that too was current throughout certain circles in the city.

The house just off the Zattere would be best. The place where Rosina Medebac had so often been recalled from the dead. If he waited there somebody would be bound to turn up sooner or later. Somebody special.

Just before turning off by Santa Maria del Rosario he felt fairly certain that he had been recognised yet again. He shouldn't have to wait for very long.

He went down the little *calle* into the square with the well and crossed with his swift limp to number 17 where he unlocked the front door and went in.

Upstairs, where it had all happened, the air was drained and depressing. Swathed in black and wreathed in incense it had been like a magic cave; now it was just a peeling room with bare boards in a damp, unsavoury house.

He lit a cigarette and fixed a bit of sacking over the window. Then he sat down to wait. Waiting was always the worst.

At first he thought there was complete silence, but then he realised it was one of those silences which contain their own sounds. The house stirred about him. There was a scraping on the stone stairs outside and a rising and falling wheeze as though the building were having trouble with its breathing; a distant bump which sounded like a dead body being dropped and a rustling, senseless whisper.

Then he began to feel as though there were somebody else in the room with him. Imagination, he told himself, the place was as bare as a pauper's coffin. But the feeling persisted until he understood who the other person was.

A girl, stabbed to death in a brawl more than two hundred years before, with long black hair and green eyes and a beauty spot on her right cheek bone.

She had been called up too much, so that now her restless soul, half materialised, haunted the room where she had been conjured up.

Merda to her, he thought; but she wouldn't go away.

He seemed to hear her whispering behind his back, but resisted the temptation to spin round because that would concede her a reality she didn't possess.

But the whispering came nearer until it seemed as though he could feel her breathing on the back of his neck, prickling the little hairs that grew there, and smell the heavy, sweet perfume hanging on the musty air.

Suddenly he couldn't bear it any longer and he whipped round on her only to find, as he had known all along, that she had gone. But in the instant of his turning, just before his eyes could verify her nothingness, he could hear a stiletto giggle.

There was another inhabited silence. She was biding her time, watching him, conjecturing how she might most effectively get at him next.

The whispering started again behind his back, and again he resolved not to turn upon it. But it came nearer and nearer, and this time it was as though her long, dead fingers were playing, mock amorous, about his face and cheeks. He stood it for as long

204

as he could and then, when he could bear it no longer, wheeled upon empty space.

Three more times she played her macabre grandmother's footsteps, and each time, as his will to ignore her snapped, there came the same ice dagger of a giggle. Then, after the third time, she didn't start again; and that was worse, for it was as though she were preparing some more subtle form of torment. After a second he realised what that torment was.

For somebody had come in through the door downstairs.

She stayed silent now, almost as though this new and real presence had arrived to take over her campaign for driving him out of his wits.

Footsteps started to come up the stone steps.

Although she was silent, he thought he could catch the faint swish of her skirt in a corner and an almost completely muffled giggle at the prospect of what was coming now.

He waited motionless in the shadow by the window as the sound of the footsteps on the stairs drew nearer as regularly as heart beats and, against his will, he found himself counting them. Nineteen. Twenty. Twenty-one. Now whoever it was had reached the top and was moving across the landing. Now the door handle was turning.

The door opened and, although there was less than a half light because of the sacking he had drawn over the window, he was able to recognise the figure which now came into the room.

'So you got away, Lion?' the figure said. 'That was really clever. And the file—where's the file?'

Still in the Lion disguise with which he had made his mock escape, but holding a gun, Peroni stepped out of the shadow by the window towards Tonino.

TWENTY-FOUR

Although it was already well on into the afternoon, the *Questura* was still in an uproar. This had continued unabated ever since Tonino had been arrested and brought in less than twenty-four hours after wrenching from the Bull the most sensational victory of the Regatta's millennial history.

All day tourists, curiosity seekers and gondoliers had jammed the normally peaceful Fondamenta San Lorenzo, together with reporters and television camera crews clamouring for a statement and the possibility of filming something other than the entrance to the *Questura*, the canal-side walk and deliberately posed gondolas bobbing up and down on the water.

To the media it seemed as though the *Questura* were maintaining an unpardonably rigid and Kremlin-esque silence. What the media didn't realise was that the chaos of speculation within the *Questura* was such that nobody would have been capable of issuing a coherent statement.

Dott. Amabile, in his smoke-wreathed heights, struggled to maintain academic rationality in a situation where it seemed as though every pupil were giving a different version of the facts. *Dott*. Tron waved and tossed in perplexity at the news (which for once *was* news to him) that it was not the Lion who had escaped, but *dott*. Peroni, and that this was linked with the arrest of Tonino. He just didn't have the Latin to cover the situation.

Only *dott*. de Benedetti and Policewoman Sofia Michelangelo were remote from the reigning chaos; they went about their business with expressions of such sublime silliness that it was fortunate their colleagues were too caught up in the whirl of it all to notice.

Those who knew *dott*. Peroni would have expected him to be flashing self-satisfaction like a police car racing to an emergency. But instead he was brooding as though, far from having achieved a Peroni triumph, he had most signally failed. This, some suspected, might have been due to Tonino's intransigence. For the hatred of all authority which the Regatta hero had briefly displayed during his first visit to the Questura was now a snarling permanency.

'You picked on me because I'm a gondolier!' he said. 'It's always the same in Venice—whenever something goes wrong it has to be a gondolier who's responsible!' He spat. '*Stronzo!*' he said.

'You didn't mean to kill the Hooker, did you?'

'I don't know what you're talking about!'

206

'You discovered it was he who told *avv*. Bixi about you, and you were so wild with rage that you hit him. And he fell, striking his head against something as he did so. But you didn't intend it to happen that way, did you?'

'I'm not answering anything!'

'You only make it worse, Tonino.' Peroni exuded Neapolitan amiability, and from behind his words promises of a deal peeped out like phony gold watches from a street vendor's coat. 'It's in your interest to help now. We've got the Lion. We've got your mother.' Tonino's jerk of fury at this made Peroni thankful the gondolier was handcuffed and guarded. 'And sooner or later they'll tell us, even if you don't.'

'Besides,' Peroni added, 'there's the whole world of the gondola—the world you did it all for. Until now that world has only been able to tell me so much, but now that I know a lot and can guess the rest, that treacherous world of yours is going to be tumbling over itself to help me.'

It was true enough; all the cards in the Lion's three-card trick were now in Peroni's hand, so Tonino's intransigence had no great importance.

Why then did Peroni continue to brood?

'I got the first lead onto Tonino,' Peroni told *dott*. Amabile, 'when I started to build up information on the Lion, the Hooker and don Amos—the three people I was convinced were direct dependents on a central organiser. I found that for several years the Lion had been the lover of Tonino's mother. It might have been a coincidence, but it was an odd one, that the man who organised the pimping at Harry's Bar should be directly linked with Tonino.'

'But that didn't necessarily mean that Tonino was your organiser,' Amabile pointed out.

'No, *dottore*,' Peroni agreed, 'and I don't think he *was* the sole organiser. I think they worked it between the three of them.'

'The facts seem to have proved you right,' *dott*. Amabile's voice sounded pedantically from far off mountains melted into cloud, 'but it was thin enough.'

'Yes,' agreed Peroni, 'until yesterday when two further pieces of information were added to my collection. First, Tonino used to be an altar boy for don Amos. And second, he was reported at one period to have been seen round a lot in bars with the Hooker. That tied him in firmly with all three of the others.'

'What would he have been doing in bars with the Hooker—apart from drinking presumably?'

'That,' said Peroni, 'takes us back to the start of the whole thing.' He was beginning to enjoy his exposition now because he felt that a shifting was imminent deep within the entrails of the volcano of the impossible. 'Tonino's father was a gondolier who died when the boy was only seven. He left him a passionate love for the gondola and a no less passionate urge to win the Regatta—things which tend to be handed down in gondoliering families. And he left him something else—the gondolier's age-old grudge against society which he believes is persecuting him. Then there was the mother's relationship with the Lion and her Bolzano origins—you remember, *dottore*, that *dott.* Muso discovered she came from Bolzano?—that would have provided a very un-Italian, un-gondoliering, un-Venetian capacity for organisation. Those are the ingredients. Then at some point the three of them decided to fuse and direct the scattered growths of gondoliering free enterprise—the touch of blackmail here, the odd bit of pimping there, the gambling and so on. And one day, looking about for likely assistants, they saw the Hooker. One of them must have realised that he wasn't quite such an idiot as he was believed to be and, given his wandering habits, could be trained for picking up useful bits of information. When Tonino was spotted about with the Hooker, I believe that was what he was doing.'

'Pure speculation?'

'Largely,' Peroni admitted cheerfully, 'though I do have a sort of indirect backing for it. The Hooker was present at Maddalena Spinelli's first meeting with the Bull, and he was the only person who is known to have observed them at subsequent meetings.'

'But she wasn't being blackmailed.'

'Exactly—that's the point. If Tonino was behind it—which he was—and learned of the affair from the Hooker—which it seems probable he did—he wouldn't have used it for blackmail. He would have let it continue peacefully—*knowing that it was going to give him a very good chance of winning the Historical Regatta!*'

From his standpoint of Friulan common sense, *dott*. Amabile considered this lunatic piece of Venetian reasoning as propounded by Naples and felt bound to concede that, given Venice as a back-drop, it might well be so.

'And what was the Hooker doing with Bixi in his office the day before Bixi was killed?'

'He was having Tonino's identity extracted from him. I don't think there's any doubt about that. By whisky, wheedling and threats. We know that *avv.* Bixi had been moving into gondoliering affairs for some time. He must have come to realise—just as we did—that there was an organiser behind them and he tried to find out who it was with the aim of going into partnership. He tried through the gondoliers who were taking Regatta bets and failed. He tried, I have no doubt, through the Lion and failed again. Then his eye fell, as theirs had done, on the Hooker. And even if the Hooker wasn't the idiot he was generally supposed to be, he was certainly no match for *avv.* Bixi. He cracked.'

'And that was the cause of his death?'

'Exactly, *dottore*. When Bixi got onto him, Tonino knew he'd been betrayed—knew that it could only have been one of four people—his mother, the Lion, don Amos and the Hooker. And then he enquired and found that the Hooker had been with Bixi on Sunday. But I don't think Tonino meant to kill him, though— I think he just struck him in rage and the force of the blow smashed the Hooker's head against something.'

'Very plausible. But why did Tonino then run the grave risk of transporting the Hooker's body by gondola to the same spot where he had left *avv.* Bixi's?'

'That's where things start to go wrong, *dottore*,' said Peroni. 'Tonino didn't kill *avv.* Bixi.'

The intricacy of the ikon was stunning; there must have been several hundred people there, as well as animals, a bewildering complexity of buildings, two wheels, a ladder and a river which, if you observed closely, wound its way about the entire lower section. At least one person was dead and several were naked; various little groups were intent upon their own activities, impervious to the multi-faceted scene about them, and the crowd by the water's edge was so dense that you wondered some of them weren't pushed in.

The ikon museum attached to the Greek church of St George on the other side of the canal from the *Questura* was the last place you would have expected to find Commissario Achille Peroni at this delicate and inconclusive moment, but he felt that it was appropriate, though he would have been at a loss to explain why.

He had been curious to visit it ever since he came to Venice, but the idea had always seemed frivolous. And then emerging from his interview with *dott*. Amabile and observing the confusion within and without the *Questura* he had on impulse come by a back way, avoiding the media people, to this first floor haven of ancient peace.

He continued to look into the ikon with its myriad figures whirling about the central, all-harmonizing Christ child, benedictory in the lap of a solemnly sweet Greek Virgin. And as he looked at it the painted characters seemed to become liquid and waver and then merge into other, more familiar characters.

Peroni began to understand why the museum was an appropriate place for him to be. For the apparent complexity characterising these ikons and resolving, if you looked at them carefully, into the most liquid simplicity was an uncannily accurate reflexion of the Bixi-Hooker affair.

There, in the ikon before him, was the Lion with the half materialised Rosina Medebac, and just over the water don Amos stuffing a bundle of betting slips into his cassock as he listened to a gondolier's confession. The Hooker shuffled over a bridge and a little further off lay dead, his body seeming to give off its foulsome odour even in the ikon.

They were all there, orbiting about the central truth which finally, at the heart of this Greek ikon, Peroni recognised. He stood staring at it until he felt as though he himself were being drawn helplessly into the scene.

He was rescued by a dry, deferential sound which it took him a second or two to recognise as a cough emanating from the soft spoken and courteous Greek custodian of the museum who had earlier given Peroni his ticket.

'If you haven't finished looking, *Signore*,' said the custodian, 'I'll be glad to stay open a little longer. But it is closing time.'

Peroni was surprised to see the ikons about him in their standing frames casting long shadows.

'No,' he said, 'I've finished looking.'

As he went downstairs, he heard a distant rumble which, still under the influence of the ikon, he took to be his own private volcano of the impossible in full eruption.

But then he realised that it was thunder.

TWENTY-FIVE

The bell-pull, which he had not observed before, was the largest and the most ancient Peroni had ever seen. Its only defect was that no bell was attached to it. When he tugged at it, it moved rustily back a few centimetres as though resentful at being woken from a centuries long sleep, but no sound of ringing, however distant, came from within. He decided to try the knocker which was of the same age and family. It was as reluctant as the bell-pull, but it grudgingly furnished a couple of thuds which echoed hollowly within.

Nobody answered. Yet the family launch was moored at the landing stage which suggested somebody should be at home. Peroni waited and then knocked again. There was another long silence, but eventually he heard a sound of movement within and then the heavy door began to creak open.

He hoped against hope that it wouldn't be Estrella. But it was. She was wearing her customary jeans and open-necked check shirt, but they were spattered with various colours of paint.

'Commissario!' she said. 'What a nice surprise!'

'Good evening, Signorina.'

'You'll have to forgive me looking like this. By an odd coincidence I was keeping my promise to you.'

'What promise was that?' said Peroni, surprised.

'I said I'd do a painting for you, remember? Well, today seemed to be the day.' Peroni caught her faint cello note of sadness and wondered why it should have sounded just then. 'I've almost finished.'

'What's the subject?'

'Come and see.'

He followed her up the great winding staircase, in spite of himself admiring the unselfconscious neatness and rhythm of her body. He knew his thoughts were going in the wrong direction, but continued to observe the flow of her as she moved up the stairs.

'Ready,' she said, standing outside the door in the long second floor corridor. 'Steady.' She looked at him with that disconcertingly knowing look of hers. 'Go.' She opened the door.

In the centre of the room was a fair-sized island of newspapers on which stood an easel and canvas.

'Go on,' said Estrella, 'don't mind me.'

It was a canal scene, quintessentially Venetian, with a gondola slanting out into the sunlight from the shade of a hump-backed bridge. It was beautiful, Peroni thought, with the glinting of the water, the light and shade and texture of the brick-work, the gondolier and the fittings of his gondola all caught by Estrella's technique of three-dimensional blobs of oil-paint. But there was something familiar about it, too, which escaped him.

'It's beautiful,' he said, echoing his first reaction.

'Don't let's exaggerate,' she said, 'but don't you recognise it?'

'There is something—but I can't place it.'

'Look well.'

He obeyed her and after a second or two understood. The picture showed that stretch of canal where he had jammed his boat with the barge of mineral water and she had rescued him.

'I had thought of painting myself clambering all over the place,' she said, spotting his recognition, 'but I thought it would have been less romantic. And more difficult, too. You'll just have to imagine me.'

'It's a wonderful present,' said Peroni sincerely.

Outside there was another, louder rumble of the thunder he had heard while coming down the stairs from the ikon museum.

'And talking about presents,' Estrella went on, 'there's another one I should like to give you.' Peroni looked at her uncertainly. 'I was wrong the other day,' she said, 'I behaved like a stupid little girl with all that stuff about the moment being here or not being here. It's always here if you want it to be. It's here now.'

She stood before him on the little island of newspapers, vulnerable and humble and offered. He stepped towards her and they stood facing each other for a second with their bodies almost touching. Then Peroni began the kiss. It was a long crescendo, and when it had almost reached its climax and they paused for a gasping second, Estrella said, 'Isn't it a bit silly kissing on a lot of old newspapers, Commissario? Wouldn't we be more comfortable on the sofa?'

'Yes, Signorina,' said Peroni, 'we would.'

And then they were on the sofa and Peroni was nuzzling her hair while his hands explored deeper into their new found land.

'Estrella,' he murmured, almost without being aware that he was doing so, and the very saying of her name was a penetration. He repeated it over and over again, no longer able to tell whether he was saying it with his lips or in his head. 'Estrella, Estrella, Estrella . . .'

And then, as though evoked by the name, a picture formed itself uninvited in his mind's eye. Blurred at first as though seen through water, then clearer and clearer, for all he tried to shut it away. Estrella in a dove-grey dress down to her ankles was standing in a bare stone room with a single glassless window looking out over desolate expanses of water, and she was talking to a man, the king Pepin who was about to attack the Venetians at Rivo Alto. Pepin had his back to her so that you couldn't see his face. But Estrella went on talking, talking, talking, and at the same time moving nearer and nearer to the king. Then as she reached him she turned him to face her, put her arms about his neck and kissed him. As she turned him towards her, Peroni saw that King Pepin's face was his own.

Scarcely aware of what he was doing, Peroni found that he had broken himself free from Estrella, was running across the large room towards the window overlooking the canal, was opening it and looking down.

The Partecipazio family launch, which had been moored there when he arrived, was gone.

After an initial surge into the waters of the lagoon, Peroni had been obliged to slow his boat to a crawl in order to avoid running aground on one of the mud banks. He hugged close to the stakes. What had she called them? *Bricole*.

The thought of her unleashed his fury again. The same fury that had gushed up black inside him when he had realised that Estrella was aping her medieval namesake in order that her father might get away. The purest Neapolitan hatred for both of them pounded through him.

The storm had begun in good earnest now. He could see huge drops of rain plopping bullet fashion into the stretch of lagoon illuminated by his headlights while jagged flashes of lightning slashed at the sky's fabric like scissors wielded by a demented tailor.

By the light of them Peroni seemed to see his volcano of the impossible, stark now in its panorama of violent death. Tonino had killed the Hooker. Tonino had organised the illicit gondoliering activities. Tonino had made the murderous attacks on Peroni.

But Tonino had not—and could not have—killed *avv.* Bixi. Because when somebody had shattered the back of Bixi's skull with a rock, Tonino had incontrovertibly been at a dinner for the competitors and officials of the Historical Regatta. Nearly thirty witnesses had twice affirmed that between eleven o'clock that night and one the following morning Tonino had not left the restaurant so much as to relieve himself.

Tonino had indeed been in Bixi's office a few hours before, summoned there by the lawyer after he had learned Tonino's identity from the Hooker the day before. The subject of the interview between the lawyer and gondolier had had nothing to do with Tonino's overcharging, but must rather have been a harsh either-or parley with Bixi pressing hard while Tonino prevaricated, promised and—the thought was ironic—surely contemplated and probably planned murder to escape from the impasse.

What Tonino can have felt when he learned the next day that Bixi had indeed been killed it was hard to imagine, but it explained his escape from Muso at the Rialto. Knowing that somebody else had killed Bixi, he hoped the police would arrest that somebody before investigating Tonino and his activities. It also indicated that Tonino had transported the Hooker's body to

Corte Balbi in the hope that his death would be ascribed to the same author as that of the lawyer.

Who that author was there could be no doubt. His motivation was more complex, but by the light of the ikon and a quick check he had made afterwards, Peroni now understood that, too.

The lagoon where Peroni's boat now chugged with exasperating slowness over the dark waters was quite deserted, such traffic as there was at this hour and in this weather being far away in the big channels. By the lightning flashes he could make out Chioggia looming black to the south and the thinner line of Pellestrina behind him.

He must have been going for quarter of an hour at this pace when he felt the soft lurch against the keel he had so much been dreading. The boat had run onto a mud shoal.

If he had done the thing officially with police launch and driver, he wouldn't have run this risk of being stranded all night in the middle of the lagoon, but the idea of where to look had only occurred to him after the official hunt had started and, as he had come to regard it as a private vendetta, he had decided to go alone. And this was the result.

He wrenched the steering wheel hard to the left (mentally refusing any concession to nautical terminology), but there was no response. He was stuck.

Cursing himself now as much as Estrella he turned off the engine and went out of the cabin. Instantly the storm pounced on him and tore at him with its claws of wind and rain while the now incessant lightning that cracked about his head like the whip of a cosmic circus master was so close that he cowered to avoid it.

There was no telling how long this could go on for; and, to make matters worse, he reckoned that he wasn't all that far from his objective, though stuck as he was he might have been a thousand kilometres away.

He contemplated getting out and pushing, but beyond the fact that the keel of the boat was sunk, he had no idea of the disposition of water and mud about him. He might sink up to his neck in mud. Or deeper. And although appearance was no longer of any moment to him, he didn't relish the prospect of drowning in mud.

He looked wildly about for inspiration and his eye fell on a boathook. At least it would serve for exploring the immediate surroundings. He picked it up and, leaning over the bows, probed into the wet darkness. On one side, the right, there was fairly solid mud. He tried the other. Mud, too, but squishier, and if he stretched the boathook out there was water, maybe fairly deep.

There was just a chance that if he pushed and levered hard enough on the right side he might get the boat back into the stream. He pushed. The boathook sunk in and he pulled it out with a squelching sound that could be heard even through the noise of the storm. He pushed out again, and this time had the satisfaction of feeling the boat shift slightly towards the water. Five minutes of this and it was drifting upon water, back once again in the stream.

Peroni ducked into the cabin and switched on the engine, nosing his craft forward and away from the mud shoal with a hasty intercession to St Janarius that he should not immediately run into another. The storm went with him like a pack of beasts roaring and buffetting at the boat.

Now he was coasting a desolate stretch of marsh on which he was just able to make out the white shapes of hundreds of gulls. He chugged in the crashing thunder towards a point, rounded it and then saw immediately ahead of him something bulking blackly against the sky. The Partecipazio Island.

As he got nearer he could distinguish the villa, crumbling and forlorn. There was no sign of the Partecipazio motor boat, but as Peroni knew that the little harbour was at the back this meant nothing.

He moored his own boat and climbed out of the cabin into the howling night. Once within the lea of the house, though, the wind dropped considerably and he was able to walk upright. He stopped for a second outside the front door, wondering whether he should knock; the situation was a sort of no man's land between a police raid and a formal call. He decided against knocking, pushed open the unlocked door and went in, closing the door behind him.

Suddenly the noise of the storm receded. Outside, where it still turmoiled, was a long way away; inside, the sudden quiet was almost tangible and more laden with menace than any thunder and lightning.

Partecipazio was sitting at one end of a long wooden table, his head in his arms, a bottle of wine and a glass at his elbow and an oil-lamp in front of him. For an instant Peroni thought he might be asleep, but then he raised his large head and there flashed across his face an expression that Peroni could not read. Then, perhaps a little wearily, he assumed his customary theatrical geniality.

'Commissario!' he said. 'Such an honour! But what can I offer you? I came here for the night so that I could get in a good day's shooting tomorrow, so I have little in the way of provisions.' The obvious falsity about the morrow's shooting lay between them like a corpse which they both politely pretended to ignore. 'A glass of wine at least?' Partecipazio went on. He took out his snuff-box, handed it to Peroni and then said, 'Ah, but I'm forgetting—you don't. An anachronistic habit. But please sit down, Commissario. Now that you are here, I must see what poor hospitality my house can afford you . . .' He half rose out of his chair.

'I've read *The Maidservant of Quality*,' said Peroni.

Partecipazio sat down again. '*The Maidservant of Quality?*' he repeated.

'A missing comedy by Carlo Goldoni,' Peroni explained.

'Ah yes, I saw in the *Gazzettino* . . .' He left the sentence suspended.

'Perhaps it might be enlightening for both of us,' said Peroni, falling into the mannered, drawing-room style which Partecipazio evoked in him, 'if we were to trace its history together.'

'You and I, Commissario? I cannot see how my poor understanding can be of assistance to the great Commissario Peroni. However, if you deem it fitting, for me it can only be an unmerited honour.' He waved his hand with the old flourish but, Peroni thought, a little limply.

'Oddly enough,' said Peroni, uncomfortably aware that he was sounding like the Marquis di Monteverde summing up for the audience at the end of the comedy, 'there's been an unusual constant in this business since the beginning. Carlo Goldoni. At first he just seemed to haunt things. And then he finally made his entrance—as he himself would surely have put it—when a manuscript of his play was stolen from the Vivaldi Hotel. I've now traced that manuscript back. A gondolier called Smiler stole it from the American at the Vivaldi who had bought it from an ex-gondolier called the Undertaker who, in his turn, got it from a canal bed hiding place where Bixi had deposited it. But where did Bixi get it from?'

'You know the answer to that, Commissario?'

'He got it from you.'

Partecipazio fetched a heavy sigh which might have been a gulp for air and then took another pinch of snuff.

'You see,' said Peroni, 'there's something that's bothered me all along about this manuscript. If somebody wanted it and believed it to be in Bixi's office, *why did they bother to kill him*? It would have been far simpler just to break in during the night. So I began to think that maybe the person didn't merely want possession of the manuscript. That they also wanted to suppress Bixi's knowledge of something in the play.

'Something in the play?' echoed Partecipazio.

'Just that,' said Peroni, 'the play tells the story of a maidservant who marries one of Goldoni's typical Venetian aristocrats and then later has a liaison, discreetly hinted at, with a dressmaker she was in love with before the marriage. Like most of Goldoni's plots, it's very thin indeed and certainly doesn't appear to say anything of relevance to a murder enquiry taking place two hundred years later. But viewed in conjunction with other facts, one gets a different impression.'

Partecipazio shifted his large body in the chair.

'The key to *The Maidservant of Quality*,' said Peroni, 'is Goldoni's *Mémoires*. From the *Mémoires* you learn that Goldoni was always putting real situations, thinly disguised into his plays. For example in *One of the Last Nights of Carnival*, the pattern designer going to Moscow is Goldoni himself going to Paris as a result of the ferocious opposition he had met with in Venice.

'But a pattern designer and a dressmaker are more or less the same thing, aren't they? So I began to wonder whether *Sior* Zulian in *The Maidservant* might not be another self portrait, like *Sior* Anzoletto in the Carnival play. And what about the Maidservant herself? Well, another thing that's very evident from the *Mémoires* is that throughout Goldoni's long and eventful life maidservants and actresses were completely interchangeable, in fact and in fiction, and that he had an unlimited enthusiasm for both.

'And then I remembered something else in the *Mémoires*. An actress, Teodora Veronese, did in fact marry into the Venetian nobility in 1744. And the man she married, I discovered this evening, was your ancestor, Anselmo Partecipazio. Five years later Goldoni mentions writing *The Maidservant* to tempt her back to the stage after her first child was born. But the play was never performed. The manuscript is never mentioned again. So what can have happened to it? Goldoni would presumably have given it to her, and it is reasonable to assume that it stayed in the family. Until you found it.'

All Partecipazio's buoyancy was drained out of him. He sat limply in the chair, arms dangling, more than ever like an enormous scarecrow, seemingly no longer even aware of Peroni's presence.

'What happened next,' Peroni went on, 'I have to guess. I imagine you immediately saw its potential value and decided to sell it to finance your gambling. But you'd read it and seen the family connection. You knew that the maidservant was Teodora Veronese, that the Marquis of Monteverde was your own ancestor and that *Sior* Zulian was Goldoni.

'The final calculation from all this is easy. There is a three year gap between the end of the first act when the Maidservant accepts the Marquis's proposal and the second when she meets Zulian again and starts her liaison with him. During those three years she remained childless, but immediately afterwards she had a son, mentioned by Goldoni in 1749. Add to this the fact that the Marquis who married Teodora Veronese was twenty years her senior and you have a practically inescapable conclusion. The father of that child was not the Marquis at all, but Carlo Goldoni. And that would make you no longer part of the great line of doges and warriors and popes. It would make you, in fact, the descendant of an actress and a Venetian playwright called Carlo Goldoni.

'The funny thing is that some people might consider that an honour, but not you. And you knew that if somebody else made the same calculations that you had made—which they would certainly do if the manuscript was sold as coming from you—the news would be splashed on every scandal sheet in Italy. After all, the story's got everything—actresses, the nobility, adultery and the literary find of the century. But if the manuscript could be sold as having no connection whatsoever with you, it would never occur to anybody to make the calculation. And you badly wanted the money. So somehow the manuscript had to be sold without seeming to come from you or to have any connection with the Partecipazio family. No easy job. And then you must have thought of getting a lawyer to handle it for you and naturally you, the gondolier's friend, thought of Bixi, the gondoliers' lawyer. You didn't know what sort of man he was.

'Whether you told him the whole story yourself or whether he read the play and drew his own conclusions, I don't know. Either way, he had you at his mercy, and I imagine he threatened you with exposure if you didn't let him keep the manuscript. So you'd got the very worst of all worlds. Unless, of course, *avv*. Bixi were to die. And so you waited for him that evening when he was on his way home and gave him his final settlement with a piece of rock which had been dug up in some street works thereabouts. Then you took his keys and went to his office and ransacked it in vain for the manuscript. And that,' Peroni concluded, 'is more or less that.'

There was a long silence inside the ancient, mouldering villa. Outside you could still hear the rumbling of thunder as the storm moved off towards Jugoslavia, and the beating swish of the rain against the windows.

'A glass of wine,' said the scarecrow Partecipazio, 'I offered you a glass of wine. Such wine!' he went on with a flash of his original self. 'A Tokai, but not the sort of Tokai you'll find in the shops, Commissario, nor even on private tables. It's specially made for the Parte—' He came to a sudden halt and looked about him bewilderedly. 'For my family,' he concluded. 'Let me get you a glass.'

Peroni watched him with pity as he limped slowly towards a large wooden cupboard with a door hanging crookedly on its hinges. But the pity vanished at the velocity of light when Partecipazio wheeled round on him with a singularly dangerous looking hunting rifle.

'Forgive this lack of hospitality, Commissario, but I have no alternative. My ancestors compel me! For it's not true about Goldoni and Teodora Veronese! Anselmo Partecipazio was the father of Veronese's child! But if the lie gets out, who will believe the truth?'

While fear churned Peroni's guts, he cursed himself for not thinking that if Partecipazio had killed once, he could kill again.

'If I were descended from a mere Venetian playwright, Commissario, no sense of family honour would run in my veins as independently of my own free will as the blood itself. Yet that sense of honour *is* alive within me! It's that which forces me to kill you!'

Tell him that other people knew the Maidservant secret? Peroni calculated wildly. That might work with ordinary people, but not with a compulsive gambler. He would just gamble you were lying. Peroni felt the bulk of his own gun against his ribs, but by the time he got to it, Partecipazio would have been able to shoot him six times over.

So had the White Lady come for him at last? Peroni wondered in a remote part of himself that was isolated from the whirling dodgem track of terror which all the rest of him had become. So far a combination of circumstances—luck, St Janarius, the Neapolitan streak—had always deflected her at the last minute. But this time . . . He saw the cavernous barrels of the hunting rifle, heard the howling desolation all about the island and drew from them no motive for hope.

Then irrationally, despite the fear, he needed to know something before the White Lady came.

'Did Estrella know?' he said, 'All this time you've been using her to check on me— did she know what she was doing?'

'Estrella?' The hunting rifle still pointed unwavering at Peroni's belly, but Partecipazio's voice swelled like a pumped organ with the old joy of eulogy. 'Estrella? She's too good, too fine, too noble, Commissario! She would never have consented to such a thing! It was only this evening, when I saw you coming, I persuaded her to hold you while I got away. She couldn't refuse me, Commissario—she loves me!'

For an instant the rifle trembled and Peroni thought he had a chance, but it steadied immediately and Peroni saw Partecipazio's finger tighten on the trigger.

221

His mind was so tensed for the imminent rifle blast that for an instant it refused to take in the sound that came next. The sound of the door opening and letting in the cracking rumble of the receding storm. And then out of the corner of his eye he saw that Estrella had stepped into the room.

'Papa,' he heard her say, 'give me the rifle.'

'No,' said Partecipazio, 'no.' And the barrels shifted towards her.

'Give it to me, papa.' Slowly she started to walk towards him.

'Stop, Estrella, or I'll shoot you, too—'

He's mad, thought Peroni, he's capable of shooting us both.

Very slowly Estrella continued to walk towards him. For the second time that evening Peroni saw Partecipazio's finger tighten on the trigger.

'Jump him!' It was the soundless yet unmistakable voice which Peroni associated with St Janarius.

Partecipazio was three metres away which made it hopeless, but Peroni jumped just the same, and only when he was in mid-flight did he remember the dream. As Pepin he had rocketed through the air to deflect the catapulted boulder. But had he been successful?

His shoulder collided with Partecipazio's chest and the rifle exploded; he couldn't tell whether the two events were simultaneous or not. The big man tottered and then toppled under the impact of Peroni's weight while Peroni himself, having grabbed the hunting rifle, slewed round towards Estrella.

She was swaying slightly with a bewildered expression on her face. But it was only when she collapsed altogether that Peroni understood he had not deflected the bullet after all.

He ran and knelt beside her, cradling her head on his knees, but at the same time still gripping Partecipazio's rifle.

Her eyes which were closed now opened and focussed on Peroni, then sought another focus and found it in her father.

'Poor papa,' she said in a whisper, 'you always do get things wrong when I'm not there, don't you?'

She looked back at Peroni. 'This'll teach me to play Estrella,' she said, her face lit with a glimmer of the old mockery.

Peroni saw her father standing above them, sane once more, his large face ugly with grief.

Then he felt Estrella move again in his arms and saw that she was looking at him with the old expression which told how she had rumbled him. 'The famous Commissario Peroni,' she said, 'triumphs ag—'

She stiffened and her eyes closed. So this was where it had all been leading to, he thought, this death in a crumbling villa on a little island lost in the Venetian lagoon.

And then he heard her voice again, weak but unmistakably of this world. 'Do you mind,' it was saying, 'lending me a clean handkerchief?'

'Do I—what?' said Peroni, totally disoriented.

'Your handkerchief,' she said, 'it will just do to bandage my shoulder.'

As he gave it to her, Peroni realised with profound embarrassment that his wild Neapolitan fancy had leapt with unerring inaccuracy at the tragic. Estrella was not dead. Thanks to his jumping her father, she had no more than a shoulder wound. With all his heart he supplicated St Janarius that she might never be aware of his melodramatic misunderstanding; her keen mockery would never let him forget it. But even as he supplicated her look told him that she knew all about it.

It told him something else, though. It told him that the frontier of the unexplored world had once again drifted up to the Island, and that presently they would cross it together.

All Futura Books are available at your bookshop or newsagent, or can be ordered from the following address:
Futura Books, Cash Sales Department,
P.O. Box 11, Falmouth, Cornwall

Please send cheque or postal order (no currency), and allow 55p for postage and packing for the first book plus 22p for the second book and 14p for each additional book ordered up to a maximum charge of £1.75 in U.K.

Customers in Eire and B.F.P.O. please allow 55p for the first book, 22p for the second book plus 14p per copy for the next 7 books, thereafter 8p per book.

Overseas customers please allow £1.00 for postage and packing for the first book and 25p per copy for each additional book.